Jove Belle

BITTERROOT QUEEN

A Bitterroot Novel

Copyright © 2017, Jove Belle
Dirt Road Books, Inc.

All rights reserved. No part of this publication may be reproduced, transmitted in any form or by any means, electronic or mechanical, including recording, print-outs, information storage and retrieval system, without permission in writing from the author. This is a work of fiction. Names, characters, places, and incidents either are the product of the author's imagination or are used fictitiously. Any resemblance to persons living or dead or to business establishments or events is coincidental.

Cover design by Jove Belle
Cover photos © konradbak and © boscorelli

Cover image content used for illustrative purposes only. Person depicted in the cover image is a model.

ISBN 978-1-947253-00-1

For Tara, who still loves me all these years later.

Acknowledgment

A few years ago, I signed up to be a part of a fundraising auction for the Golden Crown Literary Society. The winner of the auction, SJ Baker, provided the names of the main characters, Sam and Olly, a bit of the background story, and a lot of brainstorming time. Three years later, *Bitterroot Queen* is finally done. My sincere thanks to SJ for supporting a fabulous organization and for being patient with my creative process. I hope you love this book as much as I do.

Chapter One

By the time Olly hefted her duffle into the back of her Scout, the morning sun had burned off the last of the cool night air. All her gear was stowed in her vehicle, and Rampart, her border collie mix, lay on his side in the grass, panting. She wiped beads of sweat from her forehead and mentally reviewed her checklist. Packing had gone quickly, but it always paid to pause a moment. She'd learned that lesson years ago, after leaving behind an old photo of her grandmother and, on another occasion, her favorite pocketknife.

Her hair hung loose around her shoulders and drifted into her face with a gust of dry, hot air. It was long and thick and didn't get along well with the wind. She pulled a green and white snapback trucker cap from her back pocket and jammed it on her head, John Deere logo to the front. Not pretty, but totally functional.

A sales rep had given it to her a few months back when she'd been waiting tables at a roadside diner just outside of Hastings. As per her usual, she had flirted a little too much to boost her tips, and this guy thought a piece of farmer swag was a seductive gift that would surely lure her into his bed. She'd taken the hat and rejected the rest of the offer.

The next day, she'd hit the road. She'd gone from middle-of-nowhere Nebraska to middle-of-nowhere Arizona. Both were comforting in their own ways. Nebraska, with the rows of corn growing tall and straight for miles and miles was a stark contrast to Arizona, with the burnt umber plateaus jutting up amid the long expanses of dry desert. She respected the scraggly juniper and mesquite that grew in defiance of the sun and lack of rain.

Now, though, she'd been in Arizona longer than she'd planned. The heat rolling off the desert and the kindness of Mrs. Vernon, her employer and landlady in one, had combined to lull her into staying just one more day until weeks had passed. Today, though, she was moving on.

"You sure you can't stay?" Mrs. Vernon placed one hand gently on Olly's elbow. She spoke as though she'd cast Olly in the role of family rather than the short-time boarder she really was. And, because Olly had been taught to be suspicious of others, to question their motives, and to look for a hidden meaning in every gesture, the assumed intimacy made her wary. It seemed, however, that Mrs. Vernon was guileless, without any intentions beyond kindness. Of course, even after a lifetime of studying her own mother, Olly still couldn't tell when she was running a con or when she was sincere.

Mrs. Vernon, however, was a sweet woman who'd planned to spend her retirement years rocking on her porch and baking cookies for her grandchildren. Her only daughter had moved across the country before giving her any grandchildren, and she had never added a porch to the front of her house, as she'd always wanted. Simple dreams that never came true.

"Yes, I'm sure." She patted Mrs. Vernon's hand. She had stayed for almost eight weeks, six more than she had originally intended. It never took Olly long to suss out if she was in the right place or not. And this one, just like the stops before, wasn't right. Despite lingering, the quiet voice in the back of her mind got louder over time until she had no choice but to act. When she ignored that voice, it eventually transformed into thick bands of panic that constricted her chest. Wanderlust was in her blood, mapped into her genetic code, and it left her with only two choices—move or perish.

Logically, Olly knew she wouldn't actually die if she stayed in one place. Not physically. But her soul was another matter. It would wither away and leave her a shell of her true self.

She adjusted her trucker cap and reminded herself to relax. It didn't stop the clenching of her jaw or the bunching of her muscle beneath Mrs. Vernon's hand. No matter how grandmotherly Mrs. Vernon wanted to be, Olly couldn't be her surrogate grandchild any longer.

Mrs. Vernon patted her arm. "I understand, dear."

"You do?"

"Young people. Your feet have to move."

She nodded. At twenty-five, society gave her leeway. Travelling the road seemed an understandable rite of passage, one that should be sated before she reached a certain age. Would Mrs. Vernon grant her the same kindness if she were twenty years older?

"I suppose you could be right," Olly agreed, because it was the easiest thing to say. The notion that she'd eventually settle was romantic and sweet and mimicked the stories her grandmother had shared with her late at night about people who found the missing pieces of their hearts, along with their true homes. Olly didn't know of anyone who'd actually done that, though, so it fell more into the category of wishful thinking than life goal.

"I wish you would have let me repair this shirt." Mrs.

Vernon looked at the ragged edges where Olly had torn the sleeves off at the shoulder.

"It's fine." The shirt, a men's denim with shiny pearl snaps down the front, was too hot for the summer heat in southern Arizona. She'd bought it at a second-hand store a few weeks ago with plans to remove the sleeves. Before she'd gotten around to it, she'd snagged it on a nail and the fabric had torn. Mrs. Vernon had watched with horror as Olly ripped both sleeves off.

Frankly, the shirt amused her as much as it frustrated Mrs. Vernon. She liked the implication of the jagged lines and the strands hanging down, as though the shirt, along with the rest of her, just couldn't quite follow the rules.

"All right, dear. You have my number." That morning Mrs. Vernon had written out her name, address, and phone number on a piece of lined notebook paper. It'd taken much longer than it would have if she'd asked Olly to write the words for her, but she had insisted on doing it herself, curling her fingers, gnarled and misshapen with age and arthritis, around a monogrammed pen that she pushed and pulled until her name and information appeared in slanted, imperfect cursive. Then she had folded it once, carefully, and given it to Olly.

"Right here." Olly nodded and patted her breast pocket. She glanced at the time on her phone, then at the street.

Mrs. Vernon lived in a charming neighborhood that had that vibe of superiority and uniformity of post-World War II home construction—tiny by modern standards, but also sturdier, and more solid. The street in front of her house was only three blocks long and it ended abruptly two houses down. At the T intersection, a left turn would take her deeper into the neighborhood. A right turn would deliver her to the highway and out of town.

Bitterroot Queen

That was the road Olly longed for. She liked it best when the road was long and empty, nothing but smooth blacktop and yellow lines, and she could see for miles.

Mrs. Vernon had told her proudly that she loved her tiny little road. There was rarely any traffic and the neighborhood children were safe to play in their yards. And if they wanted to fool around in the middle of the street—a game of catch or maybe soccer—nobody bothered them. Olly could see how that would be an appealing selling point for some. For her, however, it stifled. She hated knowing the end of the road was close enough to reach on foot.

"Here, take this. I don't want you to go hungry." Mrs. Vernon handed her a paper grocery bag with the top rolled over as if it were a lunch bag. She had carried it carefully down the steps in front of her house earlier with Rampart at her side, nervously alternating his focus between her and Olly, who had noticed the bag earlier, but hadn't asked about it. She'd been more focused on checking her tire pressure and oil level.

She took the bag, but couldn't think of anything to say. It was probably filled with cookies that Olly shouldn't eat. Too much sugar gave her the jitters and made it hard to focus. She reached across to set it on the passenger seat, and then gave Mrs. Vernon a one-armed hug, careful not to squeeze too tight. She felt fragile in her embrace, her skin leathery and unnaturally soft at the same time. It was a little awkward. Olly was a little too stiff and Mrs. Vernon held on a little too long, but she was glad she did it. Mrs. Vernon had made many accommodations on her behalf, so it was only fair to return the consideration.

"Well...um...thanks. You know, for everything." She scratched the back of her head, pulling her hair loose in places and knocking her hat slightly askew. Instinctively, she straightened it.

"Of course, dear." Mrs. Vernon tilted her head back to get a better look at her face. She shaded her eyes from the sun with her hand. "Remember what I said."

"I will." Olly hopped into the driver's seat and turned the key in the ignition. The engine caught and rumbled to life in a way that only a 1960s-era eight-cylinder could. The tension in her chest and limbs eased with the vibration of the motor. Rampart climbed into the back seat.

"You always have a place here. Come back any time." Mrs. Vernon looked like she was going to touch Olly again. Instead, she reached into the back and gave Rampart a firm pat on the head. He rested his chin on the edge of the frame and nudged her hand when she stopped.

"Thank you for everything," Olly said.

"I won't keep you any longer." Mrs. Vernon offered her a smile, then turned back toward her house.

Olly called goodbye as she pulled away from the curb. Rampart curled into a circle in the back seat and made a contented noise that was almost a sigh. She slipped her dark aviator glasses on and pushed play on her mp3 player. It was already cued to her favorite driving mix, and Drowning Pool took over the speakers. The rhythmic drone of power chords was loud enough to drown out the rumble of her engine, and Olly tapped the steering wheel lightly as she turned out of the neighborhood. A quick stop for gas, and she'd be on the road.

Chapter Two

After spending the past two days travelling, Sam Marconi was ready to stretch her legs. And possibly sell her car. Or set it on fire and roll it off a cliff. Whichever came first.

"Please tell me we're almost there." Beth, her daughter, lifted one side of her earphones just enough to hear the answer. Faint strains of angry metal bled out from the Monster DNA headphones Sam had given her when she turned fifteen, and the look on Beth's face said she was also ready to climb out the window and start walking in the opposite direction. She was still pissed about moving and had spent the majority of the trip listening to music and not saying anything. For Sam, it had made the drive from Las Vegas feel even longer than the time they'd actually spent on the road.

She checked the GPS on her phone. Seven more miles. She patted Beth on the leg and smiled sympathetically. "Almost. Just a few more minutes."

Beth dropped her headphones back into place and returned her attention to her sketch pad. She added a few lines with her pencil, then smudged it with her thumb to soften the mark. Sam couldn't see it well enough to know what she was drawing, but if the past two days were anything to go by, it was probably another portrait of her boyfriend. That she really shouldn't have at her age, but that was a fight Sam had given up on with her.

It felt strange, after dreaming about this for so long, to think about actually arriving. Their new home was close enough that she'd be able to see it within the time it took for two songs to play. After she'd signed the closing documents via proxy, the realtor had sent the keys via certified mail, and now she was the proud owner of a small roadside motel in Bitterroot, Idaho.

Most of the drive up through Nevada and Utah had been the dry desert landscape she'd grown to hate while living in Vegas. That had continued into southern Idaho, but now they were squarely in the middle of the Bitterroot Mountains. The passing scenery alternated from tall evergreens to jagged outcroppings of rock, and the air was so clear it made her lightheaded. She was used to the smoke-laden, recycled air of the resort casino where she'd worked for the better part of fifteen years. Cracking her window here was way better than an hour at an oxygen bar on the strip.

Bitterroot was everything Vegas was not. It was an unassuming community that promised nothing, yet delivered quality. Vegas was all flash and bang. That city promised everything in bold marquee lights, but delivered very little.

She'd discovered Bitterroot when her friend Karen had moved here to work at the women's correctional facility just outside of town. She had visited for the first time when Beth was five. The quieter pace and the absence of neon had soothed her in a way she hadn't expected, so she began saving. The older Beth got, the more pressing the need to leave Vegas became. The city was on the verge of swallowing her daughter whole, and if Beth fell into the rabbit hole of Vegas's darker side, she might never get her back.

"I still don't understand why I couldn't stay in Vegas." Beth was at the age where she knew everything except that she was too young to really know anything.

The first fifty or so times Beth had asked if she could stay, Sam had answered patiently. Now, however, Beth's refusal to listen just made her tired. She knew the answer, she just didn't like it.

"We've talked about this."

"But it's not too late. Denmar's mom said I could stay with them," Beth said bitterly. "He'll pay for my bus ticket home and everything."

Sam gritted her teeth at the mention of Beth's boyfriend—she was only fifteen, for chrissakes—and glanced at her. She saw herself in Beth's auburn hair and light brown eyes. Sam's teenage years, unlike Beth's, had consisted of smoking some pot and reading novels on the banned book list. She'd never rebelled so hard against anything as Beth did against her very safe, very privileged middle-class upbringing. But it was her fault, too, working long hours at the casino so they could be comfortable. She had sacrificed time she should have been spending with Beth, and now she was trying to be a more involved parent after Beth's boundaries had already been set. She had no idea how to negotiate a truce.

Despite knowing it would only start another argument, Sam's gaze drifted to the bottom edge of the tattoo that peeked out from Beth's sleeve.

Beth covered the image with her hand and glared at her.

"Like I'd ever trust that woman to take care of you." Sam regretted the words before they were fully formed. She and Beth had reached an impasse where neither of them heard the other one anymore, and she had no idea how to fix it.

"When are you going to understand that it's my life, not yours?"

"I do understand. But fifteen isn't adult, no matter how streetwise you think you are. And I'm your mother, so I'm trying to do what's right and give us both a life where we can make better decisions. I can't just watch you destroy the life you've just begun." Sam had said it all before, but the words never seemed to penetrate. Someday, Beth would mature enough to realize that any adult who would authorize a fifteen-year-old to get a tattoo—as Denmar's mom had done for her—was not a good influence.

"Why do you hate me so much?" Beth brusquely pushed tears out of her eyes.

Sam's heart nearly broke at that. "I don't, honey. You have no idea how much I love you. I can't even quantify it."

"Whatever." Beth turned to face the window and shoved her headphones back over her ears.

Revisiting the same argument with Beth was emotionally exhausting. Sam's throat tightened and she wished, again, that she could have made different decisions earlier, that life could have offered different choices. And now here she was, trying to do the right thing and build better circumstances for them both, but deep down, she wondered if it was already too late. Her GPS instructed her to turn in two hundred yards, and she was happy for the distraction of the motel sign coming into view in the distance.

She pulled into the parking lot of the Bitterroot Queen and took a deep breath before allowing herself to look at her new home.

"Wow. What a dump," Beth observed, and for once Sam didn't snap at her for her argumentative statements.

Instead, she stared at the motel. The structure was clearly the same as the pictures—two stories, exterior entry to the rooms, an attached office with a manager's apartment to the rear—but nothing else matched. The landscape was overgrown, which she'd expected. A few weeks without regular maintenance had that effect. The rest, however, was a shock. The front wall was covered with graffiti, several windows were shattered, and the doors to most of the rooms hung open. One appeared to be missing completely. The online pictures had shown that the place was in need of some repairs, but nothing to this extent.

Instead of the thirty units ready to rent with minor TLC, Sam had a giant, gaping pit threatening to suck up every single dollar she'd saved to get her and Beth through the first year. Most small businesses failed in the first year or two due to lack of funds. Sam had planned for that, had saved enough to take them through the first off-season and into the next summer.

"What the hell..." Tears pricked at her eyes. She wiped them away angrily as she fumbled with the door handle. The message from her brain to her hands got scrambled along the way and she couldn't quite figure out how to make her fingers work. She took another deep breath and closed her eyes. When she opened them, the view hadn't changed.

Finally, she got the door open and stepped out of her car. "What the hell?" She repeated the words because no other thoughts would coalesce in her mind.

This is what a mid-life crisis looked like.

It wasn't the first time the thought had crept into her mind, but every time before, she'd been able to push it down, to silence it until it was nothing but a dull murmur behind the chaotic noise of her workaday life. Now, staring at the consequences of her decision to purchase based on the online photos without actually visiting the motel first—that voice was no longer quiet. For the first time, she had real, tangible proof right in front of her that jumping at the first available piece of property in Bitterroot might have been a mistake.

"Why'd you buy this shithole?" Beth asked, and Sam didn't have it in her to scold her daughter for swearing. It was the least of her worries at the moment.

"It didn't look like this in the pictures." Fingers of panic curled into Sam's chest. It sounded so much worse when she heard the words aloud. Yes, she'd had the building inspected and yes, she'd asked Karen to check it out for her, but she'd bought it without actually seeing the property herself. What kind of person did that?

Beth made a noncommittal grunting noise that sounded almost sympathetic and then started toward the lobby door.

"What do you think happened?" Sam searched through her purse for the keys as she followed Beth. She didn't expect Beth to know the answer, but she needed to say something to keep from screaming.

Beth shrugged and said, "Looks like a party."

"What?" The thought of her daughter causing this much damage to someone else's property while at a party made the feeling of panic ease slightly. It was a good reminder of why she needed to get Beth out of Vegas.

"That's what it looks like." Beth was far too nonchalant about her assessment. Sam wanted to be surprised that her daughter wasn't just as shocked as she was at the amount of senseless damage, but she wasn't.

"Here?" Things like this weren't supposed to happen in the middle of nowhere. That's why they had moved. Bitterroot was a small town, a place where neighbors looked out for each other. At least that's what she'd thought.

"Sure. Kids party everywhere, Mom, not just Vegas." Beth tried the door, but it wouldn't open. Sam considered that a good sign. Maybe the lobby—and the manager apartment behind the lobby—wasn't destroyed like the rest of the rooms. She handed Beth the key.

Sam did a quick inventory of visible damage from the outside, adding up doors, windows, paint, carpet, and a litany of other things. She gave up because she really didn't know anything about the price of building supplies anyway. Then, with a reminder to herself to breathe, she followed Beth inside.

Sam dropped her suitcase on the floor at her feet and set her purse on the counter. She was so tired. All she wanted to do was take a nap. Sadly, that wasn't an option. She slumped against the wall and tried to collect her wildly spinning thoughts as Beth explored their new home. The relatively untouched state of the lobby and office had given Sam hope, but that had fallen away when they entered the apartment. The party or whatever it was had clearly made its way into this part of the building. How had they gotten in without going through the main entrance?

Beth walked carefully across the living room, stepping around a spot of broken brown glass that used to be a bottle. She caught a beer can with her foot, and it skittered across the carpet. There were stains everywhere. "Are we sleeping here?"

"I don't know."

Beth nodded but didn't argue. It was a welcome break from their usual interactions. Beth had pushed her hard for the past two years, but apparently wasn't interested in kicking her while she was down. Beth opened the curtains along the back wall to reveal a bank of floor-to-ceiling windows. They were smudged, but intact. She paused and reached out as if to catch the dust motes floating in the light, and she looked out at the tree-lined mountains and the corners of her mouth curved up in a small smile. "It's actually pretty."

Sam agreed. As long as she stayed focused on the outside, it was beautiful, but the second she let herself look at the damage surrounding them, the peaceful feeling shriveled. She felt like a hollowed out corn husk, still holding her shape but with nothing within. She straightened her spine and headed toward the bedrooms with her suitcase. Beth followed. The rooms were the same size, with the bathroom in between. One room had the same view as the living room.

"Which room is mine?" Beth asked rather than tossing her bag into the room she wanted. Another kindness as far as Sam was concerned.

"I'm taking this one." Sam gestured toward the room with the view of the river and Beth nodded and turned into the other room. Sam touched her shoulder and added, "We'll set up a studio area in the living room. The light is better there."

Sam wasn't the best judge, but it seemed Beth had a talent for sketching. She also liked to paint with watercolors and oil pastels. Sam had encouraged her with the hope that it would distract her from the dangers of being a teenager in a city like Vegas. So far, the strategy hadn't worked. Sure, Beth had improved her skills, but it hadn't distracted her in the ways she had hoped.

Beth paused. "Thanks, Mom."

Sam gave her shoulder a little squeeze of encouragement. "I love you."

Bitterroot Queen

She didn't expect Beth to say it back, since more often than not, her daughter just grunted and walked away in response. Instead, Beth actually smiled. "I know." Her eyes clouded momentarily. "I love you, too."

Sam stared at her, and just as she was considering a hug, Beth walked into her room and closed the door.

Moment over.

She sighed and went into her own room. It was in roughly the same shape as the living area, stained carpet and graffiti on the walls, plus a broken window—the point of entry for the partiers? Structurally, though, everything seemed solid. No holes in the walls, the door swung silently on its hinges, and the carpet was in relatively good shape. Based on the condition of the rental rooms, it could have been much worse. She sent her thanks out to the universe and tried to decide what to do next.

The moving pod containing their furniture was scheduled to be delivered in two days, so they'd need to set up the air mattress they'd brought with them. Beth wouldn't like sharing it with Sam, but she could always take the floor if it bothered her too much. Before they could set it up, however, they needed to do a few things to the apartment.

It would be easier and quicker to do the work on their living space if the detritus of their daily lives wasn't in the way. Perhaps they should look into finding another place to sleep. Karen's house would be perfect, but Sam already had a couple of messages out to her. If she left another, she'd be pushing the boundary between eager friend and stalker. Unless Karen called back soon, staying with her for the night was out.

"Beth?" She called her daughter. "Do you have a connection on your phone?"

"Yes." Beth answered without opening the door.

"Can you google hotels in this area?"

"Really?" Beth poked her head out of the room. She looked hopeful. "Why?"

"Really. It's late. We're exhausted, and I'd like to sleep in a place that doesn't reek of beer." Sam relaxed a little for the first time since the Queen came into view. The condition of the building had thrown her, but she'd give herself the night to rest. Tomorrow, when she had a clear head, she'd tackle the problem and figure out a list of things that needed to be done before she could open for business. "We'll come back in the morning with supplies and make a game plan from there."

"Thank God. This isn't the worst place I've slept, but it's pretty close." Beth retreated into her room to collect her suitcase. Sam gaped at her back. Beth had always assured her that she slept at home when Sam had to work the overnight shift. Hearing Beth's slipped admission made her cringe. What had her daughter really been doing all those nights?

Chapter Three

The A-frame sign on the side of the highway guided Olly to the farmers' market at the center of town. Her gas tank was almost empty, but the gnawing hunger in her stomach was a more pressing issue. She'd waited too long to stop for lunch, and if she didn't eat soon, her body would make her regret that decision. Last time she'd let her blood sugar drop too low, she'd ended up binging on fast food, followed by a two-hour nap in the parking lot. She'd awoken to the night manager tapping on her window. The time before that involved public nudity and a brief stay in a New Orleans jail.

The farmers' market was small, but crowded. Rampart followed behind, just off her right heel. She picked up a package of locally made jerky and a few no-spray apples. The apple vendor also let her fill up her water bottle.

"You're new in town." He didn't ask it as a question and narrowed his eyes suspiciously. Olly stared right back, impressed when he didn't look away. Direct eye contact made most people flinch.

Instead of answering, she sliced a chunk off her apple with her pocketknife. Rampart sniffed the apple and then sat down. She split the bite, gave half to Rampart, and popped the other into her mouth. The crisp burst of flavor made her smile. The vendor returned her smile, and she relaxed slightly. She gestured toward him with the apple. "It's good."

He nodded gruffly, apparently not interested in conversation any more than she was. That was okay with her. So few people knew how to enjoy a simple moment of quiet.

She ate her apple, lingering near the stall and the strangely comforting presence of the gruff apple farmer.

"You staying long?"

She shrugged. She doubted he defined long the same way she did, and she never knew when she was going to pause in a place until it happened. "Hard to say."

She sliced off another section of apple and tossed it to Rampart. He caught it mid-air with a satisfied smack. Then she opened the jerky and fed him a piece of that, too. For good measure, she tilted the package toward the man, offering him a piece. He declined with a shake of his head.

"Got any plans?" The one downside of small towns was the locals tended to be a little nosy, even brusque old farmers.

"Not really." As she chewed her apple, she evaluated the apple seller, a slight, elderly man with crooked shoulders and gnarled fingers. He wasn't pretty, but he sold nice apples. And he had the countenance of a man who should never be counted out. She liked that.

The vendor spotted another customer trying to gain his attention. "Good luck to you," he said with a nod then left her to enjoy her meal.

She sipped her water. This town felt comfortable. She didn't know how long that would last, but she'd learned to take advantage of it when it happened. Too often, she'd pull off the highway only to be hit with an urgent wall of energy telling her to leave. If she wanted to stay, she'd need to find work.

"Come on, Ramp." She patted her leg, and he followed.

The market was lively, filling one street and spilling

around the far corner. She walked the length, weaving between the other shoppers as she fed bites of apple and jerky to Rampart. They took turns, she and him, one bite for her, the next for him. They had a good partnership.

As she walked, she kept an eye out for signs advertising available work. Sometimes, she'd get lucky and happen past a "help wanted" sign. More often than not, however, she'd notice someone struggling with a heavy load and she'd jump in to help. She couldn't count how many times that had turned into a temporary job. And temporary was as permanent as she'd ever wanted.

Luck was on her side in Bitterroot. At the entrance to the market, there was a public bulletin board with handwritten, four-by-six cards advertising different openings around town. Most were looking for long-term temporary employees to match the school year. Those were clearly aimed at college students and not a good match for her.

Two of the postings, however, looked like they might be good. The first listed various repairs needed due to storm damage at a place called Randolf Farms. Frankly, it looked more like work for a general contractor than a handyman. She didn't have a license, but she was good with her hands and she worked hard. The other card simply said "My storeroom is out of control! Help!" It was signed "Ava—Bitter Ink."

The Bitter Ink card looked new, as if it had been put up that day. The other was faded and the corners were curling over. It's possible that the job had been done months ago and the card forgotten on the board. She took them both down and tucked them into her pocket. She'd start with the newer one first. All she had to do was find Bitter Ink, and in a town this size, that shouldn't be too hard.

She finished the apple and tossed the core in the trash.

Rampart stared at the bin and issued a forlorn *harumph*. He was overly dramatic at times, but she understood. She used to feed them to him until one time a woman on the street went nuts over it. She screamed at her about what a terrible dog owner she was and how she was going to give poor Rampart cyanide poisoning. Rampart avoided the seeds, because he was smart like that, but it wasn't worth the argument.

Olly returned to the apple vendor—not that he was particularly friendly, but he was the only person in town she'd had any kind of contact with. There were several people waiting to buy apples, so she stood off to the side, in the shade, but out of the way of the customers. The vendor wasn't any friendlier to the others buying his produce, but they all seemed to agree that he had the best apples around.

When the last person paid, he turned to Olly and said, "You're back."

"Yep," Olly moved closer. "Can you tell me where Bitter Ink is?"

"You *are* new in town." The vendor scratched his head. "Ava's place is just around the corner." He pointed toward the main road that Olly had driven in on. She'd stopped before reaching the market, so at least she hadn't driven past Bitter Ink and simply not noticed.

"Thanks a lot." She started out with Rampart at her side.

"What do you want with Ava?"

"Work. She posted a card on the board." Olly inclined her head toward the bulletin board, not that she needed to. This guy obviously knew the town well.

"Ah, well, when you're done with her, I've got some work that needs done, too. If she says you do a good job, that is."

"First I have to see if she'll even hire me. Thanks for your help."

"Good luck," the apple vendor called as she rounded the corner on Main Street.

Bitterroot Queen

She paused long enough to wave, then continued in the direction he'd indicated. As promised, she found the place only a few doors down on her left. Bitter Ink turned out to be a tattoo shop. A beautiful blonde who looked like she belonged in a magazine unlocked the door and flipped the neon sign to open just as Olly approached. When she saw Olly, she smiled and pushed the door open.

"Hey there." The woman wore a white, button-down men's shirt with the sleeves rolled up and a tie knotted loosely around her neck. An unbuttoned satin vest hung open over the shirt. She had scripted lettering tattooed on both her arms, just visible beneath the edge of the sleeves. Her skin was creamy white, a sharp contrast to Olly's deeply tanned olive complexion. She smiled slowly as if she knew the punch line to something that no one else understood. "Can I help you?"

Olly fumbled with the card and almost dropped it. Eventually, she got hold of it and offered it to the woman. "Are you Ava?"

The woman glanced at the card and nodded. "I am. Who are you?"

"Olly." She extended her hand, recovered enough to remember her manners.

"Olly." Ava said her name slowly, wrapping her tongue around each letter as if she were experiencing a new food for the first time. She stepped back to make room enough for Olly to slip through the door and said, "Come on, then. Let me show you what you'll be doing."

Olly paused and glanced at Rampart. "Wait here."

He curled up on the sidewalk and rested his head on his front paws. He'd be just fine there so long as nobody bothered him. She hated to leave him in a strange town where she didn't know the people, but he had a collar and her cell phone number was on the tags.

"He can come, too," Ava said easily.

With that, Olly decided that Ava was okay in her book. She patted her leg, and Rampart hopped up to follow. "Thanks. He does okay on his own, but I like to keep him with me."

"He's a good boy. He doesn't deserve to be exiled to the front step, does he?" Ava started out talking to Olly, but she dropped to her knees to pet Rampart and finished speaking in that silly sing-song voice reserved for babies and animals. Olly didn't like it when people did that, but Rampart just wagged his tail and leaned into Ava, soaking up the attention with no regard for how ridiculous she sounded.

She finished adoring Rampart and rose to her feet. "Sorry. My wife is allergic, so we can't have a dog at home. I just have to take advantage when one shows up on my doorstep."

"Bummer." Olly wasn't quite sure how to respond. It sucked that Ava was taken, especially by someone who wouldn't let her have a dog.

Ava smiled and waved her hand dismissively. "It's okay. I love dogs, but I love Valentina more."

"Of course."

Ava led her through the front of the shop and a set of swinging doors that looked as if they belonged in an Old West saloon. They led to a room that looked to be part office, part break room, and part daycare. The space ran the width of the storefront, but wasn't very deep, maybe six feet. To the left, a glass door led to a lovely courtyard, and to the right sat a set of wooden stairs that matched the swinging doors in style. Olly hoped they weren't as fragile as they looked. An overflowing toy box and a shelf full of children's movies were tucked into the space beneath the stairs. Along the back wall, between the stairs and the glass door, were a couple of modern doors, both closed.

Instead of leading Olly to the storeroom as expected, Ava went to the courtyard. She lit a cigarette and said, "Another thing I can't do at home because of my wife. Do you want one?"

Olly eyed the pack. She'd quit a couple of years ago, but that didn't stop her fingers from itching with the instinctual need to take one when offered. Instead, she jammed her hands into her pockets. "No thanks."

Rampart ran out the door to check out the courtyard. He flopped down on a small patch of grass and sighed.

Olly rocked back on her heels, hands still firmly in her pockets, as she waited for Ava to speak. For her part, Ava seemed content to puff silently on her cigarette and watch Rampart sleep in the grass. She understood that Ava couldn't exactly give her a tour while smoking, but at the very least they could discuss the details of the job.

She gave up on waiting politely and asked, "So, where's this stockroom that needs rescuing?"

"Right." Ava took one last long drag on her cigarette, then extinguished it in a coffee can next to the door. Ava's wife, Valentina, obviously wasn't very observant if she hadn't connected the overflowing makeshift ashtray to Ava, never mind the undeniable smell that clung to smokers.

Olly moved so Ava could step inside. Rampart lifted his head and looked at Olly. She motioned for him to stay and enjoy his nap. He relaxed with another deep, happy sigh.

Ava waved her arm in a sweeping gesture. "Let me give you the grand tour. This is my office."

An oversized wooden door resting on a pair of sawhorses served as a desk. It held an ancient Windows-based computer. The monitor was dark, and Olly wondered if it even worked. There was also a small table with a set of shelves above it that held a microwave and several boxes of easy-to-prepare foods such as breakfast pastries and fruit cups. In the far corner, beneath the stairs, a teddy bear and a coloring book lay on the floor.

"Do you color?" It seemed unlikely, but the play area confused her.

Ava laughed and shook her head. "Only when my baby asks me to. Sometimes Val brings the girls by."

So, not only was Ava married to a woman, but they also had children. This small town was obviously more progressive than what she was used to.

"Girls?"

"Clara is three, Corina is eleven months. She just started walking." Ava spoke with the obvious pride of a parent.

"Congratulations." Olly didn't know what else to say. Ava's life sounded suffocating to her, but Ava obviously liked it if her tone was anything to go by.

Ava chuckled. "Thanks. Domestic bliss really is more than I ever could have wished for. I never would have believed it possible before I met Val."

Olly nodded and looked around the room. She was pretty sure she'd need to be medicated heavily in order to find anything about a wife and two toddlers blissful, but she wasn't about to tell Ava that. She still wanted the job. "So, the stockroom?"

"Of course. I was giving you a tour." Ava crossed the room and stopped at the foot of the stairs. "There's an apartment of sorts up there. It's pretty beat up, but it came with the building, and I haven't had a reason to change it."

"Do you own or lease?" Olly didn't care, but she knew it was the polite question to ask. Her mom would have asked and known the benefits of both options, all while quickly calculating how to turn that advantage in her favor. Her mom relished the game more than anyone else Olly knew.

"Own. I bought it when I moved to town. Property's a lot cheaper here than the Bay Area."

"Right."

Ava opened one door to reveal a small bathroom. "This isn't the storeroom, but you might need to know where the toilet is at some point."

"Thanks." Olly tried to keep her voice from curling up into a question at the end, but she wasn't sure it worked. All she really wanted was to get started on the storeroom, assuming, of course, that Ava actually hired her. She thought she had the job, but this was the strangest interview process she'd ever been through.

Ava did a drum roll with her hands against the wall and said, "And here's the storeroom. Ta-da!" She swept the door open with a flourish and stood to the side with her arms held out as if she were a model on a television game show.

Olly peered through the doorway, trying to make out the contents in the dim light. She stepped partially into the room, and glanced around for the switch. She found it to the left of the door and flipped it on. An overhead fluorescent tube light flickered on and off before settling in to a low buzzing that produced a pitiful amount of light.

Items were stacked everywhere in a chaotic jumble. She couldn't make out much except for what looked like an old, tattered barber's chair, a stack of lumber, and a V-twin engine from a motorcycle. Harley, maybe.

"I have some shop lights at home. I'll bring them in tomorrow so you can see what you're doing."

Olly nodded. As much as she wanted to get started today, that clearly wasn't an option. "Tell me what you want done."

"I want some shelves built along the walls. You can do that, right?" Ava looked momentarily panicked. Perhaps she'd just realized that she hadn't actually interviewed Olly and had no clue what she was capable of.

Olly half-smiled, one side of her mouth curling upward, and nodded. "Yep. I can do that."

"Oh, good. I forgot to ask." She turned back to the room and gestured toward a few items that Olly couldn't make out. "I want to sort through the stuff and separate it by work and home, keep and toss. The work stuff I want here, easy to get to. The home stuff I want to take out back and set on fire."

"Really?" Bitterroot was a small town, so maybe it was possible that their fire codes allowed for random bonfires within city limits.

"Yes, but I won't. Valentina would kill me. My plan is to get her down here and make her decide what to do with it. All I know is, I can't very well expand my front area if I have every leftover piece of our personal lives stuffed back here. But, it all starts with shelves."

"Do you have the materials?" Olly had a hammer and a small level in her truck, but she didn't have a stock of lumber or nails.

"Yeah, right there." Ava pointed to a tarp-covered pile.

Olly peeked under the tarp and did some basic calculations in her head about what the length, width, and height the shelves needed to be. She nodded slowly as the vision of the finished stockroom came into focus in her mind. "Got it."

"So, you'll start tomorrow? I'm usually here by one."

"Sounds good. I'll see you then."

Olly called Rampart on her way toward the door. There was a lot of time between now and tomorrow afternoon. Perhaps the apple guy could offer some insight on the second card as well. Two jobs meant twice the money, and that was never a bad thing.

Chapter Four

Beth stumbled out of the bathroom looking no better than when she'd gone in. Her hair was a tousled mess and her eyes half-closed. She bumped into the door frame and swore under her breath, then stepped fully into the room. She rubbed sleep from her eyes with the back of her fist and blinked. With gestures like that, Sam could almost see the little girl she used to be instead of the angry young woman she'd become. "Why am I awake this early?"

"Do you want coffee?"

"I'd kill for some."

"That's why you're up." Sam grabbed the keys from the dresser and slipped a sweatshirt over her head. Even in late summer, Idaho mornings were still cool. "Let's go."

"Can't you just bring me some?"

"I could, but hopefully we won't be coming back." Everything was packed, and she'd optimistically loaded their suitcases into the car. Hopefully, she'd see the hotel differently after a night to process what she'd found yesterday. If not, at least this place seemed to have quite a few vacancies. They should be able to get a room again that night if necessary.

"Right." Beth pushed her hands through her hair and brought it down to an almost manageable tangle. She still wore the battered Metallica T-shirt and torn jeans she'd put on the previous morning, and it was unlikely that they'd been clean then. "Can we even get coffee this early?"

Sam had thought about keeping a change of clothes out for Beth, but odds were she'd hate whatever she selected on principle.

"I hope so." She checked the time on her phone. It was 6:30, earlier than Beth had been up in months. The question about finding a place to get coffee wouldn't have come up in Vegas, but Bitterroot ran on a different schedule. She wasn't sure they could find a place open, but she had to try. The insurance office opened at eight, and she was determined to be their first phone call of the day. She had a lot to get done before that.

Beth followed her out the front door and then stopped abruptly. Her lips curled up in disgust. "God, what is that smell?"

Sam took a deep breath. The sun hung low in the Eastern sky and the only scent was fresh mountain air. "What?"

Beth glared as she shoved her sunglasses into place. "Smells like morning."

Sam laughed even though Beth wasn't trying to be funny. She opened her arms wide as if to embrace the world. "I love it."

"Ugh."

"I promise you'll get used to it. Life surrounded by neon and cigarette smoke isn't natural."

"You keep telling me that, but I don't believe you." Beth sounded almost amused. She pulled a Marlboro Red box from her jacket pocket. It was slightly crushed and only had three cigarettes inside. Beth slipped one between her lips and lit it.

Now was as good a time as any to revisit their conversation about Beth's smoking. It was another habit she had picked up from Denmar. Sam would bet her new property that his mom supplied them to her as well. But it also was yet another indication that she had dropped the ball as a parent and that hurt worse. "You know you're going to quit that, right?"

Beth took a long drag and then held the cigarette up. She studied it as she exhaled a stream of grey smoke. She blew it up and away from Sam, but the wind caught it and pushed it into Sam's face anyway. She tried not to cough. She was used to the dull, dingy layers of smoke that hung in the air in Vegas, but the direct bolt of a fresh cigarette still got to her.

"Why would I quit?" Beth continued to look at her cigarette rather than lifting her gaze to meet Sam's. Surprisingly, she spoke with a level, metered tone, rather than yelling. Sam considered that progress.

"Because your lungs hate you when you do it." Sam had done an endless amount of research about the health problems related to smoking and second-hand smoke, all of which she'd tried to talk about with Beth. The words bounced right off Beth, though, because she was still young enough to feel invincible. Sam cried anytime she allowed herself to really think about what Beth was choosing to do to herself.

"My lungs don't hate me. They hate you for making me get up so early."

Sam shook her head and decided to change tactics. If Beth didn't care about her health, perhaps Sam could make some headway with logic. "You're almost out. Who are you going to get to buy for you here?"

Beth finally looked at her. "I'm sure I'll figure something out."

So much for logic. "I won't do it."

Short of strapping Beth to a chair twenty-four hours a

day, there was no realistic way for Sam to stop Beth from smoking if she really wanted to do it, but Sam wouldn't provide her with a constant supply, either.

"I won't ask you."

Of course she wouldn't. Her fifteen-year-old daughter probably had a fake ID that listed her age as twenty-four. At least Beth wouldn't have a corner store within walking distance of home like there was in Vegas, and she was still too young to drive, if only for a few more months.

There was nothing else to say. She wasn't giving up, but it was time for her to regroup and try a different approach another day. "Come on. It looks like the office is open. Maybe we can get coffee there."

The complimentary continental breakfast really didn't appeal to Sam, but if her options were bad coffee or no coffee, the choice was obvious. And if they were lucky enough to find an open coffee stand on the side of the road, she could always dump it out.

Beth stubbed out her cigarette in the ashtray next to the lobby door. Sam shook her head, but didn't say anything. She hated that Beth smoked, but she hated a lot of other things that Beth did, too. The important part was to remember that, despite all the bumps, she loved her daughter. Not to mention, Beth was preprogrammed to run in the opposite direction when Sam pushed too hard.

As expected, the lobby had a pastry box of goodies and a pump dispenser full of coffee. She filled a cup for Beth, then one for herself. Beth selected a bear claw and an apple strudel from the box. The sign on the table said one pastry per person, and the man working the front desk glared at her. Sam smiled at him and thanked him for the coffee, but she didn't make Beth put one back. She wasn't eating one, so it balanced out if Beth ate two.

They drove to the Queen in relative silence. Sam enjoyed her surprisingly good coffee combined with the stillness of morning in Bitterroot. In Vegas, the time didn't matter. People smoked and gambled at all hours, and the sallow tint the fluorescent lights cast over their skin didn't change if it was noon or midnight. Here, the morning was crisp and quiet. She felt a reverence at the passing of time, something she'd never experienced before. Her trepidation about moving eased to a dull, manageable buzz. She had a lot of work in front of her, but Bitterroot was a pretty picturesque place to do it.

Beth wore her sunglasses and slept the twenty minutes it took to drive to the Queen. Somehow, she managed not to drop her coffee, which was impressive. When the Queen came into view, Beth pulled her sunglasses down and looked over the top of the lenses. Apparently, she hadn't been sleeping after all. "Mom, what's that?"

Beth pointed to the back corner of the lot. A blue International Scout was parked there, almost behind the building and partially covered by overgrown shrubbery. Sam frowned. If it was the same kids who destroyed the motel, they were out awfully late. Or early, depending. Either way, the vehicle clearly didn't belong there.

"What the hell?" Sam pulled slowly into the lot. She wanted to go over and tell the driver to get off her property, but she also didn't want to get murdered by a small town serial killer and then left undiscovered in the bushes for months. Maybe she should call the police. Too bad she packed up her pepper spray with all her personal belongings. It was currently in the shipping container somewhere between Vegas and here.

As she dialed the number for the local police, Beth leaned against the hood of their car, slipped another cigarette between her lips, and looked thoroughly bored as she lit it. If she was concerned about the driver of the Scout, it didn't show.

Sam pointed at Beth, disappointed that she was smoking again so quickly. "We'll talk about that in a minute."

As she listened to the phone ring, an engine roared to life. A moment later, the vehicle drove past her and out of the parking lot. The driver—a young woman with dark hair and olive skin—turned right, headed into town. The vehicle disappeared in the distance before Sam even thought about writing down the license plate number.

She disconnected the call. Sure, she could still report the incident, but what would she say? "Yes, I'd like to report a parked car. No, it's no longer parked."

She made a quick check of the property where the Scout had been parked, just in case. There was no new damage to the structure. It even looked as though the debris in the immediate area had been cleared away. Rather than the empty beer cans and pizza boxes she'd expected, there wasn't a single sign that a party had taken place in this section of the lot.

Sam glanced at her watch. She had a full hour until the insurance agency opened for business. That gave her enough time to take detailed photos of the damage and track down the inspection report that had been completed prior to her making an offer on the Queen. That was in the same storage container as her pepper spray, but hopefully the realtor, a local woman who talked fast and without pausing to breathe, would have a copy. If not, she should have the contact information for the inspector.

"What's first?" Beth didn't sound interested, exactly, but maybe willing to help. Still, it was progress after the last week of yelling alternating with pouting.

"We need to take pictures," Sam said.

"Do you have your camera?"

The camera was in that same storage container.

"No, but I have my phone. That will have to do." Sam held up her iPhone, already set to take a photo. She snapped a quick shot of Beth, much to her daughter's annoyance, and then turned her attention to the building. She should start with a broad curbside view of the property as a whole. The effect was pretty devastating.

"What should I do?"

"We also need an itemized list of all the damage. Do you want to work on that?" Sam wasn't at all sure about Beth taking on such an important job, but she wasn't about to tell her daughter that. Worst-case scenario, Sam would recreate it later.

Beth wrinkled her nose. "I'd rather take the pictures."

Beth was the artist in the family, so that actually made sense.

"Of course. That would be great. Start with the exterior, a shot of the whole building, then closer shots of the actual damage. Include shots of the broken glass and beer bottles in the lot, but don't bother with the landscaping. It looks bad, but it happened naturally rather than being inflicted upon the poor place.

"After that, go room by room. Take a shot of the exterior, including the room number. Then a shot of the room as a whole and then focus on the damage."

As Sam talked, Beth listened and nodded along. At the end, she said, "Got it."

In Vegas, she had used a digital recorder when she did her daily property walk. Then, when she got back to her office, she used speech to text software to convert everything into a document on her computer. God, that would be handy right about now, but like everything else she thought she wouldn't need, it was packed in a box somewhere. The spiral-bound notebook and generic blue pen she'd picked up at the Red Barn Market the previous evening would work for now.

Beth made her way to the outer edge of the property to begin her photo assignment, and Sam flipped to a clean sheet of paper.

Olly left Rampart in her truck and headed into the Red Barn Market. It was a little after seven in the morning and she was surprised to find the store open that early. Small towns usually closed down at six at night and didn't open back up until eight the next morning.

She'd never been to a Red Barn before, but on the inside it looked like any other grocery. She picked out some fresh fruit. They didn't have an organic section, but sprayed fruit was better than no fruit. At least that's what she told herself. If she thought about it for too long, she might change her mind.

Until she sorted out a place to stay, she couldn't cook anything, so she had to settle for foods she could eat off the shelf. She could handle the muscle kinks that came with spending the occasional night in the Scout, but she hated not being able to prepare her own food. In addition to the fruit, she grabbed a couple of packages of mixed nuts, some jerky, a loaf of whole grain bread, and some free-range, antibiotic-free sliced chicken breast.

At the checkout counter, she bumped into a spinner rack that held an assortment of postcards. She set her items in front of the cashier and steadied the rack. She selected one at random for her sister. She never had more to say to Genevieve than what would fit inside the four-inch square.

"Good morning. Did you find everything you were looking for?" The checker wore an unreasonably sunny smile and a crooked name tag that identified her as FRED.

Olly nodded slightly. "I did, Fred. Thanks."

"Oh, I'm not Fred, silly. They just make us wear this when we forget ours at home. It's supposed to be an incentive to help us remember. But I really don't care what the tag says. Everybody knows who I am. Except you, that is." The girl stood about five-four, several inches shorter than Olly, with dark hair and dark eyes that sparkled when she talked. She looked to be around sixteen or seventeen. Too young to be working instead of attending classes.

Olly nodded and made a polite humming noise to indicate she was listening. People like Not-Fred created the fabric of a community. Even though she didn't expect to be around long, she still enjoyed learning the quirky things about the individuals she came into contact with.

"I'm Rachel, by the way. Now next time you come in, you'll know for sure who I am." She finished ringing up Olly's items. "You need anything else?"

Impulsively, Olly grabbed a second postcard and handed it to Rachel. She'd send it to Mrs. Vernon. "This, too."

"You got it." Rachel brushed her fingers against Olly's as she took the card, and in addition to the smile, she gave Olly a little wink.

Olly was pretty sure Rachel was flirting with her, though odds were against it. For a town this size, one out lesbian was rare. Bitterroot met its quota and then some with Ava and her wife. Then again, maybe she'd unknowingly stumbled onto a lesbian Mecca in the mountains of northern Idaho. Olly liked that idea, no matter how unrealistic it was.

"Shouldn't you be in school?" Normally, she would never ask another woman about her age, but it seemed the quickest way to re-direct Rachel's attentions.

Rachel scanned the last item, then glanced at the clock on the wall. "Not yet. School starts at twenty after eight. My dad lets me come down to open the store until the day shift person gets here."

Olly nodded. As far as part-time high school jobs went, that wasn't a bad arrangement. "Nice." She paid and stopped Rachel from putting the items in a plastic bag. She'd forgotten to bring her reusable cloth one inside with her, but she'd bought only a few things, so she could easily carry them. No reason to add another plastic bag to a landfill.

She juggled the items around until she was able to hold them all in her arms. "Thanks." She nodded politely and headed for the door.

"I'll see you next time." Rachel smiled broadly, then turned to help the next person in line. She interacted with him in the same friendly, borderline flirtatious way. Olly's hopes for a lesbian oasis fell apart.

Ah, well. It was still a pretty town. She'd stay until she couldn't any longer.

Chapter Five

After spending the morning on top of George Randolf's barn, Olly was sore and a little sunbaked. As luck would have it, the second card from the bulletin board belonged to the farmer who'd sold her apples, and he'd been very happy to put her to work. He paid her more than promised and invited her back for another day. All in all, not a bad way to spend a morning.

With the slim stack of fresh, crisp twenties safely stowed in the compartment beneath the driver's seat, Olly headed into town to start work for Ava. As she drove, she and Rampart shared two apples and a thick roast beef sandwich, both courtesy of George the apple farmer.

She arrived at Bitter Ink thirty minutes early and spent the spare time stretched out on the grass of a nearby park with Rampart. While waiting, she scribbled a clichéd "Wish you were here" on a postcard to Genevieve. She struggled with the second card meant for Mrs. Vernon.

In the end, she settled for a few lines about how they'd arrived in Bitterroot safely and how much Rampart enjoyed the mountain air. It was weird, holding onto a connection with someone after she'd driven away, but Mrs. Vernon had been kind to her. In another world, she was exactly how Olly imagined her own grandmother might be.

As she walked from the park to Bitter Ink, she added postage from the pack of stamps in her wallet and dropped the cards into a mail collection box. She was still a few minutes early, but figured she could wait on the step until Ava arrived. Surprisingly, the front door was unlocked and Ava's voice carried from the back room. She was singing. Olly didn't recognize the song, but Ava had a mellow alto that she found soothing.

"Ava?" Olly called as she made her way to the back room. She didn't want to startle Ava. Apparently, Ava didn't hear her because she kept right on singing. Olly called her name a little louder and knocked on the door frame before stepping through the swinging doors and into the back room.

"Oh, hi!" Ava removed her earbuds and let them dangle around her neck. A bluesy melody that reminded Olly of smoky clubs and smooth whiskey was barely audible from the tiny speakers. Olly liked her music a lot harder and louder, but had to admit the song wasn't bad for what it was.

She nodded hello. Rampart, on the other hand, ran over to her, tail wagging so hard it wiggled his whole back end. The door to the storeroom was open, so Olly went there while Rampart and Ava got reacquainted. As promised, there were several shop lights set up inside, along with a circular saw, a level, a tape measure, a cordless drill, and a box of screws.

"I didn't know what kind of tools you have, so I brought mine just in case." Ava didn't look like the kind to use tools, but that didn't really mean anything. Just because she had the bone structure of a goddess and a manicure that made Olly question whether she was really a lesbian didn't mean she couldn't enjoy building birdhouses in her spare time.

"Thanks, this helps." Olly had a few tools in the Scout, but not enough for this job. She was glad not to have to buy them.

"Do you need anything else from me or are you good to get started?"

Olly realized that they hadn't discussed payment or deadlines or any of the details that usually came along with a temporary job, but she wasn't quite sure how to bring it up. Instead, she said, "Radio?"

Ava gave her that I've-got-a-secret smile. "What? You don't want to listen to me sing?"

"Um..." Olly had no idea how to answer that question. If she said she liked Ava's singing, then she'd likely be forced to listen to that instead of music she really liked, and if she said she didn't, she'd be insulting her temporary boss. Either way, she was screwed. "It's just that..."

Ava laughed, saving Olly from finishing her answer. "I'm just kidding. There's a radio over there."

Sure enough, there was an eighties-era boom box sitting on top of an equally old exercise bike. "Does it work?" In Olly's experience, just because something was old didn't mean it wasn't useful.

"It did when I put it in here five years ago. I'm assuming it still does."

Olly thanked Ava and waited for Rampart to join her in the storeroom. Instead, he stood in front of the exterior door that led to the courtyard where he'd sunned himself the day before. "Really?"

Rampart barked once, then settled onto his haunches. Olly didn't blame him. She'd rather spend the day outside, too.

"Do you mind if he goes outside?" The area was enclosed, and he wasn't the type to run off even when the opportunity existed.

"Of course not. How about I prop the door open? That way he can come and go as he likes."

Without waiting for her to respond, Ava pushed the

door open and used a large rock to brace it in place. Rampart was going to get spoiled if this job took more than a day or two. She didn't say any of that to Ava, opting instead for a simple, "Thank you."

Olly closed herself into the storeroom. She liked her music loud and power tools weren't exactly quiet, either. She plugged in the stereo and heavy static rattled the speakers. The last person to use it had left it turned on. She adjusted the tuner until she found a song that wouldn't put her to sleep. Nine Inch Nails wasn't her favorite group—she preferred Hinder or Drowning Pool—but it was certainly better than the boy bands she usually found on the radio. She wasn't looking for music she could dance to, just a throbbing bass and heavy drumbeat that she could get lost in while she worked.

With the music sorted, Olly turned to her task. She uncovered the pile of lumber to inspect what she had to work with. The stack included a decent number of two-by-threes and several sheets of half-inch medium-density fiberboard. She doubted there would be enough studs to complete the job, but there was enough to make a good start. Before she could do anything else, however, she needed to clear the space next to the wall where the shelves were meant to go.

Olly removed her button-down shirt, leaving her in a ribbed tank top. She was ready to get sweaty.

So far that morning, Sam had left messages with her insurance agent, the utility companies, the local trash company, and a locksmith. She'd also filed a police report about the damage because the insurance company would want it.

None of that satisfied the tension building in her shoulders, so she used her phone to find a local law office and made an appointment there. Hopefully she wouldn't need it, but it was better to have her bases covered.

Around eleven, she made another call to the insurance company. This time, she was transferred directly to a claims agent.

"How can I help you?" The agent, a man with a nasally voice, asked.

Sam gave him her policy number, along with the details of how she'd found the property when she arrived yesterday.

"So, you don't know when the damage was done?"

"I have a general idea, yes."

"But not the specifics?"

"Of course not. If I'd seen it happen, I would have stopped it." She took a deep breath. It wouldn't help for her to lose her temper with this guy.

"Hmm. Well, I'll email you the form you need to complete, along with a list of documentation we'll need."

"That's it?"

"For now, yes. Thank you for calling." Without waiting for a reply, he disconnected the call.

Frustrated, Sam left another message for Karen, who worked long shifts at the women's prison for several days in a row, followed by a block of days off. In some ways it was an ideal schedule, but Sam wasn't a fan. There was no way their apartment would be habitable before nightfall, and she'd much rather stay with Karen than the other hotel in town where they'd spent the previous night.

Through all of Sam's huffing and puffing and irritation, Beth had worked steadily at cleaning their apartment. In the moment, Beth seemed years older, and Sam caught flashes of the adult she might become with the right guidance. She swore to herself she was going to provide it. Occasionally, she glanced at Sam, headphones in place over her ears, and smiled. She had to give Beth credit. In spite of being a class-A pain in the ass over the past few years, her daughter was right there, scrubbing the remnants of another lifetime from their new home.

She made one more call, this one to the realtor. When the call kicked over to voicemail, Sam left a message explaining the state of the Queen and asked her to reach out to the seller.

"Mom?" Beth stared at the wall adjacent to the bank of windows with a distant, contemplative look on her face. It was the expression she got when she saw something as it could be, rather than as it was.

For all the tension between them, Sam envied her daughter's ability to visualize beauty where it didn't exist and was eager to hear what Beth had come up with this time. She left her phone on the counter and went to stand next to her. She pushed her hair out of her face and tried to see what Beth did. All she saw was an on-the-way-to-clean beige wall. She settled her arm around Beth's waist and gave her a side hug. "What's up?"

"Can I have this wall?" Beth didn't look at Sam, and when she finished the question, her lips continued to move as she silently talked herself through what she wanted to do.

"Can you wait until we're done cleaning?" She wouldn't deny Beth's request, but she really hoped that she didn't need to get started right now. They had too much to get done for a side trip to the art supply store. Hell, she wasn't even sure there was a store in Bitterroot that sold the supplies Beth needed.

She finally looked at Sam and smiled. "Yeah, I can do that."

When Beth smiled like that, like she'd burst if she didn't find a release for her creativity soon, her happiness radiated from her very pores. Sam cherished those moments and, as far as she was concerned, Beth could paint every damn wall in the place if she wanted.

"Thank you. If we finish up here early enough, we can run to the store." All of Beth's supplies, with the exception of her sketch pad and charcoal, were still in transit.

The faraway look returned to Beth's face and she nodded as she turned to face the wall again. "Home Depot. I need a lot of paint."

"Okay." Sam kissed the top of her head. Bitterroot might not have a big box store like Home Depot, but they were bound to have a hardware store that sold paint. "Soon as we're finished." She ruffled Beth's hair and headed back to the kitchen. The self-cleaning oven she'd been working on certainly wasn't living up to its promise.

"What about the carpet?" Beth asked, surprising her. She thought the conversation was over.

"What do you mean?" So far she'd managed to avoid thinking about the carpet. It looked unsalvageable to her and that was an additional expense that she hadn't budgeted for.

"Are we going to clean it or replace it?"

Sam hadn't even considered cleaning it. There were stains there that made her wonder if she should report a crime of some sort, and she was sure the possibility of contracting an STD simply from walking on it with her shoes off was far too high.

"I think it's gotta go."

"Cool. I can paint without using a drop cloth."

"Sure." Sam returned to the stove. They'd been there

for four hours, and all she'd managed to do between phone calls was pick up the debris on the floor and wipe down the countertops. At this rate, she wouldn't finish the kitchen until late tonight.

A cell phone rang in one of the bedrooms, and Sam was halfway there before she realized it was Beth's ringtone, not her own. Her own phone lay silent on the kitchen counter. She stepped out of Beth's way and tamped down a jab of jealousy. She needed her phone to ring more than Beth's did.

"Damn it." She returned to her cleaning and tried not to think about how many loose ends she was waiting to tie up.

Beth came out of her bedroom with her phone to her ear, an unlit cigarette between her lips, and a broad smile on her face that reached all the way up to her eyes. She silently mouthed, "Denmar," as she slipped through the sliding-glass door to the back patio, leaving Sam to wonder where the hell she'd found a new pack of Marlboros. She gritted her teeth and wondered if Beth's dad had been more active in her life, if it would have somehow helped. But he had his own problems, and even if he could have been bothered to help, she doubted he was capable of it.

Beth left the door cracked, the opening too narrow for the smoke to slip back in when she lit her cigarette, but wide enough to allow Sam to clearly hear Beth's side of the conversation. It was time to clean the inside of the fridge and give Beth some privacy, as much as she wanted to hear and find out how much more she should worry about.

Inside the refrigerator, Sam found a burned-out light bulb and an unopened bottle of Bud Light. She flipped open her notebook and added the light bulb to her growing list of things to pick up from the hardware store. According to the label on the beer, it was well before the sell-by date, and Sam debated the risks of drinking it. Yes, it was unopened, but who had last touched it? God only knew what that person had done or where his hands had been before putting the bottle on the shelf in the fridge. The images that conjured made her shiver. She set the beer on the counter. She'd decide what to do with it later.

As she cleaned the interior of the appliance, she caught snatches of Beth's conversation even though she was trying to tune her out.

"No, I'm not sure." Beth didn't shout, but her voice wasn't soft, either. Sam turned to see the smile on Beth's face had been replaced by a deep scowl.

Sam wished for a radio. She already didn't like Denmar and hearing Beth argue with him long distance didn't help her opinion of him.

"—test!" Beth waved her cigarette around, causing the cherry to flare up. That she talked with her hands was a sure sign that Beth was her daughter. Sam did the same thing when she was upset.

It was time to change the water in her cleaning bucket. The sound of the water whooshing down the drain, followed by the rush of tap water filling the bucket, drowned out Beth's voice. As soon as she turned it off, she could hear again.

"—asshole! It's not my fault." Beth crushed out her cigarette and hung up without saying goodbye. As she stomped to her room, Sam saw tears on Beth's face.

"Are you okay?"

Beth stopped and looked at her. She tilted her head and stared hard at Sam, as though she was trying to decide something. After a moment, she shook her head and said, "I'm fine." Her voice was brittle, but controlled. She went into her room and slammed the door hard enough to make the cupboards shake.

Sam sighed and picked up the Bud Light. She gave it a cursory cleaning with her rag, then twisted off the top. As she tilted the bottle to her mouth, she thought that any disease she might contract from the bottle would be easier to deal with than parenting a teenager.

By the time Beth re-emerged from her bedroom, Sam had finished the fridge and started on the top set of cabinets.

Beth returned to her earlier spot staring at the wall. Her eyes were puffy and red. Before she could ask what was wrong, Beth said, "Time to get some paint." Her voice was tight, but no longer held the anger from earlier. "Ready to go shopping?"

She wasn't ready by a long shot, but she had enough of a list to start with, including replacing the pepper spray she'd packed away, and Beth clearly needed a distraction. Sam ripped the page with the list from the notebook, folded it, and slipped it into her back pocket.

"Sure." She wanted to hug her, to hold her in her arms and promise everything would be okay like she did when Beth was a little girl. Except she was older now, and smart enough to know that saying the words didn't make it true, especially when the person speaking had no idea what was wrong in the first place. "How's Denmar?" she tried.

The question was as innocuous as she could make it, but Beth still stiffened, her back and shoulders rigid with tension.

"He's an asshole."

Sam hated when she swore, hated that she smoked, and hated that she looked like a grown woman before Sam was ready for it. She drew Beth into a hug without saying anything. When Beth tried to squirm away, she tightened her hold. After several moments, Beth relaxed and her body slumped against her. She wrapped her arms around Sam and buried her face in her shirt. Sam stroked her hair and made shushing sounds because that had worked last time Beth let her hold her as she cried.

"Whatever it is," Sam said, "you can talk to me. I know I don't always get it right, but I will always have your back."

Beth's shoulders started to shake, and she inhaled roughly and sobbed. Sam held her while she cried, unsure how to fix whatever her daughter was facing. Her heart ached with the weight of whatever it was and the knowledge that in some way, she held some responsibility in it, with her long hours working and difficulties reaching her.

After several minutes, Beth pulled away and Sam let her go. Beth wiped her eyes with the bottom of her T-shirt, smearing dark makeup over the fabric. "Damn, I thought I was done crying." She snuffled.

"What can I do to help?"

Beth shook her head and averted her gaze. Her expression was one of pure anguish. Sam had forgotten the harsh pain of a teenage broken heart until that moment.

"Oh, honey, talk to me," Sam pleaded.

"There's nothing you can do, Mom. Nothing anyone can do." Beth drew herself up, straightening her spine as if she was willing her emotions into a place where she could control them. "I'm going to go fix my makeup."

A knock sounded at the door. "Hello? Sam?"

Karen stood in the entryway holding a pizza and a six-pack of beer. Beth escaped to the bathroom without a word, and Sam met her at the door.

"I was wondering when the hell you'd show up." Sam took the six-pack and put it in the fridge as Karen set the pizza on the counter. When she turned around, Karen was right behind her and she almost knocked into her.

She was tall and lean, with short, light blond hair. The sides and back were combed neatly, but the top was a floppy mess of surfer chic. Karen smiled, all lopsided and sexy as she pulled Sam into a hug.

"You look great. Clearly the mountain air already agrees with you."

Sam never knew what she'd get with Karen. Sometimes, she treated Sam as a sister, sometimes as a would-be lover. Apparently, this was one of the would-be lover moments, and Sam decided to go with it. She and Karen would never work in a long-term romance, but it'd been forever since she'd shared a night with anybody and she trusted Karen not to be an asshole the next morning.

Sam straightened Karen's collar, letting her fingers linger. Touching her like this, adjusting her clothes the way a lover would, wasn't something she would normally do, but as long as she was going for it, she was going all in. Karen's eyelids dropped and when she looked at Sam, her intentions were clear.

"You look good, too." Sam played with the short hair at the back of Karen's neck. She loved the bumps that rose on Karen's skin and the shudder that worked through her body.

Karen looked at her, a wary expression in her dark eyes, but clearer than the moment before. "Yeah?" She hooked her fingers into Sam's back pockets and pulled her closer. The cool air of the refrigerator caressed her back and the heat of Karen's body pressed at her front made her think of many other things than cleaning.

She mimicked Karen's crooked smile and nodded. "Sure, why not?"

There were a million reasons why not, but Sam

couldn't focus on a single one long enough to let it override the tension building low in her belly. God, she'd forgotten how intense Karen could be.

Karen's smile blossomed to include both sides of her mouth and the soft crinkles at the corners of her eyes. She brought her head closer to Sam's, slowly as if to allow her time to change her mind. When Karen's mouth finally closed over hers, she didn't see fireworks or feel a bolt of electricity race through her body, but it was warm and soft, and so, so nice. She missed kissing as much as what came next and she sighed against Karen's lips because she was too damn happy to hold it in.

"Jesus! I leave the room for five minutes and this is what you do. Ack. Gross!" Beth made retching noises to go along with her protests.

Karen started to pull away, but Sam tightened her grip in her hair. She wouldn't let Beth dictate who she could kiss, or when and where she did it. Just because she wasn't used to seeing Sam like this didn't mean she couldn't get used to it. She pressed her mouth firmly against Karen's, and tilted her head to the side so she could feel the delicious slide of Karen's lips against hers. She let the kiss end naturally and didn't stop Karen from lifting her head away.

She gave Karen one last quick peck on the mouth, tweaked her collar, and then released her. Karen stepped out of her embrace and turned to face Beth.

"Hey, squirt! Come over here and give me a hug."

Beth didn't hesitate to close the distance between them. "I missed you." She gave Karen a bracing hug and winked at Sam when it was over. She may have said she was disgusted, but the delighted look on her face betrayed her true feelings.

"Sorry I didn't get out here yesterday to say hi. Work."

Karen shrugged as if to say, "What can you do?"

Yesterday, Sam had been on the verge of a meltdown, so it was best that Karen hadn't been there to witness her falling apart.

"It's okay." Sam closed the refrigerator and leaned against the counter.

Karen glanced around the apartment. "So," she said, rueful. "This place is a disaster. What happened?"

Sam shook her head. "No idea. Beth thinks this is the leftover remnants of a high school party."

"Jesus. It didn't look like this when I drove past a few weeks ago."

That's right. She'd asked Karen to take a look, just to make sure the photos matched the property, but that was before she'd made the offer.

"Do you remember what day you did that?" With any luck, this information would help with the insurance company.

"Sure, I took photos." Karen pulled her phone from her back pocket and tapped the screen. "I sent them to you, remember?" A moment later, she turned it until Sam could see the display. Pictures of the Queen, time stamped and dated, scrolled past in a slideshow. They were from the week prior to Sam making her offer on the property. Perhaps helpful with establishing a timeline, but not definitive evidence that the damage happened after closing.

"You're right, I have those. Thanks."

She nodded. "Sure thing." She looped one arm around Beth's neck and said, "You guys hungry?" She motioned at the pizza.

"God, yes. Mom hasn't fed me all day."

"Hey, you're always telling me that you're old enough to take care of yourself, but now you expect me to feed you? You can't have it both ways, missy."

Beth poked out her tongue, but it didn't diminish her smile. She looked happy, and it felt wonderful. She'd have to convince Karen to stay if she continued to have this effect on Beth.

"Well, it's a good thing I showed up when I did. Eat." Karen flipped open the lid to the pizza box and revealed a large combination pizza. It smelled delicious and Sam became acutely aware of how hungry she was herself.

"We don't have plates yet. Sorry."

"Who cares?" Beth pulled a slice from the box and bit off the end before the strings of cheese had broken free. She swallowed quickly and took another bite. All joking aside, Sam felt guilty about not stopping to eat sooner.

"Slow down, there, squirt. Nobody's going to steal it from you."

Beth growled and tucked her face close to her body as if she was guarding the pizza. Sam laughed and the sound was so foreign, she startled herself. If she hadn't wanted to sleep with Karen before, she sure as hell did now.

Karen selected a piece of pizza and smiled at Sam as she took a bite. She stared for a moment, watching as Karen's lips closed around the tip of the pizza. She chewed slowly, swallowed, and then poked her tongue out to lick her lower lip. Sam was officially entranced.

"Oh, come on." Beth snorted. "Stop being gross already."

Karen laughed and took another bite, and Sam turned to the fridge. The heat of a blush crept up her face, and she hid it in the cool air as she pulled a beer from the carton for Karen.

"Here." She felt stupid saying something so pedestrian, but she couldn't think of anything that didn't sound equally asinine.

Instead of Karen, Beth swiped the bottle and twisted

the top off. She smiled wickedly at Sam and said, "Cheers."

Before Sam could react, she tipped the bottle back and took a long pull.

"Hold on, squirt." Karen laughed good-naturedly, but pulled the bottle from Beth's hand nonetheless.

Sam stared at her daughter. She was only fifteen, but already so much older than Sam had been at that age.

Surprisingly, Beth didn't protest the loss of the beer. She took another bite of pizza and laughed at something Karen said. Maybe it was her worst idea ever, but Sam pulled two more beers from the fridge, one for herself and one for Beth.

Beth took it from her with a small, serious smile. "Thanks, Mom."

With the way Beth looked at her, as if she wasn't quite sure she knew Sam as well as she thought, Sam thought perhaps it had been the right decision. Time would tell, she guessed.

"All right, you guys. Eat up. We need to get that paint if we ever plan to stop living in that other hotel and start living in this one."

"What other hotel? You guys should stay with me." Karen smiled.

"Really?" Sam gave her the opportunity to back out.

"Yeah."

"Okay. We will." She smiled.

As she took her first bite of pizza, Karen slipped her arm casually around her waist. With Karen's fingers tickling along her hip and the cool slide of cold beer mingled with hot cheesy sauce in her mouth, Sam relaxed for the first time in months. Beth tipped her bottle toward them, and in that moment, Sam thought they might just be okay.

Chapter Six

Sam awoke to the thick, rich aroma of dark coffee, and in the sleep-mulled minutes between dreams and consciousness, she imagined herself back home in Las Vegas. The bed dipped beside her a moment before she felt a light touch against her stomach, followed by the press of lips to the corner of her mouth.

"Good morning." Karen kissed the side of her neck, up high in that perfect spot behind her ear. She trailed her fingers lower, skimming Sam's thigh and circling inward. God, she could wake up like this every day.

"Mmm, morning." Sam let her legs fall open. Sure, she had things to do today, but the way Karen's hand was moving up her leg felt really nice. If Karen was in the mood again after last night, she wasn't going to stop her. She'd just hurry through her shower later.

Rather than taking her up on the offer, Karen laughed and lightly slapped her thigh. "The squirt's already up. She's pacing around the living room. Something about painting a wall?"

"Right." Sam climbed out of bed. Clearly she wouldn't get any more sleep. They'd picked up the paint on the way to Karen's apartment the night before. Beth hadn't stopped talking about her plans since they left the Queen. Frankly, she'd been surprised that Beth hadn't insisted on going back last night to get started. "I guess that means it's time to get in the shower."

"Sounds like." Karen was fully dressed, wearing a snug black T-shirt and a pair of faded blue jeans with a thick leather belt around her waist. She even had a pair of black boots on and laced up. She was ready to start her day.

"What time is it?" She turned on the shower to adjust the water temperature. While it warmed up, she brushed her teeth.

Karen leaned against the doorframe, her arms folded over her chest and her gaze focused on Sam's backside. Apparently, she didn't realize Sam could see her in the mirror.

"Hey," she said. "Do I need to get dressed in order for you to answer my question?"

Karen laughed. "It certainly wouldn't hurt. What was your question?"

"Time?"

Karen glanced at her watch. "Just after seven. What's on your agenda today?"

Sam sighed. "Call my insurance adjuster. Again. I sent the claim in yesterday. Now it's in review." Until he called back, she was in limbo. "And at some point, I have to go past the high school and register Beth for classes."

Before getting into the shower, she turned and pressed her lips to Karen's. If she'd known how good a kisser Karen was, she'd have started kissing her years ago. Karen laced their fingers together and held her in place when she went to retreat. Karen deepened the kiss, working her tongue inside Sam's mouth, and her fingers moved restlessly against the skin at her hip. By the time Karen released her, Sam was breathless and ready to forget her plans for the day.

Karen nudged her gently toward the shower. "What else?"

Sam huffed and stepped into the shower. The water was perfect. Exactly the right temperature, with amazing pressure. She had used the hotel showers in Vegas for years, and had forgotten what real water pressure felt like. She tipped her head under the spray and stood, enjoying the tingle as the water pelted her skin. Eventually, she adjusted the showerhead so that she could speak without getting a mouthful of water. "I'm going to call some local contractors for bids. There's no way I can do all that work myself."

"I'll help when I can." Karen had moved closer while Sam was under the water. "You know that."

"I appreciate it, but I'll need a contractor regardless. There's just too much work. And I don't want it to look like a do-it-yourself project." Sam lathered shampoo into her hair.

"I know a guy. I could have him stop by."

As they talked, Sam lathered her body, rinsed the shampoo and body soap away at the same time, and then applied conditioner. "What's his name?"

"Alan. He's a general contractor, so it would be a one-stop shop kind of deal. He can take care of everything."

"That'd be great. I'll be there all day."

"Okay. I'll call him."

Sam rinsed the conditioner out of her hair and turned off the water. Karen handed her a fluffy brown towel as she stepped out of the shower, and Sam wrapped it around herself.

"Before you go, we should talk." Karen gestured between the two of them. "About us."

Sam paused. Last night, she'd been sure they were in the same place. She thought of this encounter with Karen as a lark. A really fun lark that included a whole bunch of awesome orgasms, but a lark nonetheless. She didn't think they were suddenly going to exchange Letterman jackets and move in together. Looking at Karen now, however, she wondered if she'd misread the situation.

"What do you mean?" It wasn't really a fair question, but she wasn't sure how to head off the conversation before it went where she thought it was going.

Karen took her hand. She looked away then back again. "Sam, you know I love you, but..."

Sam laughed with relief. Thank God. Karen was worried about hurting her feelings, not harboring a secret obsession. "Jesus, you scared me. I thought you were going to say that you want a relationship."

"I do."

"Huh?" Shit, note to self, no laughing out loud until she was absolutely certain about what Karen was saying from now on.

"As my friend. I don't want that to change." Karen twisted their fingers together, massaging Sam's with her own.

She let out a breath. "Oh, Karen. I don't want anything to change, either. Last night was fun. A lot of fun. But I'm not insane. I'm not in love with you any more than you're in love with me. No amount of naked skin time is going to change that."

Karen pulled her into a hug and squeezed hard enough to make her gasp for breath. "Thank God. I should have been more clear last night, but you just looked so good yesterday with your hair falling down and those ridiculous yellow cleaning gloves. I had no idea I have a thing for housewives, but apparently I do."

"Ha! Or the cleaning lady." Sam had looked like crap yesterday and Karen thought that was hot, which didn't make any sense. Over the years, Karen had seen her looking really, really good. She'd managed one of the major hotel and casino properties on the strip, and that came with a high expectation about appearance. Karen hadn't looked twice when Sam had been dressed and made up as if she'd stepped out of a magazine photo shoot. Yet the first time Karen saw her looking as if she'd spent the day up to her elbows in grime, she couldn't control herself. It was beyond ridiculous. "You know you're crazy, right?"

Karen shrugged. "I don't care. I won't apologize for what I think is sexy."

Relieved that their relationship wasn't somehow damaged by their spontaneity the night before, Sam hugged Karen one more time and left the bathroom. She needed to get dressed, and that had been a really strange conversation to have over a toilet.

"You shouldn't apologize," Sam said as she pulled a clean pair of jeans and a T-shirt from her suitcase. "Frankly, I should thank you. I don't even want to think about how long it had been. Last night was awesome."

"A long time, huh?" Karen helped her fasten her bra, then smoothed her T-shirt into place. "How long?" She pulled Sam close, this embrace completely different than the relieved hug they'd shared earlier. She ran her hands over Sam's back, and Sam closed her eyes briefly and let herself enjoy Karen's touch.

"Not telling you. But I will say I'm not opposed to a repeat."

"Yeah?" Karen looked like a teenage boy who'd just gotten his first glimpse of naked boob and then been promised he could touch, too.

"Yeah. But not right now." Sam stepped out of Karen's arms and finished dressing. This situation had the potential to be disastrous, but it had worked out and she was really happy with the outcome. She got to keep her friend and still have an occasional orgasm. That was a win-win.

When they finally emerged from the bedroom, Beth rolled her eyes and handed Sam a coffee in a to-go cup. "Finally."

As they were leaving, Karen reminded her about her contractor friend. "I'll see if he can come by today."

"Sure." Sam saluted her with her coffee cup and headed toward her car. She was tired of living out of her suitcase, but at least this morning's wake-up call had been pretty damn nice.

But now it was time to go paint a wall.

"Lin—" Olly tried to interject, but as always, Linda cut her off. She massaged her temples and nodded along with the phone, trying to judge her mom's rhythm. She didn't want to miss her turn to jump back in. Rampart rested his head on her thigh and looked up at her. She stroked his fur. At least he was on her side.

"I just don't understand why you won't come, Olivia. The whole family will be there. It's a celebration." Her mom spoke with an ever-present performer's lilt. She lived, breathed, and survived based on her ability to convince people of her sincerity. Or perhaps Linda's success had more to do with the hypnotic lull induced by the rhythm and cadence of her voice rather than actual trust. Regardless, Olly was immune to it.

"I don't want to reunite with two hundred of my relatives. I don't even know any of them." The thought of taking part in her mother's family reunion made her skin crawl.

Linda made a noise of disapproval. "Your heart knows them. They are family. Not to mention, your sister misses you."

She sighed. "No, she doesn't. I talked with her last week. She's fine."

In truth, Gen had begged Olly to come visit, but Linda probably didn't know that.

Bitterroot Queen

"Okay, fine. *I* miss you."

Olly didn't respond. This was why she rarely called her mom. Navigating a clear path through a militarized minefield would be easier than navigating all the traps in a conversation with Linda Jones.

"Don't pout, Olivia. It's not becoming."

"Linda, I'm not coming. Period."

"Fine. But you'll have to come home someday. You can't stay away forever."

"Watch me," Olly said under her breath.

Linda inhaled sharply, but remained silent. After a long, drawn out silence, Olly finally gave in. "Mom? Are you still there?"

"I'm here, darling." Her mom drew in a deep breath. "Tell me where you are now. I haven't gotten one of your charming little postcards in a few weeks, so I've no idea where to place you on the map."

"Northern Idaho." She didn't offer details because the only thing Linda cared about was that Olly wasn't where she wanted her.

"Idaho? What could you possibly be doing in Idaho, northern or otherwise?" Linda added just a little bit of judgment to her tone, and Olly almost laughed. One of the constant lessons of Olly's childhood—and there were always lessons—was to never make assumptions or underestimate the value of a place without first investigating.

"Not much." Olly had made the mistake of talking a town up shortly after she left home. Linda had shown up a few days later to see for herself. Another lesson learned.

"Come home. You can do 'not much' right here in New York and be with family in the process." Linda currently lived in the town where Olly had spent most of her childhood. She wasn't raised there, exactly. That happened in too many places to count, little towns up and down the Eastern Seaboard.

"Why do you want me to visit so badly?"

"I'm worried about your sister. She's barely speaking to me." The performance dropped out of Linda's voice, and she sounded uncharacteristically vulnerable.

"Shouldn't you talk to Gen about that?"

"Perhaps, but I'm talking to you about it instead."

"I'm sorry, but I really can't help you." Olly barely tolerated a phone call with Linda every other week. There was no way she could convince her older sister to do otherwise when she wasn't willing to herself.

"So, what in Idaho is more important than family?" Linda asked, the performance back in her voice. That was her standard. When she hit a wall, she changed tactics.

"Linda, I'm not coming to New York."

"What are you doing for money?"

"I'm building shelves."

"Right now?"

"No." Olly rolled her eyes. She could never tell if her mom was purposefully obtuse or if she really was just a little dumb at times. "I'm doing it for a local business. It's just a few days of work."

"You're doing odd jobs? How quaint."

Olly snorted, but didn't respond. She never expected Linda to approve.

"Have you forgotten everything I taught you? You are far too talented to be doing odd jobs."

Before Olly could respond, someone knocked on her window. The noise startled her so badly, she dropped the phone. A woman stood next to her Scout, yelling and nailing Olly's window with her keys. In her other hand, she held a canister of pepper spray. Her eyes were wide open, filled with frustration, perhaps a bit of fear, and a whole lot of fierce anger. Her hair flew around her face in a wild, auburn halo. She was scary as hell and perfectly beautiful and sexy all at the same time. For a moment, Olly was stunned into silence.

Olly held up her hand in a gesture she hoped said "hello," along with "calm the fuck down before you set that thing off accidentally." The woman, however, didn't look like she understood Olly's message. She raised the pepper spray and pointed it at Olly. What the hell? Did she plan to spray her through the window?

"Olivia? Olivia? Where did you go?" Her mom's voice was small and tinny through the phone. Frankly, Olly was surprised she could hear her at all.

She kept her gaze on the woman as she reached slowly for her phone. "Linda, I have to call you back." She disconnected the call even though her mother protested emphatically that she do the opposite. She set the phone on her dash and rested her hand on Rampart's head. He watched the woman outside the Scout warily, but so far didn't show any signs of being aggressive. He wagged his tale and continued to watch. So much for the watchdog she'd hoped he'd be when she'd rescued him in New Orleans.

On the upside, the woman had stopped banging on the window. Olly debated rolling the window down, but she didn't want to risk getting pepper sprayed. That would piss her off. She didn't know how the woman would react if she opened the door, but it was better than her upholstery retaining that nasty-pepper funk for the indefinite future.

Olly gestured at the door. "I'm coming out." She said it loud, bordering on a shout, but she wanted to make sure the woman understood. Rampart stood and licked her cheek. Olly smiled despite herself.

As she disengaged the lock, Olly noticed the woman wasn't alone. Behind her, looking more amused than frightened, a teenaged girl leaned against the side of the motel. She raised an eyebrow when Olly looked her way. Then, with a deliberate smile, she lit a cigarette and gestured for Olly to continue her interaction with the crazy woman at her window.

The day had started so simply. She woke up, called her mom, and planned to go to Bitter Ink to finish her work there. At some point, when she wasn't paying attention, everything took a sharp left. Now here she was with a lunatic glaring at her and trying to break her window with her keys.

Olly waved at the other woman and offered a tentative smile, hoping to show that she wasn't dangerous. The woman with the pepper spray pointed it at her with a menacing scowl. She definitely didn't return the smile or the wave. Great. If Bitterroot were a bigger town, Olly could simply start the Scout and drive away. But it wasn't. This town was more a village. A tiny, isolated, mountainside village where everybody knew everybody.

Rampart whimpered and nudged her in the shoulder with his nose. "I know, buddy." She rested her hand on his head again. With a sigh, she reached for the door handle. "Let's get this over with."

Olly moved slowly and deliberately, telegraphing her movements. As the door swung open, the woman took a few steps back, tripped, and then regained her footing.

The teenager laughed outright and said, "Mom, you're going to hurt yourself."

"Be quiet, Beth. Go inside," the woman said, confirming that she was the girl's mom. Not that it made a difference to Olly, but sometimes bits of information like that proved helpful.

Bitterroot Queen

Beth laughed again and a staccato streak of blue-black smoke escaped her mouth as she did. "This isn't your vandal. Seriously, Mom, you're acting like a crazy person."

Olly stepped to the side so she could close the door to her Scout. At least that way, if the woman sprayed her, she wouldn't get Rampart or the inside of her vehicle. She hoped. The soft-top was waterproof, but she didn't know if that protection extended to lung-piercing chemicals. Before she could close the door, however, Rampart jumped out.

He stood next to her for a moment, gave her a curious, head-tilted look, then walked over and sat next to the smoking girl. The girl laughed even harder and sank down next to him on the sidewalk. Rampart leaned against her, and she looped her arm around his neck. "See, even the dog thinks you're crazy."

"His name is Rampart." Olly knew she sounded like an ass as soon as she said it. Of all the ridiculous things to say. The kid found the whole thing amusing, but her mother looked dangerously close to pulling the trigger on the pepper spray. Her finger twitched and Olly really wanted her to lower the can. And what was the first thing she said? Christ. She took a breath and tried to salvage her dignity. "And I'm Olly."

She extended her hand in greeting, not really expecting the woman to accept the offer. Unsurprisingly, she didn't. After a few moments, Olly dropped her hand.

"What are you doing here?" the woman asked.

"Huh?" Why would she care if Olly called home or not? "Talking on the phone." Olly's voice rose at the end, turning a simple statement into a question. She did a mental face-palm. This was not going well.

The woman shook her head. "That's not what I meant. You're trespassing. What are you doing here?" She emphasized the last word with a desperation that didn't match the circumstances. Clearly Olly was missing something.

"Oh...um...I kinda...I'm new to the area and I haven't found a place to stay yet." Olly scratched the back of her neck. She hated explaining things like this. She didn't care if she spent a couple of nights in her Scout, but everyone else seemed to care. A lot. She gestured to her vehicle behind her. "So, I slept in here last night. I didn't figure it would matter since the place is abandoned."

And then it clicked. The motel might have been abandoned before, but it no longer was. This woman was probably the new owner. Olly looked at the building. Scrawls of graffiti covered the faded paint, and several windows were broken. No wonder she wanted to pepper spray whoever did this. Except Olly wasn't that person.

As if to confirm her thought, the woman asked, "Why wouldn't I care? Of course I care." As she talked, she gestured wildly with her hands, the canister of pepper spray flying erratically in front of Olly's face. Olly stepped to the side to decrease the chance of getting hit accidentally. On the upside, the woman had taken her finger from the trigger.

"I'm sorry," she said, amazed that she didn't stammer. "I thought the place was abandoned. Clearly, it's not."

"That's right. It's not."

"Right. So, I'll just go." Olly jerked her thumb toward the driver's side door. "And let you do...whatever it is you do here."

She snapped her fingers for Rampart as she reached for the door handle. Rampart stayed put and leaned closer to Beth. Olly stared at him. She'd never seen him do anything like that before. Traitor.

"What kind of name is Olly?" Beth gestured at her with her cigarette.

Olly shrugged. "What kind of name is Beth?"

"Touché." Beth raised her eyebrow, clearly amused once again.

Olly snapped her fingers again. "Rampart. Now," she said sharply. Rampart licked the side of Beth's face, then trotted back to Olly. She opened the door, and he jumped inside. Olly followed.

The woman stopped her before she could get the key into the ignition. "You can't sleep here. I'll call the police if I see you again."

Olly saluted her. She didn't like being treated like trash. It felt far too familiar. She had worked her whole life trying to escape that feeling. She did everything she could to not be a person who deserved suspicion. But here she was, faced with the same derisive judgment that had defined much of her childhood. Nonetheless, she smiled as she said, "Not a problem."

When she pulled out, Beth was still sitting against the building, laughing. Olly shook her head as she turned onto the highway. Her priority for the day was set. At some point, she needed to find a place to stay. A place that wasn't the back seat of her Scout in the parking lot of the Bitterroot Queen.

Chapter Seven

Olly stared at the notice board in the town square. The market wasn't open and the day was quiet except for a woman in a nearby office talking on the phone. Either the person on the other end was deaf already or would be soon if the conversation continued much longer. A sign at the top of the board said the market only opened on weekends.

She found three cards advertising places for rent. The first was a two-bedroom apartment for six-fifty a month. A steal in most cities, but more room than Olly needed and more money than she wanted to spend. The second was a house by the university. Three students looking for a fourth. And the third one specified no dogs. She patted Rampart on the head. "This is a bust, huh?"

Rampart wagged his tail and smiled at her. He wasn't bothered in the least by their precarious living situation, but he hadn't been threatened with pepper spray and he even made a new friend out of the whole thing.

She checked the time on her phone. Bitter Ink opened in five minutes. "Come on, Rampart. We'll figure this out later."

The neon "open" sign was already lit and the front door propped open when Olly arrived. A burley, lumberjack-type guy sat in the barber chair with his shirt off. Ava sat on a stool to his right, tattooing a baby's face on his ribcage. Occasionally, she looked at a photo that was affixed to the man's chest with masking tape. She

Bitterroot Queen

wore thick-rimmed, red reading glasses and her brow was furrowed.

Olly double-checked the time. No, she wasn't late. She watched Ava work for a moment. The man's face was screwed up in a grimace, but he sat perfectly still, which was impressive. She had enough tattoos, including the script on her ribs, to know how badly that area hurt. She didn't want to interrupt, but she needed to let Ava know she had arrived.

Rampart nudged her hand with his nose. He was ready to get back to his courtyard. Ava lifted the tattoo gun a fraction away from the man's side and pushed her hair out of her face with her other arm. When she turned to gather more ink, Olly said, "Hey, nice work."

Ava raised her head, her smile already in place. "Hey, you're here. I should have told you I was opening early. Boomer is leaving later today, so it was now or never."

"Not never." Boomer grinned. "Now or four weeks from now when I come back around."

Ava nodded. "Right. And we couldn't take the chance that you'd cheat on me while you're on the road."

They both laughed, and Olly decided that was her cue to head to the back. "I just wanted to check in. I'll go ahead and get to work now."

"Sure. I'll come back when I'm done."

Olly made it three steps before Ava spoke again.

"Oh, hey, you don't know Boomer, do you? Boomer, this is Olly. Olly, Boomer."

Olly turned around. She hated the formality of introductions because they felt orchestrated and false. Still, she grasped Boomer's outstretched hand and said, "Nice to meet you."

"New to Bitterroot, are ya?" Boomer had a crazy strong

grip, and Olly wasn't sure if it was normal or if she was being tested in some way. Some men did crap like that.

Olly nodded and tried to smile.

"Well, welcome." He finally released her. "I'll see you around."

"Thanks, I'll watch for you, too." Not that she would be able to miss him. Boomer was massive. She pointed to the tattoo in progress. "Really nice work."

"Yeah, isn't she great?" Boomer poked Ava, and she rocked back on her stool. Olly decided his grip was natural, not a form of intimidation. He sat forward and twisted to give Olly a view of his back. "She did all of mine. No matter what she just said, she knows I won't go to anyone else."

His back was covered with several traditional Japanese-style tattoos. Two koi circling each other in a classic yin-yang formation on the left shoulder. On his right, a samurai ready for combat with a field of golden bamboo behind him. And in the center, covering the majority of his back, a tiger and a dragon locked in battle. The lines were delicate and precise, the color bold and unmistakable. Ava was very, very good at her job.

"Nice." Work that good deserved recognition and respect. Traditional Japanese was a difficult style to master, and from what Olly could see, the portrait looked as good if not better. "Ava, what's your specialty?"

Ava shrugged. "I do everything, but I really like American traditional. And pinups are my favorite. I think." She smiled. "At least it is this week. Ask me next week and I'll probably have a different answer."

Olly planned to get a pinup eventually, but hadn't found the right artist yet. Before she left Bitterroot, maybe she should spend some time in Ava's chair. But first, she needed to finish the back room. She'd already wasted too much time if she wanted to finish early enough to search for a place to stay. Maybe the Red Barn Market would let her park in their side lot.

Ava dipped the tip of her tattoo gun into her ink cup, a sure sign she was ready to work again. Before she engaged the foot pedal, Boomer said, "No matter what you want, I promise Ava's the best one to do it."

"I believe it. I'm going to get to work. It was nice meeting you, Boomer. Thanks for letting me interrupt your session."

Boomer's response faded beneath the sound of Ava's tattoo gun sparking back to life. Olly smiled and nodded and patted her leg to let Rampart know they were moving. He stayed at her side until they reached the office area. The courtyard door was propped open. Rampart paused, looked at her, then at the courtyard. Olly patted his head and said, "Go on, then."

He ran outside, and she went to work in the storage room.

She'd completed the framework, plus the majority of the flat surfaces on the work side of the storage room. Today her goal was to finish and move all the items to the right side. She was almost out of MDF, the flat boards that had been sitting beneath that tarp. If she didn't make any mistakes, though, it would be enough to take her through this side.

Since Ava had a customer, Olly left the radio off. Boomer looked like the kind of guy who probably liked hard, fast metal, but she didn't want to take the chance. The construction sounds were annoying enough without her adding another layer of noise to the mêlée. She worked steadily, using the constant thrum of Ava's tattoo gun to guide her pace. It was different without the heavy drumbeat in her ears, but she made do. By the time Ava finished the tattoo and sent Boomer on his way, Olly had completed the first set of shelving, moved all the items to the opposite side of the room, and started on the framework for the second side. She had one piece of MDF left. Not enough to finish the job, but she had plenty of two-by-three studs to finish the bones before breaking to get more materials.

Ava popped her head in and whistled. "Looking good."

"Thanks. I'm actually surprised I haven't made better progress. It took me longer than expected to move everything around."

It might have been better that it was taking longer than estimated since she still hadn't discussed her rate with Ava and couldn't quite figure out how to bring it up. Usually, she had a much easier time, but Ava's rhythm and moods weren't easy to pin down. There was no possible way that someone was that happy all the time. Especially not with two young children at home.

"Valentina is supposed to be here any minute. I'm excited to show her your progress." Ava smiled in that generous way she had that made Olly feel special to have earned it, yet equally sure there was more behind it that Ava wasn't sharing.

"Why?" Olly cringed at her own bluntness. "Sorry, that's not really my business."

"Why, what? Why do I want to show her the shelves? Or why does she want to meet you?" Ava asked.

Olly stood the piece of MDF she was holding on the floor, holding it near her like a surfboard. "Why does she want to meet—" Before she could finish the question, two little blond girls—miniature versions of Ava, complete with the bright blue eyes and the casual grace—ran in and hugged Ava's legs. The younger one wobbled as she moved but didn't fall.

"Mommy! Mommy!" They yelled excitedly and bounced up and down.

Olly had spent very little time around children and was caught off guard by how much volume such tiny people produced. No wonder her music hadn't bothered Ava.

Ava picked them both up and swung them around with a laugh. Both girls squealed and begged for more. As she finished the second spin, a stunning Latina woman slipped her arm around Ava's waist, kissed her cheek, and took the youngest girl into her own arms.

"Hi, *mi amor*." Valentina's voice was as smooth and silky as her long dark hair.

"You made it." Ava returned the kiss to her wife's cheek, the placement a little lower and lingering, but with the same warm casualness. "I was beginning to worry."

"These two were painting pictures in daycare. I let them finish."

"Ah, yes, my little Kahlos."

"O'Keeffes," Valentina argued.

Olly had no idea what either of them meant, so she just smiled and debated going back to work.

Ava laughed. "No way are my children going to paint vaginal orchids. Not if I have anything at all to do with it."

"And grotesque mono-brow self-portraits are somehow better?"

"Infinitely." Ava nodded as if to say the subject was closed and she was thankful her wife finally saw things her way. Valentina simply shook her head and smiled. Clearly, this argument was as familiar as the rest of their relationship.

Rampart's nails clicked against the tile floor in the back room. Apparently, he'd grown tired of resting in the sun on the patio and had come in to check out what was going on. He sat behind Ava and Valentina, who were blocking the door, and looked at Olly balefully. It was quite pathetic, and Olly signaled with her hand that he should wait where he was and not charge through their legs to get to her. He sighed and dropped to the floor, his head on his paws.

The girls noticed Rampart and squealed. "A puppy! Look at the puppy! Let me pet the puppy, Mommy." They both wiggled, trying to get to within petting distance of Rampart.

Rampart lifted his ears as if assessing this new noise, but didn't move otherwise.

"Is it okay, Olly?" Ava asked, rather than simply plopping the girls down on top of Rampart. Olly appreciated that.

"Sure. He loves kids." And he did. Olly didn't know Rampart's history. She'd found him battered and far too thin, limping along a brutal section of the Ninth Ward in New Orleans a few years ago. She'd spent a good thirty minutes convincing him to trust her. He ate and drank what she had to offer, and then she'd coaxed him back to the craptastic little flat on North Rampart where she'd been crashing.

He was too weak to climb the stairs by himself, so she'd waited until he was comfortable enough to let her carry him. A few days later, they'd hit the road together and been together ever since. Olly was convinced he'd belonged to a family with lots of children at one point or another, because he loved them. He was patient and sweet and never reacted to little hands that abruptly pulled his hair. She imagined he would make an excellent babysitter. Not that she was likely to ever need one.

Ava and Valentina set the girls on the floor and they both jumped on Rampart, wrapping their arms around his neck in a tight hug. Rampart sighed, licked the baby's cheek, and rested a paw on the older girl's knee.

"Well, that's Rampart," Ava said. "And this is Olly."

Valentina stepped forward and offered Olly her hand. "I'm Valentina, Ava's wife."

They shook hands, and Olly mumbled something semi-appropriate.

"And why did you want to meet her, honey?" Ava egged her on, complete with a slight elbow jab to the side.

"Oh, that." Valentina smiled. The kind of smile that was slow and sultry and far too sexy for a storage room surrounded by two little kids and a dog. And she was smiling at Ava. Those two were clearly smitten with each other. Olly had never been smitten, but she was only twenty-five. Plenty of time for that to happen. Valentina turned her gaze to Olly. "Ava's been promising forever to add shelves to the storage room. I came by to see who is actually making good on the promise for her."

"Take a look. See what you think of the space."

Valentina settled her arm loosely around Ava's waist and said, "That's not necessary. We'll let you get back to work."

Olly felt like a voyeur. As beautiful as Ava was normally, it was magnified tenfold when she gazed at Valentina. Olly felt a sharp jab of...something. Not jealousy, exactly, because, beauty aside, neither woman spoke to her heart. They clearly belonged with one another.

Longing. That's what it was. She longed to find that connection, to meet the person who would complete her heart and make her whole for the first time in her life. She shook her head and picked up her board. Maybe one day she'd have that, but for now it did her no good to dwell on it.

"Olly," Valentina said. "At some point Ava is going to invite you to dinner with our family. I hope you'll accept."

Olly nodded. "Thank you," she said, unsure what the protocol was for an almost-dinner invitation.

Valentina smiled briefly, then turned away. She rested her palm flat against Ava's chest, just over her breast. "Walk me out?"

"Of course."

They left, and the girls followed. Rampart joined Olly in the storage room and nudged her hand with his nose. She rubbed his head affectionately. "Thanks, Ramp."

It sounded completely logical when the sales clerk recommended she buy the primer in five-gallon buckets. Every single wall in the Queen needed to be painted—and some needed to be firebombed—and there was a decent price break buying the larger container. It stopped making sense when Sam tried to lift the containers out of the back of her car. She was used to supervising and pointing at things that needed to be moved, not actually moving them herself. With Beth's help, they got the first bucket inside. She left the second in the trunk of her car. Maybe Karen could move it later. She was strong.

"Mom, not so much. You're dripping." Beth took her roller and demonstrated the correct technique. "Remember, less paint and move your arm up and down in a 'v' pattern, like this."

"Okay, okay," Sam grumbled, but she smiled. Their roles had somewhere reversed and now she was taking orders from Beth. But this was a different Beth than normal. She had a gift and took it seriously. All the disrespect, defiance, and wildness yielded to this beautiful, controlled, driven young woman. It was a powerful glimpse of who Beth might become in the future and it made Sam damn proud.

"Are you sure? I don't want you to fuck it up." Beth held the roller just out of Sam's reach.

Sam arched an eyebrow and crossed her arms. She stared at Beth, giving her a chance to realize what she'd just said. Beth crossed lines all the time, but dropping the f-bomb casually in front of Sam was new.

Beth's face went from confused to shocked to apprehensive. "Shit, I'm sorry." She clamped her hand over her mouth. "I did it again. Seriously, I'm so sorry."

Well, that reaction was new, too. Normally Beth was all bluster. If Sam didn't like it, too damn bad. But an apology? Completely unexpected. And Beth looked as if she meant it. Sam reached out for the roller and said, "I'll be careful."

Beth smiled, confusion still clear on her face. "Thanks." The word curled up at the end like a question instead of a statement, and Sam almost laughed. But then Beth gave her the roller and returned to her own wall where the beginnings of her mural were starting to take shape, leaving Sam to figure out what just happened on her own.

Maybe if she'd given Beth a little more room and not dropped on her like a hammer the second she did something wrong, Beth wouldn't have fought her so hard.

Sam gathered some paint on her roller and started again. They painted in silence long enough for her to finish the wall and move on to the next. She left the trim for later. Maybe she'd be able to convince Beth to do that part with a brush. It required greater precision and Sam was likely to make a mess of it.

"Hey, Mom," Beth said, quieter than normal.

"Yeah, sweetie?" Sam concentrated on making perfect, beige-colored "v" strokes with her roller.

"I was thinking about school..." Beth's voice trailed off.

"Oh." Sam stopped painting and turned toward Beth. She checked her watch. "I know I promised to take you today, but I didn't realize how long this would take. We'll go tomorrow, okay?" She really was a bad parent. She'd forgotten all about registering Beth for classes today.

"No, that's just it. Maybe we shouldn't go there at all." Beth bit her lip.

"What do you mean?" Sam didn't understand where Beth was going, but she had a sinking feeling she wouldn't like it.

"It's just...I'll be sixteen in a few weeks and then—"

"Stop right there. You are not dropping out of school. You will graduate and then you will go to college. This is not up for discussion."

"But I don't know any of these people, Mom. It's going to suck." Beth's voice took on the old familiar, defiant whine.

Sam turned her attention back to her wall. "That doesn't change the fact that it's going to happen. Lots of things suck. You don't get to skip them."

"I don't think I can do it." Beth spoke so softly that Sam almost didn't hear her.

She slowed her motions, but didn't stop painting. "You can do anything, Beth. You're strong and capable. Always have been." She replied with a sure, steady voice. Beth needed to understand this basic truth about herself. That kind of doubt could be debilitating. It could wind a person up until it ate away all the strength and capability.

Beth sighed. "I'm going outside."

Sam didn't look because she didn't want to watch Beth light another cigarette. She'd watched her mom and dad smoke, watched them struggle to quit, and watched as their quality of life deteriorated. She didn't want that for Beth's future, but still didn't know how to stop it. Beth was determined to make her own mistakes, and all Sam could do was be there to catch her if she fell.

"Hey, it's like a morgue in here. Why so quiet?" Karen came in from the lobby, her stride bordered on a strut, and she gave Sam a small, sexy smile.

"Hi. I'm practicing my 'v.'" She gestured at the wall. "Alan is meeting me. He should be here any minute."

"Good to know. What's up with Beth?" Karen asked.

"She's taking a break," Sam said.

"Got it." Karen didn't stop until she was close enough to kiss Sam casually on the mouth. She whispered, "Paint is a good look on you, too."

Sam laughed. Karen had some fabulously simple triggers. Her only regret was not figuring it out sooner. If not for Beth sulking on the patio, Sam would have demonstrated just how good a look paint really was on her.

Beth was sitting on the edge of the patio, knees curled up to her chest, head down. She rocked in place as she talked on her cell phone. A telltale curl of smoke rose into the air in front of her.

Sam crossed the room to the open sliding glass door. She paused when she heard Beth's voice.

"Denmar, I need your help." Beth sniffled.

Was Beth still plotting to return to Vegas? Frustration and irritation grew in Sam's chest, and she took a deep breath. She'd thought they were making progress, her and Beth. It stung to realize she'd misunderstood.

"Don't do this. Please," Beth whispered, a desperate plaintive quality to her voice. "You promised—" Beth stopped abruptly, then muttered, "Asshole." She dropped her phone in her lap, and her shoulders shook. She cried quietly, a muted sob.

Sam sighed, her stomach clenching. Whatever Beth was trying to plan with Denmar couldn't be a good idea, but there was no way Beth was ready to hear that and there was no way she was going to share it with her. She tapped the glass before sliding the door open. The patio was small, just a few steps from the door to the edge. Eventually, she planned to extend it. The view was spectacular, and she wanted to spend as much of her future as possible enjoying it. She didn't speak as she approached Beth and stood at her side. After a moment, she lowered herself to sit next to Beth.

The cigarette was burnt down to the filter with a long, precarious ash barely hanging on. Sam gently plucked it from Beth's fingers and crushed it out on the cement edge of the patio. Then she wrapped her daughter into a hug and held her. Sam rubbed her back and held her tight and made all the comforting noises that meant nothing, but also meant everything at the same time.

Eventually, Beth quieted. She pulled away and wiped at her eyes with her hands. Black mascara streaked her face, and she looked like a tragic, sad panda as she drew in a heavy breath. She released it with a shuddering sigh and said, "Thanks, Mom."

"You want to tell me about it?" Sam asked, keeping her voice as soft and gentle as possible.

"Hey, Karen. You were right. The place was easy to find," a man said, interrupting the moment.

Beth's eyes widened, and she shook her head. "No. I'm okay." She abruptly stood and brushed off her jeans. She stuffed her phone into her pocket and said, "I should get back to work."

Sam nodded and didn't push. She followed Beth inside and introduced herself. "Hi. You must be Alan."

"I am. And you're obviously Sam." He smiled.

"Nice to meet you." Sam held up her paint-speckled hands. "I'd shake your hand, but..."

"No worries. Karen said you need some work done. I'd like to give you a bid. Do you have time to walk me through now? Or should we make an appointment for another time?"

"Sure. Let me give you the tour. Beth, do you want to come with?"

Beth pointed at the wall. "I'm good."

"Yes, you are," Sam said, trying to be reassuring.

Beth rolled her eyes. "Mom..." Her face flushed pink, but she also smiled.

"What about you?" Sam asked Karen.

"I can stay with Beth. Paint a wall. Or something."

"You don't want to go with us?" Sam asked, surprised.

Karen shrugged. "Beth looks like maybe she needs me more."

"Fair enough. Beth, teach her that 'v' thing or something."

Alan picked up his clipboard with a smile and followed Sam.

As she crossed the office, Sam glanced back at Beth. She was back at her wall, her face serious and contemplative. Maybe Karen would convince her to talk, but Sam doubted it. Beth looked as if she'd put away whatever bothered her, at least for now. Sam tried to do the same as she led Alan on his tour of the Queen.

Chapter Eight

The next morning, after stopping for coffee on the way from Karen's to the Queen, Sam stood at the kitchen counter, sipping and reviewing her list for the day. The technician was scheduled to set up the internet and phone, the storage pod should arrive sometime after noon, and the insurance adjuster damn well needed to call her back. She'd turned in the form, along with all her supporting documentation two days ago. She'd give the guy until noon. If she hadn't heard by then, she'd call him again.

"What's your plan for today?" she asked Beth.

"Wall." Beth studied the blank space intently, clearly seeing something Sam couldn't.

"What is it going to be?"

Beth half-smiled. "You'll see."

"Hmm." Sam drank her coffee faster than normal. Her list didn't include time for her to savor it.

"What about you?" Beth pulled her hair into a ponytail and slipped on an oversized men's dress shirt that she liked to wear when she painted. It was covered with splotches of color.

"This morning, I paint." Sam finished her coffee and pushed up her sleeves.

It was their third morning in Bitterroot, and Sam was stuck in some sort of hellish limbo. Everything hinged on the insurance. She couldn't start work until she hired the contractor, and she couldn't hire the contractor until she heard from the insurance company. Until then, her only option was to continue cleaning and hope that beneath the grime was the dream property she'd thought she'd purchased.

"We really need to get to the school today," Sam said on her way to her bedroom. They'd finished priming the walls in the living room and kitchen.

Beth's shoulders stiffened. "Sure."

New schools sucked. Sam remembered that much, but they were unavoidable. For her, she'd switched schools every few years when her dad had gotten new orders. It had been a part of her childhood routine, as inevitable as homework and afternoon chores.

Sam made good progress with the primer, covering the walls and leaving the corners and edges for last. When she finished the last wall, she wrapped the roller in plastic wrap to keep the paint fresh until she moved into Beth's room.

"Mom," Beth called from the front room.

Sam stretched the muscles in her back, neck, and shoulders. It was definitely time for a break. "What's up?"

"That guy is here."

That guy? After she figured out what that meant, she'd review basic manners with Beth. As she entered the living room, she shot Beth a look. The effect was lost on Beth as she stood with her back to Sam, staring intently at the wall, paintbrush in hand.

The guy turned out to be Alan, construction bid in hand. "Sorry to drop by unannounced, but I thought you'd prefer to get this sooner rather than later."

Sam wiped her hands on her jeans on her way to the kitchen where Alan stood. He handed her a thick manila folder.

"Thanks."

Alan shifted from one foot to the other, but didn't move toward the exit. He darted a glance at Sam and then said, "So, what's the deal with you and Karen?"

Sam smiled, a reflex born of years of responding to seemingly innocent questions from hotel guests in Vegas. "What do you mean?"

He met her gaze, his eyes overly sincere and curious. "She said you're single, but I saw you guys kissing."

Sam shrugged. "I like to kiss her."

"But you're single?"

Sam nodded slowly. "Yes." This was interesting. Sure, she and Karen agreed that whatever they were doing together, it was casual and definitely held no romantic promises. No strings beyond the entanglements of friendship. But that didn't mean she was ready to jump into someone else's bed, regardless of how bulgy his biceps were.

"Can I take you out for dinner?" he asked with a hopeful smile.

Beth laughed, a sharp, short bark, followed by a muffled snicker. "Is he asking you on a date?"

"Yes," Sam looked at Beth.

Alan smiled wide. "Awesome. Saturday?"

What the hell? Sam retraced their conversation, trying to figure out when it had gone completely off the rails. When she'd said yes to Beth, Alan must have thought she was answering him. There was no graceful way to back out now.

Sam nodded slowly. "I can do that."

Alan smiled. "It's a date. I'll pick you up here at six."

After he left, Beth finally turned to face Sam and said, "You're kidding, right?"

"What was I supposed to say?" Sam threw up her hands in frustration.

"How about 'no'?"

"Why? You date. Why can't I? Is there an age limit?"

"No, of course not. But what about Karen?"

"What about her? Karen and I are friends. Nothing more." The words felt false as Sam said them.

"Really?" Beth arched an eyebrow. "Just friends."

Her face flushed with heat. "Yes."

Beth sighed and shook her head. "That's messed up, Mom." She turned to face the wall once more.

"Beth." Sam pushed her hands through her hair. Things with Karen were simple, easy, and fun. Somehow, with a few words, Alan and Beth had made it decidedly more complicated. "It's not like that."

"Like what?" Beth asked, her tone guarded and far too mature.

"Whatever you think Karen and I have together, we don't." She eased her way closer, but left a few feet between them.

"So you're not fucking?"

"Beth, language," Sam scolded sharply.

"Don't change the subject. I know you have been, so why would you act like it's nothing?"

"It's not nothing." Sam paused, trying to order her thoughts in a way that might make sense to Beth. "But it's not what you want it to be, either."

"But it could be." Beth whipped around, her face drawn tight with anguish. "She's good for you. Good for us. I like her."

"That's good. Karen isn't going to disappear if I go to dinner with Alan."

"You don't know that."

"Oh, Beth." Sam stopped trying to convince her and instead pulled her into a hug. At first, Beth resisted, holding her body stiff and unforgiving. Then, with a sob, she collapsed into Sam's embrace.

"I just... It doesn't suck having her around."

Sam held her, stroked her hair, and made soft sounds meant to be comforting. How had they gone from Beth up early, excited to work on her mural, to this?

Eventually, Beth calmed. She pulled away, sucked in a deep breath, and swiped her hand over her nose with a sniff. "I'm okay."

"What was that about? Can you tell me?" Sam reached out for Beth, then withdrew her hand. Beth had already shrunk back into herself.

Beth shook her head, tight, quick motions that hurt Sam with their finality.

"Nothing. I'm fine. What's the bid say?"

Sam forced herself to smile. "Right. The bid." She'd forgotten all about the envelope still in her hand. She slipped the document out and stared, shocked by the total at the bottom of the page: $712,394.63. No wonder Alan wanted to take her out to dinner.

"Jesus, is that for real?" Beth tapped the bid sheet just below the sum.

Sam glanced at her daughter and nodded, then returned her focus to the page. She couldn't stop looking at it. Seven hundred and twelve thousand, plus change. More than half the expense went to labor. She read through the itemized list carefully and everything seemed in order. Nothing was exaggerated or blown out of proportion. It just added up in a way she hadn't anticipated. She set the paper on the counter and sighed.

"Thank God for the insurance, huh?" Beth returned to her wall. Images had started to take shape, a face here, birds in flight there, but Sam still couldn't visualize the final product.

"Yeah, the insurance..." She glanced at the time. Another thirty minutes, and then she'd call. "For now, though, why don't you clean your brushes? Karen will be here any minute with lunch."

"Mmm-kay." Beth added another broad swipe of paint. Sam left her to it. Eventually she'd get hungry enough to stop.

Rather than return to her cleaning, Sam reviewed the construction bid more closely. It included windows, doors, carpet, insulation, paint, sheetrock—all of it necessary, and all expensive. A few minutes later, a paper bag labeled Bitterroot Deli dropped onto the counter in front of her. Karen and lunch had just arrived. She looked up.

"Hi." Yesterday, she would have greeted Karen with a kiss, in keeping with the new, fun physical component of their relationship. But now she felt weird about it. She smiled invitingly and waited to see what Karen would do.

"Hey," Karen said with an easy, sexy smile, followed by a light kiss on the mouth that quickly grew into more.

"Why the hell did you tell Alan that Mom is single?" Beth interrupted, her timing, as always, impeccable.

Karen gave her one last fleeting kiss and squeezed her hand before stepping away. As she pulled sandwiches from the bag, she said, "Because she is single, Beth."

"He asked her out to dinner," Beth said, her voice flat and heavy.

"He did?" Karen glanced up.

"Yeah. And she accepted."

This time Karen looked at Sam. "You did?"

Sam shrugged. "Not on purpose."

"He's a nice guy. You'll like him." Karen peeled the parchment paper away from one sandwich and offered it to Sam. "Turkey and provolone with spinach, tomato, and cucumber, as requested."

"Thanks." Sam wanted to kiss Karen again as a reward for lunch and that gorgeous smile that she kept sharing. She settled for taking a big bite of sandwich instead.

"That's it? You guys are clearly into one another, yet you're totally fine with her dating that guy?"

Karen inhaled slowly and looked at Sam. "Do you want to handle this?"

Sam swallowed hard, forcing down her sandwich before she was ready. She took a deep swig of water and then said, "I already tried. She doesn't believe me."

"Has anything changed with you?" Karen asked.

"Nope. Don't get me wrong, it's great. Awesome. Exactly what I needed. But it doesn't end with happily ever after."

Karen's smile returned. "Yeah, exactly. I couldn't have said it better." Karen unwrapped another sandwich and held it out toward Beth. "Come join us."

Beth huffed. "Not until you answer my question." Despite her protest, Beth started to wrap her brushes in plastic wrap.

"It's like your mom said. We're friends." Karen formed her words carefully, as though she was afraid she might spook Beth if she said the wrong thing. "We've been friends for a long time."

Arms crossed over her chest, Beth gave Karen a hard look. "Try again."

Sam continued to eat. It kept her from interrupting the conversation.

"Squirt, I love you, but you're asking me to explain or justify something that isn't really your business. What your mom and I get up to is between me and her, no one else."

"I'm not exactly a stranger. I don't understand why you'd encourage someone else to ask her out."

"Because they are both my friends. Alan is a good guy. If they hit it off, he'll be good to her."

Bitterroot Queen

"But—"

"Beth, that's enough." Sam finally stepped in. It was okay for Beth to ask some questions, but they were just going around in circles today. "Come eat your lunch. Or don't. But no more questions."

"Fine." Beth crossed to the island that separated the living room and kitchen, grabbed her sandwich, and stomped to her room. She slammed the door behind her.

"It's sweet, really," Karen said casually. "I didn't think she'd notice, let alone care."

"I suppose." Sam finished her sandwich. "But she doesn't want to discuss her sex life with me, so she shouldn't expect me to discuss mine with her."

Karen choked and then coughed. "Her sex life? She's only fifteen."

"Mmm." Thinking about Beth as a sexually active person made Sam's eye twitch, but she wasn't so naïve as to think it wasn't possible. Regardless of what Sam would like to think, odds were Beth had already had sex. And odds were, it was probably with Denmar. Thank God she'd talked to her about consent and condoms. If only they'd had more conversations along those lines.

"Did she tell you that?"

"No. We've talked more since arriving here than we did during the last three years in Vegas. But not about that. Though we've had talks about sex in general."

Karen gave her a one-armed hug. "Sorry."

"But this does bring us, you and me, to a crossroads." Sam had been dreading this conversation. Not because Karen would hold it against her. She wouldn't. But Sam really liked having sex with her. Once the words were out, that would be over. "We should probably stop having sex."

"Really?" Karen twirled a strand of Sam's hair around

her finger. "But I really like having sex with you."

"Yeah." Sam tilted her head, effectively lengthening the column of her neck. Sure, she just said they should stop having sex, but Karen was touching her hair, barely brushing against her throat, in just the right way.

Karen dipped her head, and the heat of her breath brought goose bumps to the surface of Sam's neck. "Are you sure?" She chuckled and placed a gentle kiss just below Sam's ear.

Sam shivered, gave herself a moment to enjoy the sensation, and then stepped away. "I'm sure." Intellectually she was, anyway. Her body, however, really wanted her to move back into the warmth of Karen's presence.

"Well, that sucks. But I get it." Karen took a bite of her sandwich and the lettuce crunched loudly.

Sam's phone rang, cutting off her response. "Hold that thought."

The number on her display screen didn't have an assigned name, so it was, more than likely, someone she didn't know. Considering how many outstanding messages she had, she took that to be a good sign. She pushed the button to answer. "This is Sam."

"Hello," the caller identified himself as an employee from the insurance company. "I'm calling about your insurance claim."

Light, floaty giddiness of relief flooded Sam's body. This was the call she'd been waiting for. Finally, she would be able to move forward. "Yes, I'm ready."

"I've reviewed your file very carefully, and I wish I had better news for you."

The buoyant energy in her chest became a little heavier. "What do you mean?"

"Because there is no clear date for when the damage occurred, there is no way to prove if it happened prior to you taking ownership or after. If it happened before you were the owner, then your insurance policy wasn't in effect yet. We can't pay for damage that occurred prior to the start of your policy."

"What about the pictures I sent you?"

"Yes, we received them, but there is a significant gap between the date the photos were taken and the day you closed. I'm sorry, but they aren't enough."

As Sam listened, she closed her eyes and tried to focus on the words, tried to make sense of their meaning. They tumbled around in her head like a confusing soup of letters with no clear form.

"I'm sorry, could you repeat that?"

"Your claim has been rejected. I'm sorry."

"Rejected."

"Yes."

"As in, no money."

"Yes."

Sam dropped her phone without disconnecting the call and slid to the floor. The bottom fell out of her world.

"Let me see if I understand this right." George, the apple farmer, stroked his chin. "You've been sleeping in your car and you don't have any place to park it tonight?"

Olly leaned back against the side of her Scout, one leg bent up so that she could rest the sole of her boot against the wheel. "Yep. That's about it."

"And you want to park in my barn?"

"Not in it, necessarily. I just need to be off the road. For safety, I'd like to be near the barn because people are less likely to mess with me if it looks like my vehicle belongs."

He nodded as though it made sense, but the confusion in his eyes hadn't cleared yet. "But why not just rent a room? Ava's got that place above her shop. She speaks highly of you. She'd probably let you stay there."

Olly dropped her foot to the ground. It was always like this when she tried to explain her situation to someone like George. He'd lived on his farm from the day he was born. The earth and trees and the sky above were written into his genetic code. He simply couldn't understand how she could survive without something to call her own. "Thanks anyway. I'll find somewhere else."

She was about to call Rampart to her when George spoke up again. "Whoa there, hot pants. I didn't say you couldn't stay. I just don't understand why you'd want to when you could put an actual roof over your head."

"I have a roof." She patted the vinyl top of her Scout. "It takes good care of me. And I'm still not sure how long I'm going to stay. I have another day, maybe two of work to do for you, and could probably scrape together some more work with Ava. That's not long enough to justify the expense of a room."

"I see. Have you checked the board again? Bitterroot is small, but you might get lucky."

"I've checked it every morning and evening. Nothing yet."

"Don't give up." George turned and started to walk away. Over his shoulder, he said, "Yeah, you can stay here. Park in the barn. Safer. And the toilet's closer that way."

George, like many farmers, had a utilitarian bathroom in his barn. Toilet, sink, shower. All had seen much better days. Still, it was better than the pay-to-use showers at a truck stop. She'd clean the place up and maybe give it a new coat of paint as thanks. "Appreciate it, George."

"You can cook me dinner tonight." George stopped after climbing the steps to the back porch. "I've got some decent steaks ready for the grill. Come in when you're ready." With that, he stepped inside. The screen door slammed shut behind him.

Olly laughed and kicked at the dirt. A flurry of dust rose up at her feet. Leave it to George to make her feel like she was doing him a favor by eating his food and taking over his barn. When she opened the door to the Scout, Rampart abandoned the dandelion down he was chasing and loped over with a big doggie smile on his face. He climbed into the back, ears up, eyes alert, ready to go. He made her life so much better. She patted his head and climbed inside.

The barn was located a hundred yards from George's house. It was relatively new, with corrugated rust-colored metal covering the sides and dark green on the roof. She liked this building. She'd spent a morning cleaning two-year-old hay out of the loft. When she'd finished, she put down a coat of weather sealant to protect the wood and keep it in good shape for many years to come.

That project had been a great deal more fun than re-roofing his equipment shed. That building had more character, and the wear of generations of work showed on every surface, but the roof was high and steep. Even with a safety harness, she had to remain on high alert. It kept her from enjoying the cool vibe of the structure and the sweet smell of alfalfa in the air.

She backed the Scout through the bay door and stopped in the middle of the large, open work space. George's barn featured four stalls for horses, along with a larger, fenced-off area for other stock animals, but no actual animals occupied the space. It held the residual scent of cattle, but it wasn't fresh. It smelled like country and hard work.

Before heading up to the house, she checked the large roll-up door opposite the one she'd entered to make sure it was locked. She also checked the pedestrian door next to it and glanced at the ladder that led to the loft, thinking she could easily upgrade it to stairs. The loft, now free of hay, was wide open and ran the full length and width of the barn. It was comfortable, and she could picture herself up there. Bitterroot felt good. It drew her in, and here, standing in a barn, of all places, she felt a bit more of that feeling of home notch into place inside her.

Another check on the plus side of her pro-con list about Bitterroot was that her mom would never want to visit. Olly wouldn't even have to hide the truth from her. Once she announced that she parked inside a barn to sleep in her vehicle in a small town that relied on a bulletin board in the center of town as the primary method of communication, Linda would mark Bitterroot off her list permanently. She liked her life to be filled with noise, complication, and most of all, people who she could bend to her will. This town offered none of those things, at least not in the quantities that Linda craved.

As she stood looking at the barn, flashes of transformation lit her imagination. She could easily picture the loft converted to an apartment, with stairs and windows and that glorious view of George's apple orchard from the second story loft door.

With her mind full of ideas, Olly set off for the house. George's steak wasn't going to cook itself.

Chapter Nine

Watts, Groves, and Pritchard Law. They weren't the only firm in Bitterroot, surprisingly, but they were the only one with a mission statement that included a shout-out to the gay community. That one little nuance made it easy for Sam to call and ask for a consultation. As a general rule, she believed that people should simply talk to one another and work together to find a resolution. She would especially like to use that approach with the Queen, but given the circumstances, she needed to know her options.

For better or worse, a lawyer could look over the paperwork from the sale, the documents from the insurance company, and the bid for renovations and determine if there were any legal grounds to help her out of this very messy situation.

Sam took a deep breath, straightened her collar, and pushed open the door.

Even though the firm was housed in a modest building, the lobby was shiny and modern, featuring a lot of stainless steel, black paint, and mirrors. The receptionist was a petite woman with an open smile. It helped put Sam at ease.

"Good morning and welcome to Watts, Groves, and Pritchard. How can I help you today?" The receptionist even managed to fill a standard greeting with warmth and confidence.

"Hello. I'm here to see Reagan Stiles. I have a nine a.m. appointment."

"And your name is?"

"Samantha Marconi."

"Perfect. If you'd like to sit, I'll let Ms. Stiles know you're here."

The lobby offered a sleek leather couch, plus a handful of modern chairs. Before she could sit, a young woman—definitely under thirty—approached, hand outstretched. Good lord, she was trusting her future to a puppy.

Sam took the woman's hand.

"Hi. You must be Sam. I'm Reagan. Come on back."

"Thanks." Sam followed her down the corridor. When they arrived at the next-to-last office, Reagan stopped and opened the door.

"Here we are." She gestured with the poise and polish of a professional spokesmodel. Reagan's office was a bit simpler than the lobby. No leather couch and the bare minimum for decorations, which included a tasteful framed print on the wall next to her degrees, various awards on the bookshelf behind her, and a small collection of leather-bound tomes. Law books, no doubt, framed by monogrammed bookends. R and S.

"Please, make yourself comfortable. Would you like anything to drink before we get started?"

Sam chose the seat closest to the door. "No. I'm fine." Actually, her stomach was a tense ball of frustration, and a drink would have to be pretty stiff to help.

"All right." Reagan circled the desk—a metal and glass monstrosity that reminded Sam of the private player's club in her old resort property—and slid gracefully into her seat. "The only note my receptionist gave me about your visit was 'property dispute.' Does that sound accurate to you?"

"In the simplest terms, I think yes." Sam wouldn't have called it that, but hearing the words, it felt pretty spot on.

"So, tell me about it."

Sam went through the details of how she came to own the Queen, the state it was in when she arrived compared to the way it was represented online, and finally, the rejection of her insurance claim. As she talked, Reagan occasionally made a note on the tablet on her desk. Sam couldn't make out the words, but she could clearly see a series of three large question marks. She had no idea if that was good or bad.

"Did you bring any documentation with you?"

Sam retrieved the file folder with the forms in question from her satchel. "Here. Copies of the police report, the closing documents for the transfer of ownership of the property, the insurance claim, the official rejection from the insurance company, and the bid from a local contractor. Oh, and I included a link to the photos and itemized list of damage. I put it all in an online album. It just seemed simpler."

Reagan scanned the documents, again jotting down notes as she went. "Have the police determined who caused the damage?"

Sam shook her head. "No, and they don't seem particularly interested in doing so."

"There's not a lot to go on, unfortunately."

"There really isn't. I suggested fingerprints, but the sheriff's deputy just laughed at that, which makes sense, I guess, since who knows how many prints are in there."

"The odds of collecting civil damages from those individuals are very low, anyway." She turned to a new page. "No response from the previous owner? That's interesting. I can reach out to him or her. I might have better luck."

"I haven't called him myself. The realtor left messages on my behalf."

Reagan finished reading, closed the file, and set the pen on top of it.

"You have a few options for how to proceed. You could bring suit against the insurance company. That's the most likely to succeed, but also the most likely to drag out over years. Or you could go after the previous owner for misrepresenting the quality of the property. Or the inspector for not pointing out the damages."

"The insurance company needs to know the exact date when the property was vandalized. Without that key piece of information, they can't determine who is liable and therefore won't approve the claim."

"Yeah, that's a pretty standard response. I have an excellent in-house investigator. I've no doubt we could determine when it happened."

A sliver of excitement skittered through Sam. "Really?"

"Yes, but you should think a moment about how much that would cost, especially considering the answer may not be what you want it to be."

Sam tamped down her enthusiasm. She hadn't discussed money with Reagan. This whole thing could be a fool's errand. At the moment, she couldn't afford much, let alone a drawn-out investigation followed by a drawn-out legal battle.

"How much would all this cost? Suing the insurance company and investigating the vandalism?"

"After this initial consultation, which is free, my firm bills at three hundred and fifty dollars per hour, plus expenses. I don't have an easy answer for how many hours this could take."

"And the investigator? I'm assuming that counts as an additional expense."

"Yes, typically a hundred and twenty-five to a hundred and fifty dollars per hour."

"Ouch."

"I know." Reagan smiled sympathetically. "If you want to pursue the case, I'll represent you."

They spent the next hour going over the points of the case. Sam asked questions, probably too many, because she didn't understand the process. She'd never been on either side of a lawsuit, and she wasn't sure if she wanted to go on record with this one. The cost alone was prohibitive.

Reagan answered her questions patiently. She was thorough and thoughtful with her words.

The conversation ended with Sam satisfied that, if she decided to move forward, Reagan could negotiate the legal aspects competently. As she stood to say goodbye, a little of the dark heavy weight that had been suffocating her eased. The band of pressure around her chest became almost bearable. Almost.

"Thank you so much for taking time for me today. I need to think about everything before I make a decision."

"Of course." Reagan shook her hand enthusiastically. "I encourage all my clients to take a night or two to consider their options. A lawsuit, regardless of how big or small, isn't something to enter into lightly. The process will upend your life, as well as the other party's. It can be traumatic, even with a good outcome."

Sam thanked her again and left. Regardless of her decision, she had a mountain of work waiting for her at the Queen, and every moment of delay was one more that she wasn't open for business. Renting rooms was the only real way to make this a success.

"Are you ready to talk about it yet?" Karen poured a cup of coffee and slid it across the counter to Sam.

Beth was up but still in the bathroom. The shuffling noises were growing louder, and Sam expected her to emerge at any moment.

"Not yet. Let's get some coffee in me first." She took a deep drink from her mug. It was too hot and too bitter, but she wasn't looking for a gentle wake-up. She needed a jolt to keep inertia from setting in. The night of fitful sleep had done nothing to help clear her mind. She was still in shock over the news from her insurance company. The logic of their words didn't help her accept the message. What the hell was she going to do in Bitterroot if she couldn't fix the state of the Queen?

Karen covered Sam's hand with her own. "This isn't one of those things that will simply go away if you ignore it."

She took a deep breath and reminded herself that Karen was her friend. She was trying to help. That didn't stop the flash of hurt and anger that flared inside her, but it did keep her from lashing out. "No, of course not."

"My offer to help still stands."

"And I appreciate that. But can we please wait until I've at least finished my coffee?" Sam raised her cup in salute and downed another large gulp.

Beth stumbled out of the bathroom. "Coffee."

Karen filled a cup and passed it to Beth.

"Go get dressed," Sam said. "I'm taking you to the school this morning." Classes had already started and there was every possibility that Sam would have let it slide again if she wasn't running so close to the top. She was angry. Not at Beth. Not at Karen. But really, really angry nonetheless. She needed to find a healthy outlet before she alienated everyone around her.

"Seriously? Mom, I—"

"No. Enough. This is happening."

Beth glared, but didn't argue. She stomped back to the bathroom and slammed the door.

"You're going to need to reinforce the hinges on her bedroom door," Karen said wryly.

Sam rolled her eyes. "Tell me about it."

"Or you could just remove the door completely. That's what my parents did when I did stuff like that."

Karen was serious, but Sam laughed anyway. The sound was unexpected to her own ears, and she laughed even harder. The outlet she needed arrived as a parenting lesson from someone who wasn't a parent.

"What? They really did."

"Oh, I believe you. But you have to admit, it's pretty funny."

Karen raised an eyebrow. "Not at the time."

"No, I imagine not. I'll think about it." Sam finished off her coffee and set the mug on the counter with a determined thud. "Now we can talk about it."

"It being the huge gap between your budget and the cost of repairs?"

Gap was putting it mildly. It was more a ravine. No, a canyon. She was standing on one side of a sheer drop and a shiny, newly renovated Queen sat on the other. No bridge in sight.

"Yes, that it."

"Do you have enough to get started?"

She'd purposefully set aside enough to carry Beth and her through the first twelve months. Sure, she could dip into that, but it would likely impact her ability to eat later down the line. "Kinda."

"What does that mean?"

"It means I have some money, but it's budgeted for other things. And I certainly don't have an extra three-quarters of a million sitting around to give Alan. That's…" She shook her head. "Without the insurance, that's impossible."

"You talked to a lawyer, right?"

"Yes. She seems great, but I haven't decided what I'm going to do yet. Still weighing my options." Sam needed to open the doors on the Queen before committing to any other financial obligations.

"Shit." Karen squeezed her hand. "Well, first things first. You have some money. We can identify the critical stuff, decide what we can do, and then find someone to help with the rest. Alan is a good guy. I'm sure he'd help on the weekends."

"No. Definitely not." She shook her head firmly.

"Why?"

"He asked me out. I don't even know if I like him. I can't have him thinking that I owe him something. I won't trade sex for labor."

"Okay, but I don't think he's like that."

"Have you ever slept with him?"

"No. I slept with his sister."

Sam laughed despite herself. She was willing to have dinner with Alan, but that was not a promise of anything more. She didn't want to confuse the situation even further by accepting his help.

"I see your point, Sam. But we could ask him."

"I can't date him if he does any work on the Queen."

"But you were willing to date him before when you planned for him to do extensive work there." Karen looked confused.

"That was different. I would have paid him. A lot. The boundaries of the relationship would have been clear."

"I still think he'd be willing."

"I'm not going to give in on this."

"Okay. No Alan. Got it. But we can still prioritize your list and set up some additional help, right?"

"Help from where? I obviously cannot afford to hire a contractor." Sam refilled her cup.

"We'll put a notice on the bulletin board in the town square. You never know. Someone might be looking for some temporary work."

"Like a day laborer?"

"Exactly. I've heard there's someone new in town. She's done some work for Ava at Bitter Ink, and for George Randolf, out at his farm. From what people are saying, they're both pleased with the quality of her work."

Sam pushed the heels of her hands into her forehead, something to counter the pressure of all these decisions.

"Tell me more about this bulletin board."

Olly picked up a red basket at the front of the store. She limited her purchases to whatever she could fit inside it. That kept her from buying more than she could afford and ensured she didn't dally while Rampart was outside waiting.

"Hey, you're back." The girl who'd helped Olly last time greeted her. She was far too cheerful for this time of day.

Olly nodded politely and said, "Hey."

"You're getting fruit, right? Grab some nectarines. They're fresh in this morning and so good. You'll love them. Promise."

"Thanks." Olly grabbed a few as instructed. She also found some fresh green beans and asparagus, so she added those to the basket as well. George insisted that she eat dinner with him. "There's plenty here," he'd said with a gruff dismissive wave of his hand. "Don't argue with me."

And so, Olly had smiled and sat down at the table to enjoy a steak with George. His breakfast selections were pitiful, so she picked up some steel cut oats, a carton of eggs, and a bag of frozen mixed fruit. She preferred it fresh, but this worked well for smoothies and George had a blender sitting on his counter. It looked to be as old as he was, but she considered that to be a bonus in appliances. Odds were it not only worked, but was powerful enough to puree a pine tree. A package of ham steaks and a gallon of chocolate milk, and Olly was ready. She headed to the checkout counter.

"Olly, right?" The cashier said as she unloaded the items from the basket and scanned them. "How'd the job at Bitter Ink go?"

"How do you know about that?"

"Small town. Everybody knows everything. Just like how you've stayed at George's place the past couple of nights. He's been in a couple of times. Can't stop singing your praises."

Knowing George, that probably meant he'd said she was all right one time. By his standards, that was high praise, but it wasn't exactly a hymn to her greatness.

"Yeah, right."

"Okay, you got me there. He almost smiled when he said your name. That's basically the same thing, right?"

Olly laughed. "For sure."

The girl finished scanning the items and looked at Olly expectantly. She hadn't hit the total button yet, so Olly had no idea how much she owed.

"What?" she asked.

"You forgot my name, didn't you?" The girl smirked.

"I did." She probably should have apologized, but couldn't be bothered. She'd met a lot of people since she'd

Bitterroot Queen

arrived. The cashier at the local grocery store wasn't her priority when it came to memorizing names.

"That's okay. I'm Rachel." She stuck out her hand.

Olly shook it. "Rachel. Got it."

"Good." Rachel pressed the total button, and Olly paid.

As she was bagging up her groceries, someone entered, making the bell above the door tinkle pleasantly. Olly turned to look out of reflex. It was the kid from the motel, the one whose mom threatened to douse her with pepper spray. Beth.

"Hey. I remember you." Beth grinned at her. "Found a new place to sleep?"

"I did. Thank you for asking." Olly returned the smile. This kid amused her. She was cool enough to not care about being cool at all. It was interesting.

Beth crossed to the small selection of office supplies and picked up a spiral notebook, a black pen, and a pack of index cards. She dropped them on the counter and said, "Can I get a pack of Marlboro reds? The box."

Rachel held out the handles of Olly's bag, prompting her to take it. She studied Olly and then turned to study Beth. "You're not eighteen."

Beth smiled. "Nope. But my money is."

"Cheeky." Olly laughed and picked up her bag. She made her way to the door. "Good luck with that."

No matter how entertaining the scene might have been, Olly had work to do. She'd promised George she'd return to paint the spindles on his porch in an hour. After her routine stop at the bulletin board in town, followed by Red Barn, she would be cutting it close. He'd been kind to her, and she didn't want to disappoint him.

An errant thought about Mrs. Vernon popped into her head. She wondered if they'd get along, George and Mrs. Vernon. She liked to think maybe they would.

"Here." Beth handed Sam the index cards. While she was a bit abrupt, she was at least civil. Her attitude had improved drastically when Karen left for work.

"Thanks." Sam slipped the small knife she kept in the console of her car under the cellophane wrapper around the cards. She sliced through the long edge and left the rest intact. With a little bit of luck, the pack would hold until she got home. She only needed one for the job notice, after all.

"Mom," Beth said, her voice soft, almost timid. "Can we talk about school, please?"

Sam dropped her head against the steering wheel and sighed. "Beth, I know you don't want to go, but school isn't something you can opt out of. You have to graduate."

"I know. I agree one hundred percent. But there are alternatives to public school."

"I can't afford private school, sweetie."

"No, of course not. But what if there's a free option?"

"Free private school? That requires a scholarship. Your grades haven't been so great lately," Sam hedged. Beth's grades had been horrible actually, with mostly Ds and Fs. When she got an occasional C, Sam said a prayer of thanks. Even so, she didn't want to tell Beth that she wasn't good enough or smart enough to get a scholarship.

"No. Free school online. There's a program called K-twelve. They do everything online and are totally accredited. They send out all the books and supplies that you need. And it's free. Did I mention that?" Beth said in a rush.

"Seriously? Where did you hear about this?"

Beth smiled for the first time that day. "Online. I searched for alternatives and found this. They work with

Bitterroot Queen

the school district. I could do this, Mom. Really. It's legit."

Sam weighed what Beth was saying. Would it hurt to let her go to school online? "What about friends? You need to meet people in order to make friends."

"I will." Beth grew even more excited. "There are a bunch of community classes offered at the college, and even more through the rec center."

Bitterroot was small. Even with the influx of students each fall, the town maintained a feeling of closeness. How many classes could they possibly offer?

"How is that better than going to school?"

"Because, don't you see, everyone in a class like that will want to be there. I'll have something in common with them."

"What about grades?"

"I'll work really hard. I promise."

Sam looked at her, skeptical. "How hard?"

"Really, really hard."

"Nothing below a C?"

"As and Bs. I can do it."

"For now, you can create our job posting." Sam handed Beth the index card and started the car. She needed to think about this. "When we get home, you can show me this K-twelve program and I'll look it over."

Beth squealed. "Yay! Thanks, Mom."

"I'm not saying yes." Sam pulled out of the parking lot and headed toward town.

"You're not saying no, either."

"True enough." Sam laughed, letting Beth's excitement draw her in. Maybe this would work. And maybe they'd find some qualified help for the renovations that wouldn't bankrupt her.

A girl could dream.

Chapter Ten

Sam studied their living quarters. The only thing that made the place almost livable was the mural Beth had been working on. Everything else was in various stages of functional, ranging from good working order (the coffee maker and the shower) to disaster (pretty much everything else). Until they figured out what to do about the floors, she refused to move anything into the apartment. Besides, Karen's bed was too comfortable for her to bust out the air mattress.

"So, tell me more about your plan for school."

After they'd finished in town, Beth had given her a tour of the virtual school she wanted to attend. While Sam still had her reservations, she had to admit that Beth's research was thorough. She'd tentatively agreed to let her pursue it, providing that she delivered on her grades as promised.

"What do you mean?" Beth asked, distracted by the flow of paint from her brush to the wall.

"When do you plan to do your school work?" Sam expected Beth to blow her off. It was Saturday after all.

"Oh, that." Beth rested her paintbrush atop a can of paint and went over to Sam. She turned on her Surface and logged into the K12 website. "I started it this morning. All I have left is this one assignment. I have to outline a persuasive essay. I'll finish it later."

Sam stared, mouth open. She'd been outside long enough to dig their gardening tools out of the storage container and then spent a couple of hours pretending to be a landscaper. When she'd stepped out, Beth had been painting, and when she returned a few minutes ago, she was standing in roughly the same place, staring at the wall.

"What—wait. Who are you and where is my daughter?"

Beth laughed. "Don't look so surprised. I started early this morning, before you were up, did a little more while you were outside, and am rolling ideas for the essay around in my head while I paint. I'm antisocial, but that doesn't mean I'm not smart."

"I know you're smart," Sam said. "Of course I do. But think of this from my perspective. I've seen your grades from your last school. Can you really blame me for being surprised?"

Beth's gaze hardened for a moment and then she relaxed. "No, I guess not." She clicked a few keys on the keyboard. "But maybe I just needed to find a different way to do it."

Sam started to respond but stopped herself. Beth's grades were a reflection of her rebellion, and like all the other things she had done, it still came back to Sam, to the kind of parent she should have been. It was like they were speaking two different languages and she was struggling to learn Beth's.

"I also found an elective that I want to take," Beth said. "It's a series of videos that teaches art theory, the use of color and contrast, technique, that sort of thing. It's free."

Unable to contain the swell of relief, excitement, and pride that flooded her chest, Sam pulled her into a bracing hug. "I'm so happy with you right now."

"Ugh. Mom, you're crushing me." Beth wiggled to free herself, but Sam only hugged her tighter.

"I can't help it. Just let me love you for a minute."

"Can you do that without collapsing my lungs?"

"Nope. Five more seconds." Sam silently counted off the seconds and even held on for a few extra because Beth didn't protest again.

When she finally let go, Beth shuffled away, but not too far. She was still close enough that Sam could hug her again if she really wanted to.

"You smell like you've been rolling in a compost pile. Why?" Beth asked.

"Because I have been. Kinda. I was working out front, weeding and such." Sam crossed to the sink and started to wash her hands. "I'm done now, though. I need to figure out how to get us into this apartment. Karen's going to get tired of us at some point."

"Nobody's responded to your help wanted ad?"

"Not yet. And I can't wait for someone to sweep in and rescue me. I'm going to do what I know how to do and go from there." She'd done the math. There simply wasn't enough money in her account to hire Alan, or any other contractor, to repair the entire property, but she could afford to have pieces done. In order to open, the exterior needed to look ready for business, even if all the rooms weren't.

She'd found an online supplier who gave a significant discount for bulk purchases. Even with the price break, the total just to do the simplest thing, such as replacing the doors, gave her sticker shock. She had queries out to a few other suppliers, wholesalers who didn't list their prices on the website. Hopefully, one of those would come back better.

Until then, she needed to work. She might not be able to do everything, but the more she figured out on her own, the less she'd end up paying someone else. Plus, if

Bitterroot Queen

she had a job to focus on, it would keep her distracted. The last thing she needed was to fall into a spiraling pit of despair over the state of the Queen.

Before heading back outside, she wiped down the counters and spread a thick, rubberized contact paper in all of the drawers and cabinets. When she'd moved into her first apartment, her mom had done this for her, and Sam had teased her about it. Now, after spending far too much time scrubbing this kitchen, she saw the wisdom behind it.

"Don't suppose you want to stop painting and come outside for a while?" Sam asked.

"And do what?"

"Tame the wild landscape. Roll around in compost. Stare forlornly at the boxes inside of the storage unit. Breathe some fresh air."

Beth tilted her head to the side and studied the section she was currently working on. It looked vaguely like a phone booth, but could just as easily end up being a bathtub full of fish.

"How long?"

"Not sure. Maybe an hour. Maybe more. Maybe less."

"Mmm, let me wrap my brushes, and then I'll join you." Beth pulled a roll of plastic wrap out of her supply caddy. She kept her extra brushes, her small tubes of paint, and a few other miscellaneous items in there.

"Thanks." Sam left her to tidy up her workspace and headed outside.

It wasn't too hot, thankfully. The altitude saw to that. Before returning to her landscaping, Sam unlocked the storage container and lifted the handle to release the top and bottom bolts holding the doors secure. Inside, there were rows of neatly stacked boxes. Near the back, out of view from the opening, was their furniture—the leather sofa Sam couldn't part with, the hutch she'd inherited when her parents died, plus a few other items.

Every day that the container sat in her parking lot cost her money. Moving their belongings inside wasn't an option yet and moving everything to a local storage unit would be a lot of extra work for very little savings. And there was no way all of this would fit into Karen's spare room. Not that Sam would ask.

By the time Beth joined her, Sam had a killer headache, but no clear solution as to what to do with their belongings. As an added layer of fun, it looked like the movers had turned her neatly sorted and separated boxes into an indecipherable tangle. The labels she'd carefully written on the fronts of the boxes weren't visible. She hoped they were just turned backward and not upside down. The only label she could read clearly said "do not open. seriously. i will kill you." Presumably that one belonged to Beth.

"Hey! That's my box of supplies. Awesome." Beth picked up the death box and carried it inside before Sam could ask, "Supplies for what?"

"Great. She won't be back," Sam muttered to herself as she shook her head and gave up. Staring at their packed boxes wasn't helping anyone. At least working in the lot made the place look a little prettier.

Just as she was turning to lock up, someone knocked on the open door of the container.

"Excuse me?" A woman—no, *the* woman, the one Sam had chased off with the pepper spray—stood just outside the container. Her dog sat by her side. "I don't know if you remember me."

"I do." Sam didn't remember her name, but she remembered the encounter. The woman was younger than Sam originally thought. Mid-twenties, maybe. Long, unruly hair pulled back in a loose ponytail. Dark eyes to match her hair. Plus a defensive stance, as though she was waiting for the next blow. Overall, she was striking, haunted, and very sexy. In other words, trouble.

"Right." The woman blushed. "It's just—" She took two rapid steps toward Sam with her hand outstretched, holding a small card. "You have work?"

Sam stared at her, wary, but didn't take the card. It was the job posting they'd placed on the bulletin board in town, so she already knew what it said.

"Hey, it's you. What's up?" Beth stood just outside the container, a smile on her face. When she saw the dog, she stopped short of lighting a cigarette. She dropped to her knees and pulled the dog into her arms. She buried her face in his fur and whispered nonsense words to him.

The woman almost smiled, one corner of her mouth lifting up at the edge. She shrugged. "Looking for work."

"You're Olly, right?" Beth looked up. "And this guy is Rampart?"

"Good memory." The woman—Olly—nodded. "And you're Beth." She turned back to Sam and said, "But I don't know your name."

"Listen, Olly, I'm not—"

"Her name is Sam. She's my mom," Beth answered for her.

"Figured."

"So, you came because of the ad in town?"

Olly nodded.

"Good. Come on, Mom. Let's show her what needs to be done." Beth stood and moved out of Sam's line of sight. The dog followed her, nudging her hand with his nose as they walked.

Sam sighed. She could hold onto their first meeting or

she could let it go and start over with Olly here and now. She certainly hadn't been at her best that day. Perhaps Olly wasn't either. "Okay, Beth is right. Let's go."

"Um, thanks?" Olly stuffed the card into her back pocket. "The card doesn't say how much..."

"Right. Well, let's take a look around, see what you think, and then we can talk money. Okay?"

Olly nodded slowly, clearly calculating something. "Okay. I suppose that works."

Sam tucked her work gloves into her back pocket.

"So," Sam said once she'd cleared the door. "Tell me about your experience."

Olly gave her that lopsided grin combined with one raised eyebrow, and it caused a strange little flutter in her gut.

"Work." She sputtered. "Your experience with construction."

"Right." Olly nodded and her smile grew. For a moment, the guarded veil lifted. "I've done lots of fix-it projects, including work for Bitter Ink, a small business in town, and for George Randolf, a local farmer. Before that, I've done just about everything, from hanging sheetrock to operating a Bobcat."

"A bobcat?" Surely she wasn't referring to an actual bobcat. What good would wild animal training do here at the Queen?

"A small tractor. They're used for leveling the ground, minor demolition, moving heavy things, stuff like that."

"Oh, yeah. Of course."

"I did see an actual bobcat once." Olly's voice took on a teasing lilt.

"Mmm." Sam had no idea how to respond, so polite noise it was.

"Yeah. Real friendly fellow. Liked to be scratched behind his ears."

Bitterroot Queen

"You're kidding," Sam deadpanned.

"Nope. I worked at a zoo once, for about two months. They let me hold one of the cubs. It was pretty awesome."

"What else have you done?" Sam allowed herself to smile, and she wondered about Olly's background and how she'd ended up in Bitterroot.

"Little bit of everything." Olly ducked her head. "But I'm being rude. We're here to talk about the job."

Sam swept her arms out wide, indicating the Queen as though it were the grand prize on a game show. "I dragged my daughter here from Vegas, only to discover that the dream property I bought was really a nightmare. Every single room is damaged." She took a calming breath. "And my insurance denied the claim. That leaves me with few resources and a huge, expensive mess to clean up."

Olly went into the first rental room they came to. The number was loose and swung in a wild arc as the door moved. After a moment, she stepped back out. "They all like this?"

"Pretty much." Sam tried to sound aloof, unbothered. In truth, she was on the verge of tears. This tour was exactly what she'd been trying to avoid all day.

"Do you have a game plan? Or would that be up to me?"

"I have—not really a game plan. More a loose idea, with a clear vision of where we are, where we need to be, and a vague concept of the work needed to get there."

"You started on the landscaping." Olly indicated the front planting beds with a nod of her head. "That's good. Giving the place a facelift, improving curb appeal, will make a huge difference. Right now, people drive by and see a derelict building. A little paint, a new sign, and some flowers will do the trick. Combined, of course, with some serious elbow grease."

The urge to hug Olly overwhelmed Sam, but she held herself back. "When can you start?"

"Right now, if you want me."

Sam bit her tongue at that and focused on a proper response. "There's just one thing." She hated to be a buzzkill, but she needed to establish clear boundaries from the start. "You still can't sleep in the lot."

Olly laughed. "Will you pepper spray me if I do?"

"Listen, about that—"

"No." Olly held up her hand. "I'm sorry about that. I should have asked. Staying here without permission was rude. I won't do it again."

"You found another place?" Sam, weirdly, felt almost guilty about kicking Olly out.

"I did." Olly smiled politely but didn't elaborate.

Rampart barked and Beth laughed. Sam and Olly resumed their tour.

"Tell me what you would do first," Sam said.

"Well," Olly scratched behind her ear, "I'd start by taking down the old signage. Then move on to the exterior paint, followed by doors and windows. Clean and replace as needed. Landscaping. Then move inside."

Sam stuck out her hand. "You're hired."

Chapter Eleven

"It's not as bad as it looks." Olly ducked her head and looked away. Her job at the Bitterroot Queen did not include consoling the owner. But the look on Sam's face, a mix of desperation and defiant independence, twisted Olly up inside. So much so that the words she normally would have kept to herself spilled out completely without permission.

When she had arrived, Sam had been standing in the lot, hands on her hips, staring at the building. She'd recovered quickly enough when Olly eased the Scout to a stop next to her. Not quick enough, though, because the heartache, regret, and immutable hope in her expression was loud enough to kick Olly right in the face.

Sam smiled, a sheepish, reluctant upturn of her lips that made Olly want to pull her into a hug. Or push her away and run. She vibrated with the mixed message as her brain yelled at her to move.

"Yes, it is." Sam sighed. "But it's mine, so I'm going to pretend you're right." She dusted her hands together, a decision clearly made. "Ready to get dirty?"

She raised her eyebrows and grinned.

"Um, that is—" Her face flushed.

"Sure," Olly said, saving her from further embarrassment. "Am I starting out here?"

"Actually, I'd really like to get moved into my apartment."

"Okay." Olly stepped out of her vehicle to stand next to Sam. Rampart leapt over the side, sat on his haunches, and nudged Olly's hand with his nose. Without thinking, she rested her hand on his head, fingers automatically scratching the fur behind his ears. "So… I'll be moving boxes?"

"Not yet. Come inside with me." Rather than moving inside, Sam stayed where she was, rooted to the ground and looking wrecked for the effort.

As defeated as she sounded, Olly wasn't ready to count Sam out. She was pretty sure this was just one vulnerable moment, a fleeting instant that would pass, leaving her galvanized and ready to take control of her world. Olly liked that Sam had invited her to take part in this journey, though she couldn't explain why.

Olly shifted her weight, restless and ready to move. Now that she had direction and purpose for the day, she wanted to get to work. Sam, however, continued to stare solemnly at the building.

"Want to head inside and get started?" Olly tugged gently at Sam's sleeve.

Sam smiled, an expression that didn't quite erase the crease in the middle of her brow. "Yeah, okay. Sure."

The apartment was littered with cleaning supplies—a roll of paper towels partially unspooled in the middle of the floor with a bottle of window cleaner next to it, a bucket of sudsy water with yellow gloves hanging over the rim on the kitchen counter, and a box of industrial-size trash bags just inside the door. From what she could see, the common areas were well on their way to livable. Except for the stained-beyond-saving carpet. And the window covered with plywood. And the shredded blinds that partially obscured the view of the river through the sliding glass door.

Olly moved to the middle of the room and waited for Sam to offer some direction.

"It was a lot worse when we got here."

Based on the tour Sam had previously given her of the rest of the property, Olly believed her. She nodded, unsure what to say.

Without inviting Olly to join her, Sam made her way across the room to a closed door. After a moment, Olly followed.

Sam hesitated with her hand on the knob. "This is my room. We can start here." And then she opened the door and entered.

The room was stark, bare walls and floors. The walls had been primed, but the shadow of a large penis was still visible on one wall, spray-paint art left over from an unauthorized party. Another wall was covered with layer after layer of sprayed-on initials and names, muted by the primer but not obscured. The sliding doors to the closet hung haphazardly, the louvered slats broken and crooked. The carpet stank of mildew and beer and piss.

"Where have you been sleeping?"

"With a friend." Sam gestured toward the apartment at large. "We've been working primarily on the kitchen and bathroom. When the primer didn't work in this room, it stifled my enthusiasm for painting. I'm afraid the sheetrock needs to come down."

Olly was done talking about the work that needed done. She lifted the closet doors from the metal track, stacked them together, and carried them to the backyard via the sliding glass door that gave Sam's room the same view of the river that they enjoyed from the living room. She dropped them unceremoniously and returned to the room.

"Do you have more primer? Paint?"

"Primer yes. We bought ten gallons. Paint no. Not for this room, yet."

"You should get some. Enough for this room and Beth's. I'll keep working here. Oh, and get a box of mud."

"Mud?"

"Yeah, it's the stuff they use with drywall. Comes in a box about this big." With her hands, Olly mimicked the shape of a box about twelve by twelve by twelve. "Just ask someone. Tell them you need drywall mud."

"Okay." Sam hesitated, her brow drawn down. "What will you do?"

"Everything else." Olly smiled, already in motion, moving toward Beth's room. "Beth, if there's anything in here that you don't want me to find, you should put it away now," Olly announced before opening the door.

"Nah, all my good stuff got left behind when we moved." Beth didn't even glance away from her work.

Olly entered and repeated the process. As she removed the things inside the room, Sam discussed the situation with Beth.

"Apparently, I need paint. Do you want to come with me?"

"For what?"

"My room and yours," Sam said.

That got Beth's attention. She covered her paint and wrapped her brushes in flimsy plastic. "Yeah, no way you're picking the color for my room."

After dropping the closet doors outside, Olly joined them in the living room. "Get another five gallons of primer. We'll need to do that a couple of times, at least. Plus all the supplies. Don't worry about masking tape. I'll have all the trim and outlet covers off before you get back."

Bitterroot Queen

After a record-breaking dash to the hardware store, Sam and Beth returned with five gallons of primer and two gallons of paint—a neutral eggshell for Sam and a purple so dark it was almost black for Beth. A car Sam didn't recognize was parked near the lobby entrance, next to Olly's Scout.

"Rachel's here." Beth sounded almost excited.

"Rachel?" It took Sam a moment to place the name. "The girl from the market?"

"Yeah, she's awesome." Beth hopped out of the car and yelled, "Come on."

They found Rachel and Olly in the backyard, standing over a pile of long, skinny boards. Olly held a piece of paper with some sort of diagram on it. Periodically, she would point at the paper, then at a specific board. Rachel nodded, smiling at Olly like a puppy in love. Rampart lay stretched out on his side in a small patch of sunlight.

Sam detoured long enough to drop the paint in the appropriate rooms, then made her way out back. Beth was already there, staring at Rachel the same way Rachel was looking at Olly.

"What are you guys doing?"

"I'm just getting these two lined up." Olly turned to greet her with a lazy half-smile that made Sam's stomach drop. "Then I'll be in to start painting with you."

"Oh yeah? What are they doing?"

While she'd been gone, Olly had converted the damaged closet doors into a makeshift worktable. It was crude, but functional. An orange extension cord snaked across the grass from the table to an outlet in the living room.

"They're going to sand and paint all the trim."

"Really?"

"As soon as Rachel gets back from a quick trip home.

You're borrowing her sander."

"My dad's sander, actually."

"Right."

"I'm going with her." Beth tugged on Rachel's arm and pulled her back inside.

"How did you rope her into this?" Sam asked.

"She just showed up. I'm not one to turn down free labor."

"You're amazing." Sam shook her head. Olly was so far removed from the person Sam had originally thought. Most people wouldn't have asked about work after the property owner threatened to pepper spray her. Sam admired that and had to admit that the project was going to be a hell of a lot easier with Olly than without. Plus, Olly put her at ease. Made her believe that she wasn't completely insane for buying the Bitterroot Queen and that this crazy life experiment might actually work out. Not to mention, the rate Olly quoted her was unbelievably less expensive than hiring Alan would have been.

Olly tilted her head and regarded Sam. "Thanks." She said the word softly, almost a whisper, and Sam was caught in the bare vulnerability in her eyes.

Then, with a curt shake of her head, Olly walked briskly away, head tucked into her chest. "I should get back to work. Where's the paint?" Her words trailed behind her like a kite that had lost the breeze.

Stupid, stupid, stupid.

It was such a simple situation. Olly wanted to impress Sam with her work, show her that she was worth retaining for the duration of the work on the Queen. For once, she wasn't flirting, wasn't trying to distract herself from the muted gray wash that colored her life. Between the camaraderie with Ava at Bitter Ink, the affinity with George at Randolf Farms, and the building ease of spending time at the Bitterroot Queen with Sam and Beth, Olly had forgotten to fortify herself. As much as she toyed with the idea of staying, she knew she'd eventually leave this place. She always did.

She wasn't sure what had happened between them, but she knew it was something. It wasn't a moment, like the kind that populated every single trade paperback romance her mom had bought off the supermarket rack when Olly was a kid. It was more a prelude to a moment. Sam had given her a simple compliment, the words leaving her mouth casually, as if without any real thought or consideration. Still, Sam seemed to have seen her and that made Olly vulnerable, an emotional state she'd never learned to cope with properly, despite the years spent in its company.

On the heels of her response—thanks—a single thought raced through her, filling her chest with thrumming, anxious energy. Run.

She made her way into the bathroom and closed and locked the door behind her. She stood at the sink, trying to sort out her thoughts. This reaction—the overwhelming compulsion to get away at the slightest hint of an emotional connection to another human being—this wasn't normal. God, when she stopped to think about how very messed up she was, she really hated her mom. Fuck. Sam probably thought she was a freak. Hell, she was right.

A light knock sounded at the door, followed by, "Hey, are you okay in there?" Sam asked in a subdued voice.

Olly stared at herself in the mirror and forced herself

to breathe. One long, slow inhale, followed by an equally long and slow exhale. "Yeah. I'll be out in a minute." Her voice sounded almost normal.

A soft thud sounded, followed by a faint scraping noise, as if Sam had leaned against the door and then slid down.

Olly continued to breathe deeply, focusing on the way her body moved with the act, the way the air circulated through her. Eventually, her heart rate slowed, and she splashed some cold water on her face. *Stupid*.

Olly gave herself another few moments to center herself, mentally repeating the mantra that had guided her during the months and years that followed leaving Linda's home. She wasn't really vulnerable. Not truly. She could climb into her Scout and leave right now. Or tomorrow. Or next week. She had the power to shape her own life, the power to step away at any time. She was okay.

Finally, with her heart rate back to normal and her hair pulled back in a loose ponytail, Olly turned the knob to open the bathroom door. As suspected, Sam sat on the floor with her back to the door. She scrambled to her feet.

"Hey there. I was worried."

"Don't be. I'm fine." Olly moved past her, into Sam's bedroom where the distraction of painting waited for her.

The primer went up quickly and the penis faded more. Another coat might just be enough. Olly stretched and smiled at Sam, trying to regain some of the camaraderie they'd shared earlier.

Sam studied their progress. "What next?"

"While this dries, we can do the first coat of primer in Beth's room."

"We might have to postpone that, depending on the time. I have a date tonight."

As she spoke, Sam's cheeks turned a lovely shade of pink. Olly was struck, in that moment, with the strange and unbidden desire to be the cause of such a blush. She took a half-step toward Sam before the meaning of the words registered.

Sam had a date.

Tonight.

Olly stopped dead, one foot suspended in midair. "Oh." She forced herself to lower her foot, painfully aware of how awkward and strained the moment had become. To give herself something to do, she picked up the pan of paint and the roller. "That's okay. I can start without you."

She tried to smile, but was certain it was more of a grimace.

"It's actually a miscommunication."

Olly looked at her, wondering what that meant.

"He asked the same time Beth said something and I said yes to her, but he thought I said it to him—it's ridiculous. Never mind. Frankly, I think I'd have more fun here with you, painting."

He. What the hell? Sam set off Olly's gaydar in a major way, and she was rarely wrong about such things. Not that it mattered, really. Sam could date whoever she wanted. "You can't think that way. If you do, your date is destined to fail before it even begins. Even though it was a weird misunderstanding, he could be the man of your dreams." She hoped not.

"I'm pretty sure he's not. But I'm still going to dress like he might be."

"Then I'll leave you to it. I'm going to check on my impromptu labor force, then move to Beth's room."

Sam nodded. "Sounds good. I'm headed to the storage

pod to find a date-worthy outfit. Wish me luck."

"Try not to get lost in there."

Olly turned to take the paint supplies to Beth's room, and Sam brushed past her on the way out the door. In her absence, the air felt thicker and the room less inviting. She dropped off the paint and went to the backyard. "How's it going out here?" she asked.

Beth was talking on her phone, her brow drawn into an intense scowl. Rachel rested on the edge of the cement patio, staring at Beth with a strange expression on her face.

"Good," Rachel said, turning her attention to Olly. "We finished a few pieces. Let me show you." She stood, brushed her hands over her backside, and made her way to the makeshift sawhorse table. One side held a neat row of newly sanded lengths of trim. As she'd instructed, they hadn't gone all the way to the bare wood, but rather they'd removed the top layers of paint, leaving it smooth and ready for a fresh coat.

"How do you feel about using the sander only? Would it be easier with a paint scraper? Or even paint remover?" Olly hated the chemicals involved in paint stripper, but she also knew it was a serious time-saver.

"I brought a scraper." Rachel held up the tool. "My dad insisted. He was right. It helps a lot."

"It pays to listen to your parents." The lesson wasn't universally true, especially not for Olly, but generally, parents were well-intentioned and kids learned if they listened.

"What are you doing out here? Where's Sam?"

Olly glanced at the door leading to Sam's room. "Getting ready. Apparently, she has a date."

"A date?" Rachel asked.

"With some guy."

"Seriously? A dude?"

"Yep."

"Sucks. Sorry." Rachel punched Olly lightly in the arm.

"What's that supposed to mean?"

Rachel rolled her eyes. "Not like I haven't seen you checking her out."

"That's crazy. And anyway, what about Beth? What's going on there?"

"Nothing. She's on the phone with her boyfriend."

"Sucks. Sorry," Olly repeated, without including the physical contact. "At least she doesn't look very happy about it." She gestured toward Beth who looked even less happy than she had a few moments ago.

"Yeah, whatever. I'm going back to work." Rachel picked up the sander and turned it on, effectively blocking any further conversation.

Olly followed Rachel's lead and went back inside to prime Beth's room.

As Alan held the chair for her, the waiter lit the candle in the middle of the table. Between the soft glow, the linen napkins, and the ankle-length apron on the waiter, Sam decided this was one of those restaurants. The kind where the staff deferred to the man at the table, where they brought her food and drink based on his order, and where the tab made most men think they were owed something at the end of the night.

All in all, Sam wished she'd stayed at the Queen, painting the walls and eating pizza without the expectation that was no doubt building in Alan.

"This is nice." Sam flipped open her menu, paused for a moment, and then forced herself to meet Alan's gaze.

"Any recommendations?"

"I really don't know. A buddy of mine told me about this place. This is my first time, too." Alan squirmed and adjusted his tie. His hair, slicked down with product and combed to the side, reflected the flicker of the candlelight, giving it the strange polished look of patent leather.

"Really?" Sam asked.

"Yeah." Alan smiled sheepishly. "Truth? I'm more of a pizza on the couch kind of guy."

Sam smiled, a real one rather than the forced, polite version she'd used with him so far. This was the first thing he'd said since picking her up that actually appealed to her on any level. She looked around and inspected the overly formal setting more closely. "Then why all this?"

Alan shrugged. "I wanted to impress you."

"And you think this is the way to do it?"

"Isn't it? I mean, you're from Vegas, so I figured this is what you're used to."

"True, but I left Vegas and chose a place that's as far removed from it as possible." Sam didn't point out how this place, the fanciest in Bitterroot, was a far cry from what Vegas had to offer.

The sommelier appeared at Alan's side with a bottle of red wine. He displayed it formally with a white linen towel draped over one arm. Without looking at Sam, he gave Alan a speech about the characteristics and quality of pinot noir.

"Um, sure, I guess." Alan glanced sideways at Sam, a questioning look on his face.

"Very good, sir." The waiter turned to leave.

"Actually," Sam interrupted his progress, "can we get two pints of whatever you have on draft? An IPA for me, if you have it. Alan?"

Bitterroot Queen

"That sounds great."

The waiter looked as offended as Alan did relieved.

"As you wish." With that, he turned and walked away. This time, Sam let him go.

"You don't like wine?" Alan asked.

"I love wine, especially the one he offered. But it retails for around three hundred and fifty dollars. I can't afford it at the moment." Sam left the part about not letting Alan buy her such an expensive drink unsaid. Maybe he preferred a quiet night with pizza and a movie, but that made her more suspicious of his choice of restaurant, not less.

"Wow. I had no idea. Thanks."

Sam studied him, in his dress shirt with the top button undone, his hair gelled and shiny, and his jacket stretched tight across his shoulders, easily a size too small. Why was she here? Her arrangement with Karen was so simple. And hot. No pressure or expectations. Just orgasms. Really fabulous orgasms.

Then there was Olly. She knew less about her than she did about Alan at this point. Still, she was drawn to her. If it were Olly, not Alan, sitting opposite her right now, she would find the whole production and the effort sweet and charming rather than calculated and presumptuous. The thought intrigued her, but also made her stomach squirm with something indefinable.

"Alan," Sam caught Alan's gaze and held it, "you should know, I'm not going to sleep with you."

"I—" Alan choked and sputtered. "I—That's...um..."

The waiter returned with their drinks, and Sam took a deep drink of her very tasty, not terribly expensive beer. It was going to be a long night.

Chapter Twelve

The next morning, Sam made a quick trip to Red Barn Market and picked up a few fresh veggies, some bread, and deli meat. Even though the kitchen was in working order, more or less, she still wasn't ready to start cooking elaborate meals. Sandwiches were the perfect solution. There was only so much pizza and takeout she could eat.

At least her "date" hadn't gone as badly as she had thought it would. Alan turned out to be as nice a guy as she thought, even after she told him she wasn't going to sleep with him. Once they got past that, they talked about Bitterroot and some of the things that went on in the area. He told her about his business and described, with great pride, some of the projects he had completed in the area. All in all, it went okay and maybe she had a friend out of the deal. Maybe she'd even hire him in the future for smaller and much less expensive projects.

When she pulled into the lot, Olly was already there, working with her long-sleeved flannel tied around her waist. The tight tank top revealed well-defined shoulder and arm muscles, along with a tapestry of colorful tattoos. The view hit Sam at a visceral level, a sharp bolt deep in her gut.

Jesus. She'd managed to navigate her entire career in Vegas without lusting after her employees, and here she was doing just that. She didn't know whether to blame it on the fresh mountain air or the way the sun glinted off the sheen of sweat covering Olly's skin. With an impressive act of will, Sam looked away and focused on safely parking her car.

The lot looked much improved from earlier that morning when Sam left for her appointment. She'd been gone for just over two hours, and Olly hadn't been there when she'd driven away. Still, she'd pruned and leveled the top edge of the overgrown shrubs that lined the front of the building. Now they looked almost inviting.

Once again, Sam was struck by how powerfully Olly impacted their efforts. Because of her, both bedrooms were habitable, with fresh paint, a facelift for the outlets and light fixtures, and, perhaps most important, Olly had ripped the carpet out, leaving behind worn hardwood floors that she planned to finish with a durable sealant. That had to wait until later, though. The rooms were livable and that was enough for now.

Rampart lay a few feet away, relaxing in the sun, possibly asleep. As Sam pulled to a stop, he popped up and moved over to sit next to Olly. He nudged her hand with his nose, and as she stroked his head, Olly turned and looked in Sam's direction.

Olly gave her a quirky smile and a short wave. She set the long shrub trimmers on the ground, brushed the dirt and plant debris off her shirt and pants, and came over. Without breaking her motion, she scooped the grocery bags out of Sam's hands and started toward the main entrance beside Sam. Rampart kept pace a half-step behind.

"Hi. I hope you don't mind that I got started without you," Olly said as she shuffled the bags until she could open the swinging door with one hand. She held it open for Sam, and then, after signaling Rampart to wait outside, she followed Sam through the lobby and into the kitchen. She set the bags on the counter.

"No, I don't mind at all. It looks like you've made some great progress."

Olly pulled the front of her shirt up to wipe the sweat off her face. Sam definitely did not stare at the defined ridges of her abs. In fact, she would deny it emphatically if asked about it.

"I figure I've got a good two days of work on the front landscaping. And that doesn't include planting or laying any kind of ornamental filler."

"Ornamental filler?" Sam unpacked her groceries, lining them up to make sandwiches in a bit.

"Hey. You have food." Beth appeared from the direction of her bedroom. Her hair was pulled back in a loose, unkempt ponytail, and she was wearing a pair of bright red footy pajamas that Sam had given her two Christmases ago as a joke. They didn't quite fit, and the fabric pulled tight around her shoulders, chest, and belly. Beth grabbed the bag of chips and popped it open. "Yum."

"Are you planning to get dressed anytime today?" Sam asked out of habit. Parents were supposed to ask questions like that, to remind their kids of things to help them grow into functional adults.

"Yeah, right after Olly tells me about this." She gestured vaguely toward the designs on Olly's arms.

"Some other time, Beth. I've got to get back to work. Your mom isn't paying me to tell you about my wild youthful exploits." Olly started toward the door.

To Sam, Olly looked like she wasn't much older than Beth, so if her youth was misspent, she was still in the process of misspending it. Not that her work ethic reflected that so far.

"Wait," Sam said. "You were telling me about planting beds and ornamental filler?"

"Oh yeah, that's just a fancy way of saying bark or mulch or pretty rocks. I worked at a nursery one summer." She shrugged.

"Do I have to decide on that now?"

"No. In fact, I recommend against it. Trimming everything down and weeding is good for now. The rest should wait until after the exterior is painted and the doors and windows are repaired. Otherwise, we might trample over the work and just end up redoing it."

"Good. So what is your plan for the rest of today?"

"Prune the back of that hedge. That way we'll be able to paint the wall easier. Then I'll start on the rest of the lot, especially out along the road. That will make a big difference in terms of curb appeal. Unless you need me in here." She inclined her head toward the carpet in the living room, the last big project before they could truly get settled.

Everything she said made sense. "How long will the lot take, do you think?"

"I should have enough time to finish pruning today. Then tomorrow, I'll tackle the weeding. Looks like someone got a good start on that already."

"That was me." Sam had spent the better part of a day pulling weeds to work out her frustration. It had helped a little.

"If it's okay, I'd like to start a compost bin with the plant matter rather than putting it in the dumpster. With all this beautiful southern sun exposure in the back, this place really needs to have a veggie garden. Fresh compost would help nourish it. Plus, gardens are really beautiful." Olly's skin tinged pink and she looked down and away. "I think your guests would like it."

That was the closest Sam had ever come to a genuine "aw, shucks" moment. It was adorable. And then what Olly said sank in.

"Garden?" Sam hesitated. She wasn't eager to add another project to the insane amount of things she needed to do already. It was impossible to conceptualize.

"Yeah, Mom. That would be great. Fresh veggies. I'll do it. I can totally picture it."

Of course Beth would want a garden. The aesthetic of it surely appealed to her, but how enthusiastic would she be after she realized how much work it was?

"I don't know." Sam drew the last word out. She hated to say no, but wasn't prepared to commit to the work herself.

"You don't have to decide today. Just let Olly do the compost thing, and we'll go from there. Okay?"

"How much will that cost?"

Olly adjusted the ball cap she wore and scratched the back of her neck. "It'll take me an hour or so to build it, so a lot less than it would cost to have it hauled away in a dumpster."

An hour of labor, plus construction supplies would definitely be cheaper than putting it in the dumpster. The cost of having it delivered gave her palpitations, and then, after it had arrived, she learned about the cost of having it emptied. Still, Sam hesitated. The direct money savings wasn't likely to offset the cost of her own future time and effort spent maintaining something like a compost bin. She'd never been a gardener and wasn't sure she was ready to start.

"I'll leave you to think about it." Olly backed away from the counter. "I'll get back to work."

"Don't you want a sandwich?" Beth offered.

Olly glanced at Sam, then back to Beth. "Another time, Beth."

Bitterroot Queen

Beth set the chips on the counter. "Oh come on. Mom, tell her it's okay for her to eat with us. She's not exactly the hired help."

Sam almost laughed. That was exactly what Olly was in this scenario. More than that, though, if she continued to be this helpful, she was their goddamned savior. Before Sam could affirm Beth's invitation, Olly made it to the door that separated their apartment from the lobby.

"That's okay. I brought my lunch." With that, she stepped through the door.

"Why didn't you stop her? We can spare one sandwich, can't we?"

"Yes, of course. But she clearly didn't want to stay."

"Hmph." Beth picked up the bag of chips and said, "I need to get dressed." She started toward her room.

"Why are you in pajamas?"

"I was doing school work online. Didn't see a reason to get dressed," Beth answered without turning around.

"Do you want a sandwich?" Sam called after her.

"Yeah, in a minute." The bedroom door closed behind her, a bit quieter than the last few times.

Sam put together a plate of sandwiches for Beth, cut in triangles because Beth liked them that way, or rather, she used to. When she was six. After she finished eating, she'd leave another message with the realtor, asking her to contact the previous owner. Again. She'd given up on getting an actual response, but she continued to seek one on principle. Also, she needed to contact Reagan, her potential new attorney. As much as she couldn't afford to pay the fees, she couldn't afford to simply let the insurance company off the hook. The longer she thought about their refusal to pay out her benefits, the angrier she got about it. Even if it took years, as Reagan cautioned, it would eventually be worth it. She hoped.

By the time she finished on the phone, she'd need some sort of therapy. Schlepping boxes around would be the perfect solution. At this point, the container was about half empty. They'd brought in all the boxes labeled "bathroom," "Sam's bedroom," "Beth's room," along with most of the "kitchen" boxes. That left far too many "living room" and "misc" boxes. Beth was dangerously close to finishing her mural, the last domino that needed to fall before the carpet could come up. Instead of waiting, Sam would bring the boxes into the motel lobby and sort them there. The container could then be picked up and Sam could mark it off of her list of expenses. Good. She had a plan.

"Come on, Ramp." Olly patted the side of her leg. A sandwich would have been nice, but she wasn't really hungry yet. Besides, she'd made a deal with herself that she would finish the back side of the shrubs before taking a food break. She had at least an hour, maybe two, before that would happen.

She did take a moment to drink some water and dump her flannel into the Scout. She'd started off cool that morning, but was sweating way too much now. She stripped off the tank top, too, leaving her only in her razorback sports bra.

"What do you think? Should we stay in Bitterroot for a while?" Her initial panicked urge to run away had settled to the back of her mind. Bitterroot spoke to her in a way she'd never before experienced.

Rampart looked up at her, his eyes full of devotion and a sincere curiosity.

"Is that a yes or no?"

Rampart barked once and wagged his tail.

"You like it here?" She took another drink of water and checked Rampart's bowl. It was still half full, but she didn't want him to run out. She dumped the last of hers in to top it off.

Rampart barked again and sat down.

"George is a pretty good guy. And Bitterroot feels really good. Doesn't it?"

That morning, over eggs and toast, George had offered her the use of his spare bedroom. More than that, he didn't freak out when she stiffened and didn't answer immediately. He was a gruff, crusty old guy, but he totally got her. She couldn't remember that ever happening with anyone else. As further evidence, he had brushed off the offer and replaced it by saying she could use the loft in the barn, if she wanted, and convert it into an apartment.

The whole thing filled her with an unfamiliar feeling of warmth. In some far recess of her mind, she was almost willing to call it a feeling of home. Since she'd never really had that, she couldn't say for sure. But it felt good. Not scary. Not like a trap. There was a ton of work to do here at the motel. Maybe while she was doing that, she'd give the loft a test run. Maybe pick up some furniture. Did Bitterroot have a Craigslist? Or was that bulletin board their version of online postings? Probably.

"What do you say, tonight, after we finish up here, let's set up the hammock in the loft and spend the night up there? We'll have to figure something out for stairs. That ladder is a little steep for you."

Rampart barked agreeably in response.

She put her water bottle in the Scout, adjusted her hat, and tucked the wayward strands of hair back up under it before she returned to the hedge.

She worked at a steady pace, stopping occasionally to check that her edges were straight. A line of shrubbery that was pruned wider in some spots and narrower in others would be tragic, and she didn't want Sam to think she'd hired the wrong person, especially not when she was contemplating an extended stay in Bitterroot. She needed the work if that was going to happen, and there was plenty of that at the Queen.

When she was about halfway down the length of the hedge, an oversized Chevy truck pulled into the lot and a tall woman got out. She wore denim jeans and her legs seemed to go on forever. Her hair was cut short and combed back on the sides, and she wore a tank top similar to the one Olly had abandoned earlier.

She smiled and walked toward Olly rather than the entrance to the lobby. "Hi. You must be Olly. I'm Karen, a friend of Sam and Beth." She extended her hand.

Olly wiped the sweat and dirt from her palm onto her jeans and shook her hand.

"Nice to meet you."

Rampart stood at attention at Olly's side, watching Karen. He wasn't on alert, but he wasn't relaxed, either. "This is Rampart."

Karen knelt and offered him her hand to sniff. Then, after he seemed satisfied, she patted him on the head. "Hey, guy. Nice to meet you, too. Beth told me all about you." She scratched Rampart behind his ears one more time and then stood.

"Looks like you're making some good progress here." As Karen spoke, she surveyed Olly's work and nodded thoughtfully.

"I do my best."

Karen held herself in a tight, controlled manner and gave off a decidedly male energy. Plus, Olly's gaydar was pinging madly. Another lesbian. Another plus in the pro column for Bitterroot.

"I'm on my way into work and just wanted to stop by and say hi."

The way Karen lingered an extra moment or two made Olly wonder if she'd meant to say hi to Sam or if she was just there to check Olly out.

Olly shuffled her feet, uncomfortable with the feeling that she was being sized up. "Okay, well, I'll get back to work." She held up the pruning shears as if that explained everything. "It was, um, nice to meet you."

Karen laughed and said, "Same here." With that, she turned and went to the lobby. Olly went back to work, a little unsettled, but glad that Bitterroot seemed to have more gay people than she ever would have suspected.

"Ugh," Beth said as she handed Sam yet another box labeled "misc." They'd been working for an hour, give or take, moving boxes into the reception area, and there were only a few boxes left in the container.

"Hey, I'll take that." Karen dropped a kiss on Sam's cheek and took the box in one smooth motion.

"What are you doing here?" Sam picked up another box and followed Karen inside. They'd propped the door open for easy access. Beth followed.

"Just stopped by on my way to work. I can't stay." Karen set the "misc" box on top of a stack of "living room" boxes.

"Sheesh." Beth set her box on the correct stack and then relocated Karen's.

Karen punched Beth's shoulder, a light, teasing shot. "Sorry 'bout that."

"Whatever." Beth rolled her eyes, but couldn't quite hide her smile. She headed back to the container for another load.

Sam turned to Karen and pulled her into a deeper kiss. "I'm glad you're here, even for a minute."

"I'll help you with the last of the boxes, then I have to run."

Two more trips back and forth and the container was officially empty. Sam walked Karen to her truck, kissed her goodbye, and then followed Beth inside.

"I need to finish some school stuff," Beth announced as they cleared the threshold, as though she thought Sam had some complicated and sinister plan to distract her.

"Good." Sam studied the boxes.

After arranging pickup of the moving pod, Sam went to check on Olly. She was finishing up the back side of the shrubbery. There were several small piles of trimmings lined up on the sidewalk in front of the hedge.

"This looks pretty good."

"Thanks." Olly removed her cap and wiped sweat from her brow with her arm. "I love stuff like this. Taking something that's all wild and in disarray and turning it into something neat and orderly. It's satisfying."

"I never thought of it that way." Sam caught herself staring at Olly's arms, at how her tattoos interacted with the bulge and taper of her muscles. It was captivating. Apparently, she was into tattoos. This was news to her.

Olly shrugged and dropped her hand to her side. Rampart was there immediately, nudging her for pats. Olly scratched his head absently. "I don't really care what the job is, so long as I can see my progress at the end of the day."

Bitterroot Queen

"What's the plan for all this?" Sam gestured toward the debris. Sure, Olly had mentioned a compost bin, but Sam really had no idea what that meant in terms of practical execution.

"That depends on you. I can put it in the dumpster when it arrives, or I could set it aside for now and build a compost bin later on."

"Okay, do that."

"Sure thing." Olly shifted her weight from foot to foot as though standing still was unnatural to her. "Do you need me to do something else? Or can I start on the beds?" She jerked her chin down to indicate the weeds at their feet. Even with the time Sam had spent out here, there were still far too many things growing in the planter beds that shouldn't be there.

"Actually, can I get your help inside for a minute? It's time to tackle the carpet in the living room."

"Sure." Olly led the way to the entrance, her gait a confident, loping movement that held an almost wild, kinetic energy. Once again, she held the door open for Sam with a polite nod and a smile. Rampart sat just outside the door without being told. Good dog.

"Thanks." Sam ducked inside, pausing just long enough to return Olly's smile.

The entry from the office into the apartment was filled with empty boxes that needed to be broken down. Without asking, Olly picked one up and flipped open a knife that somehow made it from her back pocket to her hand without so much as a flash of metal. She cut the taped edges and flattened the box. She picked up a second, all the while watching Sam with a polite look on her face.

"What do you need help with?"

Sam laughed. "The boxes, apparently."

Olly finished the second box and dropped it on top of the first. "I like to keep my hands busy, but I can stop." She stared at Sam, her gaze deep and penetrating, as if she were looking for a greater meaning that went beyond boxes and shrubs. For a moment, Sam was captivated, but then Olly smiled and laughed self-consciously and the spell, as it were, was broken. Sam turned to face the living area, her back to Olly.

"Any suggestions for this carpet?" She swept her hand out in an expansive gesture. Now, in addition to the strange, thankfully unidentifiable stains, the floor was also speckled with various shades of paint.

"Well," Olly drew the word out. "Clearly, this carpet needs to come out. I can do that pretty quick, if you want."

"That would be great, but what about after that?"

"What do you mean?" Olly's voice was louder this time, closer. Just over Sam's left shoulder.

"What do I do for a floor after the carpet is taken up?"

"Depends on what we find. This place was built in the forties, so there's likely hardwood in here, same as the bedrooms."

"That would be great." Pleased at the prospect, Sam whipped around to face Olly, who was closer than expected. Olly took a startled step back, and Sam blushed and put a hand on her arm to steady her.

"Yes, it would."

"Do you think it's oak?"

Olly frowned, clearly thinking. "In this area? More likely to find Hemlock or some sort of fir. Maybe cedar, but that would be weird."

Sam hadn't realized there were options beyond oak when it came to hardwood floors. "Huh. What's in the bedrooms? Will it be the same here?"

"Hemlock, and this is likely to be the same. It makes sense for the era."

"What about the guest rooms?" Sam asked, on the verge of being excited.

"The same, probably."

Fizzy, happy energy sparked inside her. This was the best news she'd had in weeks. Not that she had a clue about dealing with hardwood. Thankfully, it seemed as though Olly knew what to do—just like everything else so far. Whatever the process, it had to be cheaper than installing new carpet in each room. And it was prettier.

"So how do we remove this?" Sam should have paid attention when Olly pulled up the carpet in the bedrooms, but the job had been gross and Olly hadn't pressed her to help.

Olly picked up another box. "First, we have to clear the floor." She broke down that box and started on the next. "Do you have plans for these boxes?"

"Dumpster?"

She shook her head, an amused smile growing on her face. "No, don't do that. I'll take care of them."

"What does that mean?"

"Cardboard makes excellent compost, after the tape is removed, obviously."

Nothing about that was obvious, but Sam smiled and nodded and set to work clearing Beth's paint supplies out of the corner. As she shuffled everything to the back patio, a half-empty pack of cigarettes fell out of a canvas bag full of paint brushes. She slipped the pack into her pocket. Beth might have others, but now, at least, she didn't have these.

"Okay, what's next?"

Olly had finished with the boxes and moved the stack of flattened cardboard into the lobby.

"Now we pull."

She flipped that knife open again, and Beth stepped out of her room at the same moment. "Whoa there, killer. No weapons on school property," Beth said as she held up her hands in mock fear.

Olly laughed. Not the reserved, semi-polite laugh that she afforded Sam. This laugh was deep and rich and moved through her whole body. It was startling and breathtaking at the same time.

"You're just in time, kid. We're getting ready to commit homicide on the carpet."

"'Bout time. It's been asking for it since we got here." Beth smiled, full of teeth and sweetness.

"It's usually best to start in a doorway or at a wall," Olly said, her voice full of amusement. "So, here is good." She indicated the break between the kitchen and living room.

The floor in the kitchen wasn't much better, Sam thought. It had what looked to be the original linoleum floor, worn and cracked and pulling up at the corners. Carpet first, though.

Olly knelt and slipped her knife under the edge of the carpet. With small, controlled motions, she loosened the tacks. Eventually, when she had the whole seam undone, she gripped the carpet and stood. It came away from the floor easily, with a loud crackling and tearing sound.

"Now we roll it up." Olly pointed toward the sliding glass door on the other side of the room.

Sam moved in line with Olly and motioned for Beth to help. With the three of them working together, the carpet was easy to maneuver. Rolling it, however, disturbed all the latent funk and whatever else that had built up in it over the years.

"This is nasty." Beth grimaced and turned her face away.

"It's definitely not awesome," Olly agreed, also grimacing. She pushed ahead, outpacing both Sam and Beth. Occasionally, the sides of the carpet got held up, and Olly moved from side to side, pulling it free from the strip of nails that held it down, which made her muscles flex in really fabulous ways.

Sam was so distracted by this view that she didn't notice that Beth had fallen way behind until she said, "Mom..."

Sam turned. Beth sat flat on the floor, hand on her stomach, face pale.

"What's wrong?" Sam moved to her side.

"I don't feel so great."

"Bathroom." Sam urged Beth to her feet and nudged her in that direction.

Beth closed the door behind her, and the sound of retching followed.

"Wow. What's up with her?" Olly had stopped working and stood with her hands loose at her side, a confused expression on her face.

"Maybe the smell of the carpet."

"Possible." Olly regarded the carpet doubtfully, as if she couldn't understand but wasn't prepared to argue about it.

Beth appeared in the bathroom doorway. She wiped her mouth with the back of her hand. "I'm going to lie down for a minute, okay?"

Sam started to follow her, but Beth waved her off. "I'll be fine."

"Okay. Let me know if you need anything." There were few things that made Sam feel as helpless as when her daughter was ill, especially if she didn't understand why. She waited until Beth had retreated to her room then continued working. She and Olly removed the rest of the carpet and then dragged it out of the building to the dumpster via the lobby.

"This was pretty simple," Sam said. "Gross, but simple."

"Most things are easier to remove than to put up in the first place."

Back in the apartment, Olly stared at the wood floor. As far as Sam could tell, it was in decent shape. But she wasn't an expert.

"What do you think?" Sam asked as she stood next to her, trying to figure out how she saw the floor. For instance, did she appreciate the beauty, or did she only see the work needed to make it even more beautiful?

"Yeah, I love being able to breathe new life into something old and neglected, like these floors."

"I never really thought about it." Sam had spent too much time in Vegas, where everything was flashy and disposable.

Olly looked at her, an idea taking form on her face. "How do you feel about reclaimed materials? On my drive into Bitterroot, I passed a hotel in Missoula slated for demolition. It's derelict, but still gorgeous. I could talk to the contractor about pulling some stuff out of there. I bet he'd go for it. They usually do."

"You've done that before?"

"Once or twice. It's fun, actually."

Sam didn't know how she felt about reclaimed material, but she was learning to trust Olly. That was enough. "Yeah, sure. Why not?"

"Awesome. I'll see what I can do to make that happen." She pulled her phone from her back pocket and checked the time. "For now, though, it's getting pretty late. Do you want me to remove those tack strips tonight? Or wait until tomorrow morning?"

Bitterroot Queen

Sam sighed. She wanted them gone now, but didn't want to keep Olly from her life, either.

"If you'd rather wait until tomorrow, I'll finish up outside. If you want it done tonight, I'll leave the yard debris until morning." Olly nodded toward the door.

"So, either way, you're not rushing to get out of here?"

"No. I hate leaving things undone. I'd finish both, but I promised George I'd be home in time to fix dinner. He worries when I'm late."

"George?"

Sam had no idea who George was. What role did he fill in Olly's life? Why did he worry? And why did Sam care?

"George, the apple farmer." Olly looked at her expectantly.

"I have no idea what that means."

"George was the first person I met here in Bitterroot. At the farmers' market. He sold me apples and refilled my water bottle. And he told me about the job postings on the bulletin board."

"So, George is the reason we met?"

"Not quite. We met because you have a thing about people sleeping in your lot."

Sam's face flushed with heat. "Yeah, I really am sorry about that."

"Don't be. You clearly had some damage done to your property. And you were totally fierce, defending it like that." The slight teasing glint in Olly's eyes didn't diminish the compliment.

"Fierce?"

"Yeah, like a straight-up Amazon warrior."

"You're teasing me."

"Maybe. But you definitely scared the crap out of my mom. I had to call her three days in a row because of the way I hung up on her that day."

"You were talking to your mom? Oh, crap. Now I'm doubly sorry."

Olly laughed. "My sister says it was good for Linda. She tends to think of us as commodities to be traded rather than people she's responsible for nurturing."

"Linda? That's your mom?"

"Yeah."

"Does she live around here?"

"Upstate New York."

"Is that where you're from?"

"You have lots of questions." Olly smiled. "I'm going to start demanding answers from you in exchange."

"Okay. My mom's name was Viola. My dad was Archer. They never came to visit me, either, but they did fix me and Beth dinner every once in a while."

"Where are you from?" Olly asked.

"Ah, you never answered that question."

"Upstate New York." Olly gave her that crooked grin that short-circuited Sam's ability to think.

"Las Vegas."

The banter between them felt good, trading questions and learning little bits. If the ridiculous smile that was making her face ache was any kind of indication, Sam liked it. A lot.

Chapter Thirteen

Olly studied the loft. She'd worked steadily over the past week—whenever she wasn't at the Queen with Sam and Beth—to make improvements on the space.

First, she'd checked the roof for leaks. The corrugated metal, which she loved when it rained, was in good shape, as was the shiplap beneath it. When she finished inspecting the roof, she'd found several rolls of attic insulation with an R value of 49, in addition to some rolls of R-21 for the walls, electrical wire, boxes, outlets, light fixtures, and a roll of vapor barrier. All good stuff.

The supplies were stacked neatly in the middle of the barn with a note: *Let me know when you are ready to do the plumbing and sheetrock. ~ G*

Installing the insulation was by far her least favorite activity, but also necessary. Old barns such as this weren't built for energy efficiency. In summer, they were hot as hell and equally cold in the winter. The insulation required her to wear long-sleeved shirts and long pants, and still, no matter how careful she was, she always ended up with fiberglass strands all over herself. It itched with a crazy fury.

If things had been left to her, she would have picked out an ecofiber insulation, the kind made of recycled denim. It was dusty as hell to work with, especially if she used a blower, but it was much better for the environment, had greater sound dampening and insulating properties, and didn't make her want to scratch her skin off. But she didn't bring it up, because George was being so helpful, and since he'd provided the insulation, she was going to use it.

She was finishing off the last section of the ceiling when George joined her in the loft. Rampart barked from his post at the bottom of the ladder, alerting her too late that someone was coming.

"Looks good." George inspected the area as if he hadn't seen it before. "You're right. It does feel good up here."

Olly folded open the corner side of the insulation and stapled it in place. Six quick, precise hits with the swing stapler and the roof insulation was finished. She descended the ladder, skipping the last few steps and dropping to the floor of the loft with a gentle thud.

"Yep. It's coming along. Thanks for the supplies." She hadn't talked to him about that yet. Not really. There were a few other things she wanted, but was hesitant to bring it up. When Sam paid her, she'd have enough to buy some supplies on her own.

"What's this?" George indicated the scramble of electrical wires poking out from one section of the wall, opposite the ladder. She'd strung all the wiring, including all the boxes, prior to starting the insulation. Before the sheetrock, she'd fill in the appropriate outlets, switches, and fixtures.

"Oh, that." Olly brushed the insulation from her legs and then stripped off her gloves and long sleeved shirt. "I'd like to put a breaker box there."

"Yeah?" George looked around the room, tracing a pattern in the air with his finger that followed the path of the wiring. "Where'd you learn to do this?"

"Stepdad number three was an electrician. I'm not licensed or anything, but it'll pass."

"Anything you can't do, kid?"

Olly laughed. "I'm sure there is."

"Well, when you find it, let me know."

"Will do." Olly checked her phone for the time. She'd promised Sam she'd be over by nine to start the exterior paint. She could chat with George a little longer.

"What kind of box do you want?"

"Huh?" It took Olly a moment to realize what George was asking. "For the load center? You don't need to worry about that. I'll pick it up."

"Are you sure?" George asked.

"Sure. It seems only fair, what with you letting me stay here and all." Olly still wasn't willing to commit to a time frame, but she knew one thing was certain, the busier she was, the more likely she was to stay. When she was idle, her thoughts got away from her until, eventually, she had no choice but to move on. It was inevitable.

George nodded slightly in acknowledgement. "Have you given any thought to heat?"

Olly had given it a lot of thought, actually. She was loath to use wall heaters, as they were inefficient and drew a lot of electricity. Her hope was to make this space as self-contained as possible. She had a couple of ideas, but wasn't sure how George would feel about them.

"Yeah, I've been meaning to talk to you about that."

"I figured. You're always thinking about something. What's on your mind?"

"Do you know what geothermal heating and cooling is?"

George scratched the top of his head. "I remember hearing something about that a few years back, but couldn't tell you what it means."

"It's an old practice that got forgotten somewhere along the line. Basically, it's a system that draws from the earth to maintain a stable temperature. Requires a lot of digging and pipe."

"How much digging?"

"Enough that I don't want to do it with a shovel." Olly glanced at her phone again. Time for her to get moving.

"I've got that Ditch Witch. Is that big enough?"

"That's the right idea, but it doesn't go deep enough, unfortunately."

"I'm sure we can come up with a backhoe if that's what you need." George smiled conspiratorially, as if he and Olly were plotting a great adventure.

"Sounds good." Olly patted his shoulder. "I'd like to use a combination of geothermal, a rocket stove mass heater, and a series of ceiling fans, but I'll have to tell you more about it at dinner. Sam is expecting me soon and I need a quick shower to get the insulation off before I go."

"Sure thing. Of course. About that, do you plan to add a shower up here?"

She went back and forth on that. She certainly didn't need a shower when there was already one downstairs, but the next person, assuming George rented the apartment after she left, might appreciate it.

"Maybe. What do you think?" As she talked, she gathered up her things, a towel, change of clothes, wallet, phone, keys, and hat. Rampart was already downstairs and ready to go.

George walked with her toward the ladder. "I think it might be nice. Proper stairs, too."

Olly laughed. George had been so standoffish when they'd met, now he doted on her like a loving grandfather. It was adorable and surprisingly didn't feel suffocating at all. That was an odd turn of events.

After they made it down the ladder, George continued

on toward the open equipment door, and Olly headed toward the small, functional shower room. Once again, she was struck by how okay she was with the exchange. Everything that Olly put in place in that apartment was one more little root taking hold in this community. Conversations where George alluded to her future didn't frighten the hell out of her. The feeling, a curious mix of contentment and belonging, settled in her chest in a way that made her feel safe and warm.

While she waited for the water to warm up, Olly sent a quick text message to her sister.

She hit send before she could talk herself out of it.

I think I found it.

Olly didn't explain what "it" was. Gen would know. They'd certainly talked about it enough. On her sixteenth birthday, Olly had driven away from Linda's house and Gen stayed behind. Since then, Gen had asked the same question every time they talked. What was Olly looking for? For nine years and more stops than Olly could remember, her answer had always been the same. She would know it when she found it.

It? Seriously?

Seriously.

*I decided it was a myth a long time ago.
I'm shocked.*

Olly laughed. She missed Gen and she almost regretted leaving her behind. It was for the best, though. If she'd stayed, she wouldn't have been able to almost forget the person Gen became to please their mom. She embraced the con, bent and twisted until she virtually disappeared, leaving behind a grifter Linda could be proud of. In spite of that, Olly remembered the girl who shared her secrets, who protected her, and who encouraged her to reach for what she wanted, even if that was simply to drive for a decade in search of something. That's who she texted, the sister who was her champion in a world of sliding standards.

> *Me too. But it's here and it's real.*
>
> *Should I tell Mom?*
>
> *Don't you dare.*
>
> *Don't worry. Your secret is safe with me.*

A moment later, before Olly could send off her reply, another message from Gen came through.

> *I'm happy for you.*
>
> *I am too.*

Gen had changed a lot in the past few years. So much so that Olly worried that she was making a mistake by sharing any of this with her. But it felt so good, being in Bitterroot, and who else could she confide in? Who else knew her well enough to get it?

Bitterroot Queen

"Are you sure you know how to use this?" Sam asked, the instructions clutched in her hand as though the slight breeze might snatch them away permanently.

"Yep, I'm sure." Olly continued to set up. She'd caulked the cracks and taped off the trim yesterday. Then, to simplify today's work, she had asked the man at the paint counter to pre-strain the paint. It was something they did upon request but didn't advertise. The only thing left was to insert the feed tube into the five gallon bucket, plug in the machine, and pull the trigger.

"But you didn't read the instructions."

That wasn't true. She'd read them over three times the previous day, plus she'd used this exact machine a couple of times before. She didn't believe in being unprepared to work. Frankly, she would have preferred to spend the day sanding and finishing the floors in Sam's apartment, but the industrial sander wasn't available until the weekend. Painting the exterior was a good second choice, assuming Sam let her start soon.

Beth stood off to the side, petting Rampart, cigarette dangling in her other hand. The ash had grown unrealistically long, and Olly was pretty sure she hadn't taken a drag from it since she'd arrived.

Olly set the spray nozzle on the small impromptu workstation she'd fashioned from two paint buckets and a stack of flattened cardboard. She faced Sam fully and said, "Yes, I did. I know how to use it. I promise."

"But Beth doesn—"

"I can teach her."

For some reason, Beth wanted to learn how to use the sprayer. Fifteen-year-old girls, even artists, generally didn't sign up for menial labor, and Olly wasn't about to turn it down. Showing her would slow the process a bit, taking time to go over the way it worked, but that was okay. Olly liked Beth. She liked her spirit, and how even though she and Sam were often at odds, she sensed beneath that a fierce loyalty to Sam and a craving for her guidance, which Sam was still trying to figure out how to give her without stepping on her toes. Linda had never been that way, had never asked Olly her opinion or tried to understand her. As far as she was concerned, Olly was a stranger in her life, tied only through genetics and the misguided sense of obligation Linda tried to foist on her.

"Mom," Beth said with a sigh but also a smile as she stubbed out her cigarette on the heel of her boot and then tossed it into the trash bin. "It's okay. Go work on the website or something." She picked up the spray gun and kept her fingers far away from the trigger as Olly had instructed.

"We really do have this. No problem." Olly pried the instructions from Sam's grip with a grin. She had developed an easy way of interacting with Sam. She flirted just a little, spoke with candor, and laughed often, things she enjoyed doing anyway. And when that wasn't enough, she flexed her arms. That always distracted Sam from whatever she'd been focused on. It had taken her a few days to pick up on that, but once she did, she sank her teeth into it. Sam was crazy sexy, glamour and polish, even in her work clothes, but Olly had seen her gaze linger on her arms much longer than necessary and though she was a little uptight to be Olly's usual type, that was okay. She was beautiful, had spectacular breasts, and she blushed every single time she caught Olly checking her out. It made for a fun work day.

"Um, okay," Sam stammered. "I'll be inside." As predicted, a pretty flush of pink spread over her cheeks. As she stepped inside, Olly wanted to call her back, press her lips to Sam's, and taste—

Beth slapped her arm. "Stop trying to break my mom."

"Ouch. Don't hit. I'm delicate."

"As if."

"Besides, your mom's pretty tough. She's been through a lot, and she'll get through a lot more. I admire that."

Beth stared at her, as if seeing her for the first time. "What do you mean?"

"It's pretty ballsy to make a change like this. To try to make a better life for you and her. She bought a place she'd never seen in person, found what she did, and rolled with it. She didn't give up. That's the definition of ballsy."

"You seem pretty ballsy yourself."

"Maybe. I think your mom might have me beat in some departments, though." She grinned. "Let's paint."

She led Beth to the far corner of the building, the paint hose uncoiling lazily behind them, where she painted in slow, even swipes, letting the color coat the building. The key was to let the paint guide her, and not try to force it to do otherwise.

"You ready to try?" She held the sprayer out to Beth. "Don't fight the paint. It's like a mutual agreement kind of process."

"First, I need to ask a favor." As she spoke, Beth pulled a folded sheet of paper from her pocket and offered it to Olly.

"What's this?" Olly opened the page to find a well-drawn sketch of the Queen, featuring a large, negative-space metal sign with back lighting on the exterior section of wall in front of the office.

"I designed this, but don't know anyone around here who does metalwork. I don't know anyone, really, except you and Rachel. Can you help me find someone? I want to surprise my mom."

Olly studied the drawing. It showed a fair amount of skill. In contrast to the free-flowing mural she'd painted in their living room, this had been done with careful precision. It showed a level of discipline that Olly hadn't attributed to Beth. She folded it and tucked it into her own pocket.

"I can ask around. George seems to know everyone." And if George didn't have any suggestions, she'd swing past Bitter Ink and ask Ava.

"What is it with you and that apple guy?"

"That apple guy gave me a place to stay after your mom threatened to mace me." Olly grinned.

"Like she had any choice, what with you lurking around like an up-to-no-good punk." Beth grinned back.

"Lurking? I was talking on the phone. Right in plain sight. There was no lurking, young lady."

"Oh, okay. Whatever."

Olly laughed. "Yeah, yeah. I'll see if I can find someone who works in metal. Speaking of, you're a decent artist, you know that?"

Beth shrugged. "Yeah, of course."

"What are you planning to do with it?"

"My art? Probably nothing." Beth stared in to space, a wistful look on her face. "Artists don't make shit."

"Ah, the ever important money."

"You say it like it doesn't matter."

"Look, I'm not going to lie. Money can be a good thing to have. It pays the bills and can take care of some things. But it's not everything. There are artists out there doing what they love and making enough money to have the kinds of lives they want. Ultimately, it comes down to what you love, what brings you joy. If art is your thing—

Bitterroot Queen

if that's what you absolutely have to do and it's your passion—believe me, you'll find a way to make it work."

Just then, Karen pulled into the hotel parking lot, her big truck tires crunching loudly on the gravel and kicking up dust. She gave them a polite wave and then headed into the lobby, no doubt in search of Sam.

"What's the deal with her?" Olly regretted it as soon as she said it and almost winced. It was none of her business.

"She and my mom are friends from way back."

"Just friends?" Olly tried to make it sound innocent.

"Why? Jealous?" Beth smiled, a wicked gleam in her eyes.

"What? No." Olly paused. "I don't think so, anyway." Or was she?

"Yeah, whatever," Beth said. "They hooked up a few times after we moved here, but I think that's over now. Or, if it's not, they are being way more careful around me than they were."

"You don't want them to hook up?" Olly wasn't sure why she cared who Sam was hooking up with or why it was important that Beth didn't want her to do it with Karen. It was all a little twisted up in her mind. Beth acted older than fifteen, making it easy for Olly to think of her as a friend. But Sam was Beth's mom, and that meant Olly definitely shouldn't be asking Beth for the inside scoop on Sam's sex life.

"I thought it was cool at first. Karen is great. She's really good to my mom, and they seem really happy together."

"Oh." Ouch. That also explained the weird territorial vibe she got off Karen.

"But then, my mom said yes when that dude asked her out, plus she said she and Karen aren't even dating."

"Speaking of that dude, any idea how the date went?" If the date was a bust, maybe she could up her game a little, flirt more, and see what happened. But the new information from Beth about Karen might preclude that.

"I didn't ask." Beth shrugged. "She didn't say anything about it, but she hasn't gone out with him again, so it was probably not great, but not totally bad. I can usually tell when that happens. She gets into a mood."

Olly nodded and did what she always did when reality made her head hurt. She went to work. She finished the section she was painting and then handed the sprayer off to Beth. With a little luck, Karen would be long gone by the time they finished making their way around the building.

Chapter Fourteen

Sam stared at the floor. There were a few stains visible, even after they'd been worked over with a giant industrial sander that made Sam's arms quake from simply watching Olly use it.

When she shut off the sander, a haze of dust settled over everything in the room. Olly's dark hair took on a blond hue, and her face had a distinct raccoon effect from her protective eyewear and face mask. Sam giggled and then clapped her hands over her mouth to stop herself. Olly had given up her Saturday for this. Laughing was not the best way to say thank you.

Olly gave her a mock-scowl, then shook her hair out. It puffed out for a moment before she deftly pulled it into a ponytail. "That'll teach me not to forget my hat when operating this thing."

She dug her ballcap—that dreadful green thing with mesh sides and a tractor on the front—from her back pocket, knocked off the dust, and jammed it on her head. Sam giggled even harder.

Beth poked her head out of her room. "Is it safe to come out yet?"

"Yeah, if you don't mind a little dust." Olly smiled, her gaze lingering on Sam for a moment before she turned her attention to Beth. "You look nice."

Startled by Olly's observations, she looked at her

daughter. She wore a pair of ripped jeans, black motorcycle boots, a white tank top, and a pair of suspenders. Her hair, which had been a longer version of Sam's own auburn mane last time Sam had seen her, was shorn almost to the skin on the sides, with a longer section at the front that fell dramatically over her eyes. It was dyed a shockingly bright pink.

"Um, thanks." Beth shuffled uncomfortably.

"What's up with—" Sam gestured exaggeratedly at Beth, "all that?"

"Time for a change," Beth said with a shrug.

In the middle of staring at Olly's arms, watching them flex and contract in a symphony of movement that kept the sander in check while also making the tattoos on her arms come to life, Sam had left Beth to her own devices. It had only been a few hours, but that was obviously enough time for her to do a major makeover on herself. Dammit.

"Bold change," Sam said mildly, trying to sound neutral. There was no point to belaboring it, since Beth had already done it, and besides, it wasn't a battle worth fighting. Not when the two of them were finally starting to communicate with more than the occasional grunt or growl.

"Do you like it?" Beth tugged on the long lock of hair covering her eye.

"I do," Olly said without looking up. She was brushing the dust off the sander with a handheld broom.

Sam took a moment to study Beth objectively. Yes, the change was shocking, intentionally so. But it worked. Like everything else that had happened since she bought the Queen, this was a clear visual break from who Beth had been in Vegas.

Bitterroot Queen

"Yes." Sam nodded slowly. "I do."

Beth smiled, a radiant beam reminiscent of the little girl she'd been, like when Sam pushed her higher and higher on the swing at the park in the rare moments she had time to spend with her. A deep pang of nostalgia settled in the pit of her stomach, and she suppressed the urge to pull Beth into a hug.

"That's a good look on you, too," Beth said, deadpan.

Like everything else, Sam was covered with a thin layer of sawdust. It was the finishing touch to the paint-splattered jeans and the threadbare T-shirt left over from her college years with "UNLV" on the front. "Thanks," she said with a grin. "I worked hard on it. Anyway. Plans tonight?"

Olly finished clearing the dust from the sander and pushed it out of the room before Beth answered.

"I'm going out."

Sam tried not to frown. "Out? Like a date?"

"Maybe."

Okay, time to parent. Without being an ass. "So...what about Denmar?"

A light pink blush rose on Beth's neck and cheeks, and Sam realized that she hadn't heard Beth mention him in a couple of days, nor had she overheard any phone conversations between them. Damn. She'd been so caught up in working on the motel that she maybe missed some of Beth's cues.

"He's being an asshole," she said dismissively.

"Okay. Did you break up, then?"

Beth looked down. "No, not really." She shrugged. "I don't really know."

Sam hoped it had ended with him, but she wasn't going to push her to do it. She moved to pull Beth into a hug, and Beth shrieked and stepped out of reach.

"God, Mom. You're covered in sawdust."

Sam stepped back, smiling. "So who are you going out with?"

"Rachel."

Oh. Sam's brain stuttered to a stop. The way Beth was acting—blushing, stammering, changing her hair, and putting on clean clothes—it seemed as though this was a date, or that Beth wanted it to be. But this was the first time Beth had shown any interest in another girl. Before this, she'd been very determinedly straight, to the point of announcing it multiple times when she was angry at Sam for whatever reason. Maybe her baby wasn't as straight as she claimed.

"Oh," Sam said, unsure how to proceed with this revelation.

"It's not a date," Beth said in a rush.

"Are you sure?" Sam would have left it, but Rachel gave off a decidedly queer vibe, and Sam's gaydar was rarely, if ever, wrong.

Beth shrugged again. "I don't really know. She just said there's a party and asked if I wanted to come. She's picking me up at seven."

"A party?" Sam arched an eyebrow. "And you're just telling me this now?"

"Relax. It's just a small group getting together at some guy's place to watch movies. Besides, I'm not really interested in drinking much these days."

"Some guy? Who?" She ignored the comment about drinking.

"A friend of Rachel's from school. It's okay. He's legit."

According to Rachel? Sam didn't voice that. "Will his parents be home?"

"I don't know, but Rachel promised me it would be really low-key. No wild night to remember or anything like that."

Bitterroot Queen

"Okay, you already know how I feel about things like this, and I know that I wasn't always the mom you might have needed or wanted. I also know that you've gone to a lot of parties that I don't know about. But this is a different place, and I'm trying to be better."

"Mom—" she said, the familiar angry teen edge to it.

"But you've also been working really hard and helping out a lot. So how about this? In the future, will you please let me know further in advance when you plan to do things like this and give me information on the place and time and people going? This is a small town, after all, and things work differently. Can you do that?"

Beth regarded her for a moment. "Yeah. So can I go, then?"

"Like I said, you've been working really hard, and I think you should have some fun. But let's set some ground rules."

"Seriously?"

"Yes. Make sure you have your phone at all times and if anything makes you feel uncomfortable, or anything's weird, leave and call me. I don't care what time it is. Your safety is my number one priority. Got it?"

"Okay," she grumbled but she sounded relieved, too.

"All right. So is this a date with Rachel?"

"I don't know."

"She didn't say?"

"Not really. But I do like Rachel a hell of a lot more than Denmar. He's being a jerk."

"Hmm." Sam didn't want to curtail Beth's new—friendship? Romance?—but she also wanted her to be careful and she wasn't sure how to broach that without setting Beth off.

"It'll be fine, Mom. I promise. And if I need anything, I'll call you or Olly."

"Olly?" Sam asked in her best mom voice. And since when did Beth talk to Olly?

"Yeah, she's cool. And she'd totally kick ass if somebody tried to hurt me."

For some reason, Sam could envision Olly doing that. "Okay, well, I guess it's good for you to have two people you can call instead of just one if there's trouble. What time does this party end?"

"I'm not sure. I'm pretty tired, though. My mom has turned into a slave driver, you know, making me work all the time. So I'll probably come back around midnight. Is that okay?"

Sam nodded. "One more thing."

"Jesus, Mom."

"We'll discuss your language later. Right now, you should probably find out if this is a date or not. And, if it is, and you plan to explore that with Rachel, you need to talk to Denmar. Lord knows, I'm not his biggest fan, but it's not fair to him or you or Rachel for you not to talk it out and properly end things with him if that's what you want. You can't just break up by virtue of never speaking again. You're better than that."

"Okay, okay. Sheesh." She rolled her eyes but flashed a smile before she went back to her room, leaving Sam to stand in the dissipating dust, wondering what the hell had just happened.

Olly parked the sander in the lobby, careful to position it out of the flow of traffic, where no one could trip on it. Rampart looked up from his napping spot behind the counter, then dropped his head back to his paws when he realized who it was.

"Hey, Ramp."

Between the still unpacked moving boxes and the detritus left over from the previous owner, the lobby was a haphazard mess, so she started organizing the chaos a bit. Besides, Sam and Beth were talking about mother-daughter things, and they deserved some privacy, though she needed to check in with Sam about what was on the agenda for later. It was almost seven, and she had other things she needed to finish that night. Earlier that day, before she'd left to come here, George had shown up with a truck full of lumber and talked about a set of stairs leading from the barn floor to the loft above. She was eager to get started on that project.

She heard a second door closing in the living quarters and took that as a sign that it was safe for her to return. She brought the broom, dustpan, and an empty box with her.

"Hey." Beth lounged against the kitchen counter.

"Kid." Olly set the box near the back patio door and started to work. "What's the occasion?" She nodded toward Beth's outfit and her new hair. "I do like it, by the way."

"You do? Thanks." Beth smiled in a way that lit up her face, something Olly had only seen a couple of times before.

"Yeah. The outfit suits you, and the hair is fun. Artistic. So, whatcha doing tonight?"

"I may or may not have a date."

"Huh. Well, good luck with that." Olly scooped up a pile of dust with the dustpan.

"You're not going to ask what that means?"

"Nah. Unless you want me to, I guess. You can tell me if you need to."

"You aren't like other adults."

Olly shrugged. "I guess not. Why would I want to be? Most people live very limited lives. I want more."

"More means living out of your car?"

"Sure, if that's what it takes. I like to see different places. Experience things at a native level. Can't do that if you're stuck in one place."

"So, you're planning to leave Bitterroot?" Beth sounded... hurt, maybe.

"Dunno. I expect so, but who knows the future for sure? George is really cool, and I like his place. I'm remodeling the loft in his barn, turning it into an apartment."

"An apartment in a barn? Why?"

"Why not? It's a good space. And I think George hopes that I'll stay when it's all done." As she talked, Olly continued to work. She made steady progress, and her box was just about full. She'd need another before she finished.

"Will you?"

"Maybe. It'd be a first, but I'm not ruling it out."

"I hope you do."

Olly stopped and turned to face Beth. She smiled. "Thanks, kid. I'll keep you posted. Now, you were going to tell me about your might-be-a-date plans for the evening." She started on the next section of floor.

"That girl, Rachel, invited me out. To this party at some dude's house. I said yes."

"And she didn't say if it was a date or not?" Olly wasn't surprised. Kids were awful at communicating their emotions. It was too much pressure, or at least it felt like it, and teenagers were terrified of being vulnerable. Still, kudos to Rachel for extending the invitation. She knew about Beth's boyfriend back in Vegas and still took the initiative.

"Nope."

"And you didn't ask?"

"Nope."

"Why not?"

Beth hesitated. "I...I'm not sure what I want the answer to be. I love my boyfriend. At least I thought I did." She sighed and stared at her boots. "I don't know anymore. He's being such a jerk since I moved, and it's hard, you know, not seeing him every day like I used to."

"What's he being a jerk about?"

"Everything. I think he's fucking my friend Jenny."

"That is definitely jerk behavior." Olly tried to sound nonjudgmental, but it was hard. She was all in favor of people defining the terms of their relationships however they wanted. Open relationships, polyamory, monogamy, whatever worked for the people involved. It pissed her off, however, when people broke the agreed-upon rules of their relationship. Even young people needed to learn to define those with each other. If Beth thought he was sleeping around, that meant he hadn't actually talked about it with her, and that sucked.

"It is, isn't it," Beth said flatly. "I really should break up with him."

"Well, you should definitely talk to him, at the very least. To clear your head about it, anyway."

"Yeah, but not tonight. Tonight, party with Rachel." Beth smiled, but it didn't make her look any happier.

"But not a date," Olly said firmly.

"No?"

"No. Not if you're still in a relationship with Denmar. That wouldn't be cool."

"No, it wouldn't be. You're right."

"But that doesn't mean you can't have fun."

"Right. Speaking of fun, can I call you if things get out of hand? I mean, I'd call my mom, but she'll just overreact. I'd like to have a backup plan. Just in case."

"And what do you think will go wrong?"

"It's a party. Anything could happen." Beth stared at her, expression solemn.

"Okay. Do you have my number?"

"Not yet." Beth held out her cell phone. Olly took it, added her contact information, and then handed it back.

"Be safe, kid."

"I'm trying." Beth went to the front door. "I'm going to wait outside for Rachel."

Olly watched her go, hoping that kids her age in Bitterroot didn't do the stupid shit they did elsewhere. It was probably a vain hope, but Beth seemed to have common sense, at least. She worked steadily for a few minutes, until Sam entered from the bedroom. She'd cleaned off the sawdust and put her hair up in a messy bun. Auburn strands had escaped and framed her face. It was a subtle, simple change from earlier, but the difference was almost as startling as Beth's change. Olly stared, transfixed.

"You look beautiful," Olly blurted, and bit back a groan. That might have been too forward. But something...what was it? What was she feeling, and what was this strange pull that kept her gaze on Sam and made her want a whole lot more?

"Really?" Sam glanced down at herself. She still wore the same work jeans and holey T-shirt she'd had on all day. "Okay. I'll take your word for it." Olly couldn't stop staring, and it was a very bad idea that she was standing in the same room with Sam. She wanted to do things she had no business doing. At all. But still, she moved closer.

"Thanks." Sam looked up then. Her eyes widened and her breath hitched.

Olly noticed. Oh, how she noticed. And somehow, she had closed the distance between them until she was close enough to touch. Her fingers itched to move, to gloss over the bare bits of Sam's skin barely visible through the worn spots in the T-shirt. The slightest motion, just a little tip forward, and she would be able to bury her nose in the crook of Sam's neck, to inhale her scent and taste the goose bumps that were forming there.

"Olly." Sam's voice was breathy and hesitant. There was a compelling invitation mixed in with a weak warning. She tilted her head up slightly, leaving her throat exposed.

Olly stared at her, burning in places that had been coming alive since she'd started work at the motel. And then reality smacked her in the head. She was making a move on Sam. The woman who had hired her to do a few jobs. Who might be involved with Karen. She took a step back.

"Uh." She cleared her throat. "Sorry," Olly said, her face flushed with embarrassment and something indefinable. Shit. What the hell was she thinking?

Sam reached for her, but Olly moved away. She needed to regroup, to think about what she was doing.

"I'm, um, going to check on Beth." Olly fled to the lobby and out into the parking lot, Rampart on her heels, where she filled her lungs, drawing deep and letting the evening air clear the fog in her brain.

Beth stood, hunched against the wall with an unlit cigarette in her hand. "What's going on?" she asked. She glared at the cigarette for a moment longer and then returned it to the pack.

"Nothing." Olly's insides were still shaking. Her reaction to Sam wasn't completely out of left field. After all, Sam was hot as fuck, and Olly wasn't blind. Plus, she liked her. But that didn't explain the intensity of her reaction. Before tonight, she'd teased and flirted, but this was next-level shit and she had no idea where it had come from. Or maybe she did and she wasn't ready to think about that.

"Nothing?" Beth arched an eyebrow. "Then why do you look like you're about to hurl?"

Olly wrapped one arm around her belly. Now that Beth mentioned it, her stomach was threatening to send all her insides out. She shrugged weakly. "Something I ate, maybe?"

A car pulled into the lot, and Beth pushed away from the wall. "That's my ride."

"Have fun." Olly walked with her as far as the Scout and stopped.

"Yeah, thanks. Later."

With a nod, Olly climbed into her vehicle, waited half a moment for Rampart to join her, and then started the engine and drove away, thoughts muddled and heart racing. What the hell had she done? Would Sam even want her to continue working for her? She groaned. Of all the stupid things she could've done, this was one of the worst. She thought this was it, that Bitterroot might be a place for her. And she went and did that.

Nothing to be done about it now. And there were other projects waiting for her attention that would distract her. At least for a while.

Chapter Fifteen

Olly parked just outside the barn. Since she'd decided to sleep in the apartment rather than her Scout, she preferred to leave the Scout in the driveway. That kept the place from smelling like a commercial garage. Inside, she found a new stack of building materials. There was stove pipe, fire brick, and several lengths of timber. In other words, exactly what she needed to start on the stairs and the heating system.

"That Sam kept you late tonight," George said when he entered the barn behind her.

That Sam. Olly had been trying not to think about her, focusing instead on the work she had to do here. "Yeah. We were sanding the floors. Hemlock. Beautiful grain." She walked the length of one of the long boards she would use to create the runners for the stairs, dragging her finger over the surface as she moved.

"I'm not trying to rush you. I just want this stuff here, on hand when you're ready for it."

"Sure." Olly nodded, focusing on the grain of the wood as variations of stair plans gained purchase in her mind. "What do you see here? One long run? Or a modified spiral?"

There was more than enough length to the floor of the barn to accommodate a long run, and that's what she envisioned, but would adjust to match George's plan.

"Up to you. If you want a spiral, I won't stop you. But a traditional flight seems more practical."

"Mmm. It does." Olly grabbed her tape and took some quick measurements. A little bit of math and she was ready to mark where to make the notches in the runner. She jotted a few notes on a piece of scrap paper and reached for her carpenter's quick square.

"So, did you eat yet?"

"Not really hungry." She marked off the first step and then stopped abruptly. "Shit. Are you? I can fix something for you now."

"I already ate. Was going to bring you a plate."

So far, their dining arrangement had been casual. When she was around, she cooked for George. She enjoyed doing it and he was willing to let her. When she was gone, he took care of his own meal prep. Maybe they should discuss a more formal arrangement to avoid any possible confusion.

"I'm good. Thanks anyway." Olly went back to marking off steps. She'd definitely have enough time to cut out the first one and perhaps the second.

"I drove past the motel today," he said. "You've made quite the difference."

Heat flushed Olly's cheeks. She hoped she hadn't made a difference right out of the job with her ill-advised, aborted come-on. "You think?"

"I know."

"Thanks." Olly finished making the notches, looked at the length of the run, and then went back to her calculations. If she split it at the midpoint, she could include a level rest point that would also make the stairs more stable. It was common to have a landing such as that when a set of stairs changed directions midway, but not so much when it was one direction. Defying convention, she decided to insert the break.

"What are you doing there next?"

"Probably putting down a coat of finish in the living quarters. They're still living out of boxes until the floor gets done. It's not ideal." She grabbed the jigsaw. It wasn't her preferred tool, but it would get the job done. "Wonder if she'll let me use something like linseed oil on it."

"That'd be nice," George said.

"Yeah." She stood with the saw in her hand. She itched to keep working, to distract her mind and body from...everything. She leaned against a sawhorse, resting her weight on one hip. A paper in her pocket crinkled and she pulled it out. "Oh, hey, I've been meaning to ask. Do you know anyone who does metalwork? Or custom sign-making?"

The hand-drawn design Beth had given her had been riding around in her pocket for the last few days. She unfolded it and showed the picture to George.

"This for that lady? Sam?" George glanced at the paper with a sniff.

"Yeah. Her daughter designed it for her."

George slipped his reading glasses onto his face and took the paper. "Oh, yes. This is very nice. You could check with the blacksmith. Quinn. Ava knows how to get ahold of her." He gave the paper back to Olly.

"Is she that hard to reach?"

"She's—" George paused, a thoughtful look on his face. "Private. Work goes to her through a broker. But Ava is a more direct route."

"I'm overdue for a trip to Bitter Ink anyway. I'll stop in to say hi sometime this week."

"Need any help with those stairs?" George scratched the back of his neck.

"Nah. I'm going to feed Ramp, notch out this one run and then head up to sleep."

"Okay. I'll let you get to it, then." George made his way out of the barn with a slow, measured pace, his shoulders hunched slightly from carrying the burdens of a lifetime.

Olly set to work making her cuts and trying—unsuccessfully—to get thoughts of Sam out of her head.

Olly was six and Gen was nine. They had climbed so high in the cherry tree that there was no way their mom could get to them. As Linda stood at the base of the trunk, swearing and yelling for them to get down, Olly stared at the sky and laughed and laughed. She loved being up there, so high it felt like she could almost touch the clouds.

Gen watched their mom, a wary expression on her face. She urged Olly down. "It's time to go inside. Mom's real upset."

Olly ducked Gen's reach and tried to climb higher and higher and higher.

Then, just like that, she was falling down, down, down.

When she landed, her left arm gave a sickening pop-crunch sound, and pain shot like lightning through her body. She didn't like this, her mom glaring at her, her arm hurting, and Gen calling down that she was stupid. She wanted to go back. Go back to touching the clouds and not hurting.

For a moment, she floated up, drifty and happy, but then her mom snatched up her other arm. She pulled hard, her fingers pinching and digging in until she couldn't tell which arm hurt the most.

Bitterroot Queen

"Hurts," she tried to say, but the words came out strangled and wrong. She couldn't make her voice work, and still her mom was squeezing and dragging her toward the house.

Her mom's voice, screeching and menacing, melded with the tinkling sound of rain that changed again to a bouncy piano tune. Each time her mom opened her mouth, another note came out.

Then the music stopped and her mom faded and the tree loomed large above her.

A moment later, the dream disappeared completely, and Olly sat bolt upright, clutching her left arm and trying to clear her head. The break hadn't healed right and bugged her sometimes when the weather changed. It didn't hurt as much as it had when she fell, or for the two days after when her mom had insisted nothing was wrong and she needed to stop faking it. On day three, she'd taken her to the doctor. The X-rays had sent Linda to parenting classes and Olly and Gen to foster care for six months while Linda figured out how to be a good mom.

The piano music sounded again.

She pressed her palms to her temples. The music was definitely coming from outside her head.

Her phone. She fumbled with the few belongings on the makeshift bedside table constructed from a series of stacked wooden milk cartons. It took a moment, but she eventually came up with her cell.

"'lo?" she said, her voice rough with sleep. "Hello," she said, a bit clearer this time.

"Olly?"

"Yeah." She rubbed her eyes. What time was it?

"Olly? Can you come get me?"

"Beth?" Just like that, Olly was awake. "Where are you?" She didn't ask what had happened. The fact that

Beth had called meant something was wrong, the details of which could wait until later.

The night was cool and crisp and did absolutely nothing to dispel the tension and anxiety gripping Sam's chest. After Olly had gone home for the night, Sam had taken a long, hot bath, changed into some comfy jammies, and curled up with a hot chocolate and her Kindle. It'd been so long since she'd had even a moment to read.

Midnight came. No Beth.

Another hour. Still, no Beth.

Sam tried her number; it went to voicemail.

At that point, she gave herself permission to worry. She realized now, in retrospect, that Beth had spent many, many nights away from home, either at a party or out with Denmar. That didn't make this night any easier. Should she try Olly? She kicked herself. It was late and Olly had left on strange terms. That was another issue that was digging at her, what to do about the moment they had shared earlier that day. So, it felt weird calling her at this hour. She wasn't family, after all, and Sam barely knew her. What could she do?

Maybe she should call the police. And say what? Her daughter was at a party. No, she didn't know where. God, what the hell kind of parent was she that she didn't have these details? In the future, that would be a new rule, too.

At two in the morning, Sam started to pace. She walked the length of her bedroom over and over, and when that was no longer enough, she moved to the living room. She walked from the corner by the rear, sliding glass door, out to the front lobby, where she would stare out into the night, willing headlights to appear. After a few moments, she reversed direction, returned to her starting point to repeat the trip back to the lobby.

A long forty-five minutes later, the headlights she'd been watching for appeared.

Olly's light blue Scout swung into the lot, pulled to a stop in front of the lobby, and Beth tumbled out. She staggered toward the entrance, her steps clumsy and awkward. Olly walked next to her, a hand out to steady her, but somehow Beth stayed upright. As they approached, Olly's expression was one of worry and sadness. Beth reached for the door and missed, her hand swishing away uselessly. Sam stared at her, incredulous. Beth tried again and managed to knock her knuckles against the handle. Before she could try a third time, Sam yanked the door open from the inside.

"Beth! For God's sake, where have you been?"

Beth smiled at her, sloppy and happy. "Out. At the party."

She moved past Sam and into the apartment. Olly stood just inside the circle of light that the lobby offered.

"Thank you," Sam said, wanting her to stay but also knowing it wasn't appropriate to ask.

"Yeah. Talk to you later." She waved and returned to her vehicle. She pulled out into the night, back into her own life. Sam owed her. And why the hell hadn't Beth called her?

"It's nearly three in the morning," Sam said to her. "I thought we agreed that you'd be home at midnight." She was dangerously close to losing her temper.

"We did?" Beth turned suddenly. "Whoa." She gripped the counter. "My brain is sloshy."

Sam gripped her shoulders. "What. Happened."

"Huh?" She scrunched up her nose. "Oh, Rachel took me to this party, and I explained that it wasn't a date, couldn't be a date, because I have a boyfriend, even if he is a complete dick about this whole pregnancy thing." Beth flopped down on the floor.

Sam's brain stuttered to a stop. Pregnancy thing? What the hell? Beth wasn't old enough to be having sex—not that being too young stopped teens from hooking up—let alone getting pregnant. Why the hell hadn't they had more conversations about sex?

"And she was bummed, you know? Because she wanted it to be a date. And then we got to the party, and I told the guy that I wasn't drinking. He said no problem and brought me a non-alcoholic drink. Punch, I think. I drank it, and he laughed and brought me more. I think he might have been lying. And Rachel and I danced, like close slow dances, and it felt really, really nice. So, when she tried to kiss me, I let her. I shouldn't have, because it wasn't a date. But I don't even like Denmar now, and she felt so good."

Beth's voice faded to static-filled white noise that crowded everything from her mind except for one word. Pregnancy. Pregnant. Beth was pregnant? The question ran through her head on a loop, pushing everything else out. She couldn't make sense of anything.

"And I don't think I'll go there..." Beth continued as if she hadn't just thrown Sam's entire world off its axis.

"Beth," Sam said, sharper than she intended. "Stop talking."

"Because he's an ass, but Rachel is really nice and she smells like raspberries and her hands are soft."

Sam knelt in front of her and shook her, maybe harder than she intended. "Beth. What pregnancy thing?"

Beth looked at her, her focus sliding to her after her eyes landed on Sam. "Huh?"

"You said pregnancy thing. Who is pregnant?"

"I said that?" Beth closed her eyes and shook her head. "I didn't mean to say that."

"But you did." Sam forced herself to breathe through the band of panic that closed around her chest. "Who's pregnant?"

Beth opened her eyes, and for a moment, the clouded haze cleared from her eyes. "Mom." She started to cry. "I'm so drunk. Don't listen to me. I'm sorry. I didn't mean it. I didn't mean any of it." Big, sloppy wet tears slid down her face, and she sniffed and wiped her nose with the back of her hand.

Sam pulled her into her arms and let her cry until her shoulder grew damp and her sobs gave way to a series of ungraceful hiccups. Beth hugged her and then pulled away. Her face was a wreck, covered in black smears of makeup, snot, and red splotches. She pulled the hem of her own shirt up and wiped away the mess. When she was done, most of the snot was gone, along with some of the makeup.

"Come on, sweetie." Sam helped Beth to her feet and led her into her bedroom. It was a disaster of moving-in progress—hastily unpacked clothes, unmade bed, and haphazard stacks of boxes along one wall.

Beth fell onto the bed with a grunt. Her eyes drooped, and she moved with a rubbery lack of definition. Sam removed Beth's shoes and tucked her in. The rest could wait until the morning.

"I'm really sorry, Mom," Beth said, her voice far away and sleepy.

"It's okay." Sam patted Beth's leg. Any talk they needed

to have would wait until morning, when Beth was sober and Sam was rested.

Sam was at the door, ready to turn off the light, when Beth mumbled something.

"What was that, baby?" Sam asked.

"I didn't mean to get pregnant."

Chapter Sixteen

Sleep, as it turned out, never came for Sam. Those words—*I didn't mean to get pregnant*—rolled through her brain on a constant loop. She stood in the open doorway to Beth's room long enough to lose track of time. In slumber, her daughter looked so sweet—innocent, even—and Sam just couldn't reconcile the two.

When she wasn't staring at Beth, she was on the computer, doing research. She found the nearest abortion clinic, which wasn't as far away as she expected. Unsurprisingly, she couldn't find a single one in Idaho, but there was one just over the border in Missoula. It was one of two located in Montana, and she was thankful to be so close to the almost-progressive college town.

An abortion. That was as hard for Sam to think about as Beth being pregnant. Her daughter had been careless with a grown-up decision and was now faced with an even more difficult choice. And, ultimately, Sam shared responsibility, too. If she had been more present, if she had taken more time to really talk to her, and to provide the guidance Beth needed, she might not be in this situation. Sam ached for her daughter's future, and a large part of her hoped Beth would let Sam make her an appointment at the clinic.

But what if Beth wanted to keep it? Then what? Sam wasn't prepared to be a grandmother. Or was she? Did it even matter? Shit. This was on her, too, and ultimately, she would support Beth with whatever she decided to do.

Then, because she suddenly had this potential grandchild to worry about, Sam searched online for prenatal care. She found an obstetrician in town who had kind eyes. An online profile wasn't enough to tell if she would judge Beth—and by extension, Sam—or not, but Sam stared at those eyes and tried to divine if this woman would take care of Beth.

She looked up prenatal vitamins and added fifteen different brands to her shopping cart on Amazon.com before she gave up and decided to let the doctor tell her what kind to get. If Beth decided to keep the baby.

At one point, she reviewed their insurance policy. The cost of her COBRA benefits had been enough to make her seriously consider not taking the option. Now, she was overwhelmed with relief that she'd filled out the paperwork. People had babies without insurance. It happened, but she couldn't imagine the mountain of paperwork and debt collection notices that went along with that kind of expense. Her policy covered all prenatal care but considerably less after the baby was born.

Eventually, the sun came up, and Beth slept on. Sam moved to the kitchen. Coffee would help clear her mind. Hopefully.

As she waited for the machine to stop dripping, Karen came in via the lobby.

"Morning." Karen greeted her with a smile, a container of fresh fruit, and a brown paper bag from the bakery.

Sam took the bag and looked inside. Croissants. Karen definitely knew the way to Sam's heart. If buttery, flakey, French bread didn't seduce someone, clearly that person was already dead. She took one out, ready to stuff it in her mouth as she usually would, and realized that her stomach was strung through with tight knots. Eating, even something she loved, was out of the question.

She dropped the croissant back into the bag. "I need to wake up before I eat anything." She tried to smile, but somewhere between being happy to see Karen and drowning in the events of the past few hours, the message got crossed and her smile came out more as a pained grimace.

Karen's expression clouded. "Glad you're awake. I worried I was too early."

The coffee maker finished, and Sam grabbed a second mug from the hooks that lined the underside of the cabinet. It gave her a good excuse not to look at Karen for a few moments while she calculated her possible responses.

As she poured, Sam said, "Nope, I've been up for a while."

"Everything okay?"

Karen was an old friend who knew Sam better than most. If she couldn't confide in her, who could she? Still, her brain was too rattled, too sleep-deprived, and too shell-shocked to fully comprehend the meaning of Beth's announcement. She was not ready to say the words "Beth's pregnant" aloud. Saying it would add a level of reality to the situation that she couldn't handle just yet. As it was, she felt like there was still the possibility that she'd misheard. Or misunderstood. Or maybe Beth was joking or saying stupid things because she was drunk.

"Yes, of course." Sam forced herself to smile. "So, what's up with you this morning?" She hadn't seen much of Karen this week, so her arrival was unexpected.

"I wanted to see you." Karen moved closer. Close enough to touch. "We haven't talked about your date with Alan. How'd it go?"

"It was okay," Sam answered, carefully. "We had dinner and then took a nice walk through downtown. It was—" Sam struggled for the right word to describe the evening. In the end, she settled for a repeat of "nice."

"Nice? Why doesn't that sound like a good thing?"

Sam looked up at her, expecting warmth and comfort and mild excitement to fill her as it had the last time she'd been this close to Karen. She got two out of the three—warmth and comfort. No thrill of anticipation. She took a sip of her coffee before popping open the plastic clamshell container full of fruit.

"It was fine." She selected a piece of melon and ate it without elaborating on her answer.

"Come on, Sam, give me something here. Will you see him again?"

"I doubt it."

Alan was nice enough, in a milquetoast kind of way. He was kind and friendly and not terrible to look at. He was sturdy and staid and the kind of man most women wanted to marry. All of that stability and good intentions did nothing for her, though. No sparks with him. Not even remotely.

"I'm going to interpret that as a no, then," Karen said, tone flat. She grabbed a croissant and dunked it in her coffee. "That's okay, though. Nothing says you two have to fall in love and get married or anything."

Sam choked on her coffee. When she finally stopped coughing, she said, "Is that what you thought would happen?"

"No. I mean, Alan is a great guy. Women fall for him all the time, so it might have occurred to me as a possibility." Karen's cheeks turned pink, and she stuffed her croissant in her mouth.

This was an interesting turn. Karen had encouraged the date, but now it seemed that she hadn't been as supportive of them getting together as she presented herself to be.

"And that possibility bothered you." Sam tried not to smile, but amusement bloomed in her chest. Karen was jealous. Which was sort of funny, but maybe not after all. Another complication.

"No," Karen said vehemently as she sprayed crumbs across the counter. Between the two of them, breakfast was going to end with Sam wiping down the cabinets and sweeping the floor.

"Are you sure?"

"Maybe," Karen mumbled, her head turned away.

"What was that?" Sam had heard her fine, but she couldn't help but push for more. In that moment, Karen was adorable, like a thirteen-year-old boy who didn't know what to do with his first crush.

Karen looked her in the eye and said, "Maybe. I didn't expect to care, but it bothers me, okay?"

Sam placed her hand over Karen's. "Yeah, it's totally okay."

"So, are you going to see him again?" Karen asked, a hopeful smile teasing at the edges of her lips.

"No." Sam shook her head, letting her own smile take over.

"Good." Karen palmed the side of Sam's face and worked her fingers into the hair at the base of her neck. With a soft caress of her thumb over Sam's cheek, she dipped her head and gently kissed her on the mouth. When the kiss ended, Karen eased back slightly and rested her forehead against Sam's. "Okay?"

Sam nodded and surged forward into another kiss. She wasn't in love with Karen, and the look in her eyes meant they needed to have a serious conversation about what they were doing, but in that moment, Karen provided exactly the distraction she needed. This, she understood. It made sense, unlike the messy tension building between her and Olly. And rather than obsessing about Beth and pregnancy and what the hell they were going to do, she let herself simply enjoy what Karen had to offer.

Waking up in the barn was life-affirming for Olly, especially after last night. As the sun rose, the loft filled with light, along with the small sounds of animals on the rise and the scent of fresh morning air. It was, hands down, the best alarm clock she'd ever had.

The worst, by far, was her phone. She was glad, however, that she was in the habit of leaving the ringer on and turned up. If not, she might have missed Beth's call for help. That kid had been messed up, too altered to focus on anything and talking without any kind of filter. She was going to have a banging headache this morning. And a major fight with Sam.

Rampart stood and stretched before making his way to Olly. She slept crossways in her hammock, with one of her feet dangling over the edge. He licked her leg and barked a happy good morning.

"Ready to get started, Ramp?"

She got to her feet and scooped him up into one arm as she made her way over to the ladder. Carrying him up and down would probably seem silly to some people, but she loved Rampart way more than she cared about what those people would say. Hopefully, she'd be able to finish the stairs, if not today, at least by the end of the week.

When they made it to the ground, she propped open the door, and Rampart rushed outside, a happy dog smile stretched across his face, which made her laugh.

She paused on her way to the restroom to evaluate the work she'd done the previous evening on the stairs. As much as she wanted to finish them, she also wanted to make the forty-five-minute drive to Missoula to check out the hotel she'd seen on her way into town. And if she stopped by the Queen to check in on Beth and Sam, that would be okay, too. Of course, she was operating on the assumption that she was still working for Sam after what happened. For now, she'd go with that.

As a compromise, she would finish cutting the runners and then head out. If she got back early enough, she could put the landing up, and maybe even start on the bottom set of stairs. Decision made, she patted the wood and headed off to take care of her morning rituals.

Around eleven, Olly pulled into the gravel lot in front of the Bitterroot Queen. She sat there, hands on the wheel, trying to calm the ridiculous pounding of her heart. Perhaps this was a bad idea. Or perhaps she should suck it up and go inside.

Beth had been so trashed the night before that she could barely stand on her own and she'd talked nonstop in that slurred, happy, almost present way that drunk people did, complete with an I-love-you-man moment. Not that Olly had been any better at fifteen, but she also hadn't had a concerned mom at home waiting for her. Seeing the expression on Sam's face had been the hardest part.

Realistically, Beth might still be sleeping. That didn't

change that Olly needed to see her and verify that she was okay after a clearly rough night. She also wanted to check in with Sam, and make sure she was okay, too. But Beth provided a nice cover for that.

Rampart jumped from the backseat to the front and nudged Olly with his nose. She pushed her hand into his fur, roughing it up and rubbing his neck briskly, in the way that always made him happy.

"You want to go in? Huh?" She buried her face in his fur and hugged him. Fortified, she straightened and said, "Yeah, let's just head in and get it over with."

Olly was surprised to find the lobby door unlocked, so she knocked loudly on the glass as she entered. Surprising Sam seemed like the worst idea ever, especially after the pepper spray incident. Sam met her at the door to the apartment, and oh, God, she looked gorgeous, even with the dark circles under her eyes and furrowed brow.

"Hi," Olly said and even she could tell that it sounded goofy and maybe a little stupid. God, was she going to be like this around Sam forever, now? And how inappropriate was that, given what had happened?

"Hey, what's up?" Sam held the door open and leaned against the inside wall, leaving plenty of room for Olly to enter. Similar to their first meeting, Sam's body was filled with a cagey anxiety, and Olly almost asked where her pepper spray was.

"Just checking on Beth. She okay?" Olly kicked the bare wood with her boot. It was easier, she realized, to talk to Sam if she didn't actually look at her.

"She fell right to sleep." She paused. "Listen, I'm really glad you came by because I wanted to thank you for bringing her home. Also, I'm sorry that happened. I don't know why she didn't just call me."

Bitterroot Queen

"Who knows? She was pretty messed up. I'm just glad she was able to call one of us."

"Thank you. I mean it. It means a lot to me. More than I can say."

Olly nodded and heat rushed to her cheeks. "You're welcome. So, is she awake?"

"I am now." Beth stood in the door, makeup streaking her face. She wore an oversized shirt that had slipped off her shoulder.

"How are you feeling?" Olly asked, sympathetic but still worried.

"Like hammered shit." Beth took a couple of steps toward the kitchen and stopped suddenly. She closed her eyes and pressed her fingers to her temples. "Movement is bad." After a moment, she opened her eyes and eventually shuffled her feet enough times to make it to the far end of the island.

"You were in pretty bad shape last night," Olly said quietly. Sam tensed, and Olly hoped she'd at least give Beth a little space to talk about it.

"Yeah, I don't know what the hell happened. Everything was mellow, and nobody pushed me to drink after I said I didn't want to. Then, the next thing I know, I can't even put together a sentence. I don't remember much after that."

Normally, when a teen said she hadn't drank but somehow ended up drunk, as if the alcohol magically transported itself from her cup and right into her bloodstream, Olly was the first to call bullshit. She wasn't that far removed from her under-age drinking and partying stage and knew very well the types of things that happened in that environment. Yet, something about Beth's demeanor, her frankness perhaps, convinced Olly that she was probably telling the truth. She looked at Sam.

"That doesn't sound right. You want me to check into the party?"

"And do what?" Sam asked, her voice filled with weariness.

"Ask some questions, find out what happened, and then make sure it never happens again." Olly kept the answer simple, tried not to sound as angry as she was.

"No," Beth said with clear authority.

"I wasn't asking you."

Sam sighed. "I don't know. Beth needs to make some changes. She needs to decide to keep herself safe." She stared at Beth with a strange intensity.

Olly snorted. "She might have some street smarts, but she's still a kid."

"We all have to grow up sometime." Sam shrugged as though that explained everything.

"Yeah, but what if somebody at the party drugged her? How do we just let that go?" Olly asked, surprised by how much it mattered to her and confused about when, exactly, they'd become a "we."

"And what if Beth drank more than she realized and came home drunk? Her track record with parties, alcohol, and the truth is spotty at best." Sam glanced sideways at Beth as she spoke.

"I'm right here, you know," Beth said. "So quit talking over me."

"Yes, but that doesn't change anything." Sam shook her head. "Were you drugged? Against your will, that is?"

There was clearly more to Beth's history than Olly knew if Sam's immediate conclusion was that Beth had taken whatever it was willingly.

Beth glared at Sam for a moment and then turned away. "I'm going back to bed."

Bitterroot Queen

"That's great. No reason for you to wake up and take a little responsibility for this mess."

In response, Beth growled and slammed her bedroom door, leaving Sam, Olly, and a heavy, uncomfortable silence behind.

Olly cleared her throat. "Sam, just let me look into it. Somebody deserves a serious ass-kicking if they were putting something in the drinks."

"Maybe, but at this point, I really have no reason to believe Beth didn't do this to herself," Sam said with a calm undertone that made Olly want to shake her.

What the hell was this? If Linda had taught Olly anything, it was that retribution should be swift and painful. Anything less and the lesson wouldn't stick. "Fuck this," Olly said, frustration winning over tact.

Sam touched her arm. "Wait."

Olly stood, frozen in place by the light touch of Sam's two fingers burning through her skin and right down to the bone. She swallowed hard. It was so inappropriate to feel this. Especially now, in the middle of this family drama. It occurred to her that she might actually be including herself in "family" and that added to her confusion.

Beth reappeared, still looking as though someone had kicked her in the gut repeatedly. "It's my life. I'll decide who needs their ass kicked," Beth said, as if her opinion was the necessary end to the conversation. She was wrong, of course.

"It's your life to a point. And frankly, you've made a spectacular and alarming mess of it," Sam said. "So, no. You don't get to decide anything about how it's handled."

"What? It was just a party. I told you, not a big deal." Beth spoke with a quiet, measured tone, biting off each word at the end. Clearly, her hangover did not like to argue.

"And maybe if you'd been around more, I'd have some idea how to do things right. Not that you'd know."

Ouch. Olly started to back away, toward the door. This was definitely not her scene and not her baggage.

"Yes, Beth. You also told me other things. One in particular stands out," Sam said flatly, but her gaze was fixed on Beth, a keen glint in her eyes.

The color drained from Beth's face. "I did?"

Olly stopped, looking from Beth to Sam and back to Beth. This didn't sound good.

"You did." Sam nodded, a definitive motion that said this part of the conversation was over for now, but far from finished. "We'll talk about it later."

"Mom..."

"Later," Sam snapped. After a deep breath, she turned toward Olly. "You never did say why you stopped in. Was it just to see Beth, or is there something else I should be worried about right now?"

"Worried?" Olly stammered, caught up in the intensity of Sam's glare. She followed Sam's example and sucked in a lungful of air. "No, nothing to worry about. I'm, um, headed to Missoula to check out that derelict hotel property and find out about getting some materials from it. If that's okay." And if I'm still hired, she finished silently.

"Really?"

"Yeah. So when I'm done, I'll let you know what I find out and we'll go from there. But I did want to make sure Beth was okay."

Sam paused, head tilted and brows drawn together. After a moment, she said, "That's really sweet. Thank you."

"Sure." Olly nodded, awkward and unsure of what to do with the way Sam was studying her.

"What hotel?" Beth said.

"Huh?" Olly was caught up with staring at Sam and didn't have the mental faculties to figure out what Beth was asking.

"The hotel. What's the deal with it?"

"It's being torn down and I thought I might be able to salvage some things from it for here."

"So where is it?" Beth asked.

"Missoula."

"And you're going today?"

"Mmm-hmm."

"Good. I'm going with you." Beth rushed back to her room—stopping once to grab her head and moan with pain.

Sam whipped her head around and glared at Olly, then back in the direction Beth had gone. "Beth, we need to talk."

"We can talk after," Beth called from her room.

"Fine. I'm coming, too." Sam grabbed her purse and keys from the kitchen counter.

Shit. Olly bit her lip. She couldn't read the tension well enough to know where it was coming from and how long it would take for it to be turned on her. All she knew was, just like that, her solo road trip had somehow become a group outing.

Chapter Seventeen

The drive from Bitterroot to Missoula was silent. Usually, Olly didn't mind that, but usually it was just her, Rampart, and some very loud rock. This trip, she didn't even have music. When Olly had pulled onto the highway, she had turned on her music, but at the first mosh-pit-worthy scream, Beth had cried out and clamped her hands over her ears. With a sigh, Olly had turned it off. Beth then spent the rest of the ride slumped in the back seat, staring sullenly out the window. Her complexion shifted through various shades of green.

Sam alternated between glaring at Olly and Beth. Olly kept her gaze determinedly on the road. Shit like this—family drama—was high on her list of reasons for leaving Linda in her rearview mirror. And everybody else. This was why she didn't stay long in one place. Getting attached generally came at a price, and for the first time since arriving in Bitterroot, her insides itched with the need to move, to seek whatever came next. She bargained with herself, reasoning that Bitterroot had been great until this. Maybe it would pass. She could give it a little time and let the dust clear on whatever was causing the tension. But if it didn't, she was out of here.

They entered the city of Missoula, and a few minutes later, Olly announced, "This is the place." She flipped on her blinker and turned into a gravel lot.

A faded sign marked a four-story brick building that took up most of the block, with the rest dedicated to parking. The thought of getting inside there, of what she might find, sparked some excitement, which helped her focus on something other than the tension in the vehicle. She loved stuff like this, the old and falling down. She loved the stories and the possibilities. And she loved taking something full of someone else's memories and starting it on a renewed life. Most of all, she loved the way it felt in her hands, the idea that, without her, the glory of reclaimed materials would dissolve into nothing more than a trash heap on its way to a landfill.

She smiled at Sam, so happy with these prospects that she momentarily forgot about the situation. Sam looked startled, then her face relaxed and she returned the smile.

"Let's go." Olly got out and walked to the back of the Scout. After collecting her tool bag, she told Rampart to wait. Odds were he'd be cooler in the vehicle, which was parked in the shade with the top off, than inside the hotel.

Sam followed, but Beth didn't move.

"Come on," Sam said, the irritation back in her voice.

Somewhere along the line, Beth had stuck one of Olly's trucker caps on her head, and she pulled it down over her face. "I'll stay with Rampart."

"No, you'll come inside with us." The steel in Sam's tone left no room for argument, but still Beth didn't move.

Olly placed her hand lightly on Sam's arm. "We don't know what kind of shape this building is in. The owners are opting for demo, so it's probably pretty wrecked. That's why Ramp is staying out here. Might be safer for her not to go inside."

"Fine." She sighed, a full body exhale that left her shoulders slumped and her mouth pulled down in a frown.

"Whatever," Beth muttered as she curled up on the bench seat and spooned her body around Rampart, holding him close with her face snuggled into the fur of his neck. Dogs, especially Rampart, had an inexplicable ability to soothe simply by virtue of his presence.

"Come on." Olly gently took Sam's hand and tugged until she fell in step with her and it was both comfortable and exciting, feeling her fingers around hers. Sadly, when they reached the front door, Olly forced herself to let go. The touch of Sam's palm, cool and smooth against hers, left her with warm, melted toffee seeping through her system.

They stood together on the steps, where Sam stared at her, a bemused smile on her face. Olly realized after a prolonged moment that she was staring, too, and no doubt wearing a stupid, happy grin. She laughed, dispelling the energy built up inside her, and tested the front door. It was unlocked. Technically, they were trespassing, but she didn't mention that to Sam. She just wanted to get a look around before contacting the construction foreman.

"Careful." Olly held the door open and pulled a Mag Light from her tool bag, which she handed to Sam. "The power's off."

"Thanks." Sam turned the flashlight on and went inside.

Olly dug out another light, a smaller version of the one she gave Sam.

The interior showed clear signs of vandalism, with spray paint tags, torn wallpaper, and a grand chandelier that lay in a crashed heap in the foyer. The sight of it, broken and unusable, made Olly inhale sharply. It had been far too beautiful in a former life to be so abused now. It deserved better.

"Looks like the same assholes from the Queen were here, too," Sam said. "So, what are you looking for?"

"Anything we can save and use."

"Use for what?"

"Saving your Queen," Olly said, already distracted by the hand-turned spindles on the staircase. She was definitely taking those.

"This stuff?" Sam's voice squeaked. "I mean, I know you said there might be things here to reclaim, but—"

Olly turned back, inventorying the brass light fixtures and the dusty tiffany windows that separated the lobby from the dining room. "You can't see it?" she asked.

Beth was a startlingly good artist. For her to have that kind of talent, Sam must have some kind of vision of what this could become.

She sighed. "All I see is dust and cobwebs. And mess." Sam swept her light over the room in a haphazard arc.

"Really?"

Sam squinted at the wall of Tiffany windows, as if they were coming into clear focus in her mind. She looked away with a shake of her head. "Really."

"Weird." Olly didn't point out that Beth would have been better company for this project. That kid would be as excited as Olly about this stuff.

"Tell me what you see," Sam said.

Olly hesitated. "Okay. Let's go down here." She started toward the guest rooms on the first floor and stopped when she reached room one. "Okay, look at this." She tapped the number on the door with the tip of her flashlight. "This is old-school craftsmanship. We'll take all the room numbers and use them throughout the Queen."

She set her tool bag on the floor, to the right of the

door, and found a flat-edge screw driver inside. She used it to unscrew the number and handed it to Sam. It was solid, heavy, and clearly created with pride.

"See how it feels in your hand? Like it's something that will be here long after we're all gone? Things like this, these are the touches that will make your motel elegant in the long run. Sure, it's a little dusty and tarnished, but this is brass. It'll polish up nice. People will appreciate this."

Sam bounced the "1" in her hand, and a smile started to form on her face. "I think I get it."

"Good." Olly placed the number, along with the matching screws, in a zipper pocket inside her bag.

"Show me something else."

Olly met Sam's grin with one of her own. She pointed with her screwdriver and said, "Look up. See that window? Picture that in one of the rooms."

It was a half-circle leaded glass window, probably made by the same craftsman who made the Tiffany windows out front.

Sam scrunched up her nose. "Over the door?"

"Possibly. The door to the bathroom, maybe. Or you could use it as a wall decoration. Or as a see-through break in the wall between the main room and the bath. Or maybe you take all the windows and use them as a border around the planting beds out front. Or maybe you hand them to Beth and ask her to create a sculpture." She smiled. "The point is, you can do anything you want with it. It's beautiful, and it still has life left. And with goods like it, all it costs is a little bit of time, patience, and care. That's not so much, when you think about it."

She left the money savings implied rather than pointing it out explicitly. Sam was smart enough to draw that conclusion on her own. The excitement that Olly had felt

Bitterroot Queen

as she'd pulled into the lot suffused her once again. She loved everything about a place like this, the warmth of the wood and the glint of light off the glass.

"Where did you learn all this?"

"Stepdad." Olly opened the door and stepped inside without mentioning that it had been stepdad number four of six. Her mom targeted men as if they were marks to be conquered and then disposed of.

"Oh?"

Olly pursed her lips and nodded. At some point, she would have to unpack all the baggage that came with her family, especially her mom and the seemingly endless number of men that had populated Olly's childhood, but that was not on her to-do list for today.

"We'll take the doors too, along with the hardware." She ran her hand over the surface of the door, letting her fingers travel through the dust, trying to map out the grain that had long ago been sanded smooth. According to the contractor, this property had fifty-two rooms. Even if half were damaged, that would still leave enough for the Queen. She turned to evaluate the rest of the room.

"Please tell me we're not taking those drapes." Sam shone her light on the far wall, illuminating floor to ceiling heavy velvet drapery, dark red with an intricate dark paisley pattern woven throughout.

They were lush in a way that made Olly wonder if this place had been more than a hotel. If it had been a brothel, that would also explain the expansive front room. It would have been the main parlor where clients were greeted and entertained prior to heading off to the rooms. The thought made Olly smirk.

"We might." Olly crossed the room and pulled the material aside. Dust billowed up in her face and something scurried over her feet. Hopefully, Sam didn't notice that. Olly waited for the dust to settle before saying, "And we might take these windows." She pointed at the wall switch and outlets. "We'll definitely take those switch plates. Come on."

"How, exactly, are we taking any of this? Your Scout isn't going to cut it."

Olly grinned. "I thought we'd put everything in the trunk of your sedan."

Sam glared, but it didn't have any heat in it. "Funny."

"Kidding. We'll rent a truck, obviously. U-Haul to the rescue." Olly led the way to the en suite bathroom. It was floor to ceiling subway tile, the old style that was a slightly different size and hue than the ones available from big-box hardware stores nowadays. Along the far wall sat a classic claw-foot tub. And the plumbing fixtures for the tub were brass and crystal. Despite years of use, followed by years of neglect, they shined in the low light.

"Oh, wow," Sam whispered.

"Is that good or bad?"

"I'm not sure." Sam laughed.

"I love this stuff. But I'm not sure we can use any of it. The tile, if we can get it off the walls, would be awesome to use, but the tubs, beautiful as they are, aren't really suited for a modern motel. People shower. And those who take baths want a jetted tub. The fixtures, though...we might be able to do something with those."

"That tub is gorgeous."

"Yeah, maybe we can take just one for your apartment. They really are impractical otherwise." Olly retreated to the main room.

The walls were a combination of expensive—but old and falling apart—wallpaper and wainscoting. The paper had pulled away from the wall where it met the chair rail. Olly pulled on the section and revealed the shiplap beneath. She smiled. This was good stuff.

"See this?" She indicated the exposed wood. "We'll take this and use it on the walls in the rooms. It cleans up awesome and looks great with a coat of whitewashed paint. And the floor. We'll take what we can of that, too."

Olly led Sam upstairs. The rooms were much the same on the second and third floors, but the fourth was different. There were only four rooms, executive suites. This is where the money had stayed. And, as nice as the other rooms were, this floor made Olly salivate.

As they inspected the rooms, each slightly different than the last, she took mental notes about the available materials and where she could use them at the Queen. Sam seemed more or less nonplussed about the entire experience until they reached the last bathroom on the top floor. Like the other three suites, the floor was covered with marble slab, but the shower grabbed Sam's attention.

"What the hell?" She stared, eyes wide with wonder.

Olly could hardly blame her. She'd only seen a shower like this a few other times. There was brass piping circling the enclosure at various heights, with multiple showerheads, including four wide rain style, placed overhead. There were multiple faucets as well, to control the flow of water to the whole contraption. Back in the day, it had been the height of luxury.

"Oh, we're taking this. Somebody wants it." At some point, maybe Sam would want to add an executive suite. Or maybe they'd sell it and use the money to buy something more practical for the Queen. Regardless, it was too precious to leave it to be demolished.

Sam nodded. "Agreed."

As they retraced their steps back to the ground floor, Olly tried to order her thoughts. She wanted to prolong the high she felt about the prospects available to her with this building before the tension between Beth and Sam could destroy that happy energy.

With hesitation, she asked, "So, want to talk about what's going on with Beth?"

Sam looked at her sideways, splitting her attention between Olly and the steps they were descending. "Did she say anything to you last night?"

Sam didn't seem like the type of parent to go nuts over her kid having a little too much fun at a party. Not that she'd like it, but her reaction, like something was buzzing beneath her skin, irritating and scaring her at the same time, didn't really add up.

"A little. She was pretty out of it. Talked about her boyfriend, about moving here, and about how much she loved me, man." Olly tried for the joke, but Sam didn't look amused.

"That's it?"

"Why? What else is there?"

"I'm—" Sam shook her head. "I can't really talk about it. Not yet."

"Okay." Olly allowed the change of subject. "So. This building is a total goldmine."

Sam smiled wistfully. "I wish I could share your enthusiasm, but all I see is dirt and work. I have enough of that at home."

"Then I suppose you'll just have to trust me."

They reached the foyer, where Olly stopped. She looked at Sam, trying to keep her expression open and inviting, something she wasn't comfortable doing as a general rule. She preferred that her thoughts, feelings, and other secrets remain just that—secrets. She placed one hand on Sam's arm, midway between her shoulder and elbow, and squeezed gently.

"I'm going to help make the Bitterroot Queen everything you dreamed it would be. I promise."

Sam swayed, leaning into Olly's touch, and they stood like that for several moments, simply staring into each other's eyes.

"I believe you." Sam exhaled softly and finally turned away.

Olly followed her out into the bright light of day, electricity and other things traveling along her nerves.

Chapter Eighteen

Until now, Sam had never been to Montana. Objectively, it was beautiful. Riding in the car had a lulling effect, and she was so tired, since she'd been up all night, and the adrenaline from worrying and anticipation of the impending conversation with Beth had settled into the back of her mind. She was left with warmth from the sun seeping into her chest and the weight of life behind her eyes.

The bone-deep exhaustion gave way to sleep on the way home. The last thing she remembered was looking up at the big, wide sky filled with fluffy white clouds, and she didn't wake until Olly pulled into the lot at home. Perhaps it was the crunch of gravel beneath their tires or maybe it was the soft curse that Olly issued, she couldn't be sure.

She stretched to clear the sleepy, syrupy feeling from her body and mind, and smiled at the memory of her dream. She'd been in bed with Karen, enjoying those soft, slow kisses that Karen was so good at, when out of nowhere, Karen morphed into Olly. The kisses grew more heated, more demanding, and so much more exciting. When she was awake, logic told her Olly was far too young, but asleep, she apparently had no such hesitation. She sighed happily.

"Good dream, Mom?"

Beth was fully awake in the back seat with Rampart draped over her legs. She managed a tentative smile.

"You're up. Good." Seeing Beth left no room for the soft pleasure of her dream. She was suddenly wide awake and all the good feelings from it dissipated, replaced with the hard reality of what they both faced.

Beth's smile fell. "I'm sorry about last night." She didn't offer any excuses or rebellious arguments, which was a welcome change, but Sam wasn't as concerned about Beth breaking curfew as she was with the secret she'd revealed.

"How's your head?"

"Olly gave me some ibuprofen, so it's not pounding quite as hard."

"You need to drink water. Alcohol dehydrates you, and that makes you feel sicker."

"I will."

It wasn't until Sam turned her attention to Olly that she realized they were stopped at the very outer edge of the lot. Olly kept her gaze focused intently on the windshield, a small scowl creasing her brow.

"What's wrong?" Sam followed Olly's line of sight. Someone was seated on the sidewalk in front of the lobby. "Who's that?"

Even when she first met Olly, when Sam had threatened to pepper spray her, she'd never seen Olly look unhappy. Cautious, yes. Serious, sure. But never this weird emotion that she couldn't quite pinpoint. Wary, maybe? Possibly angry. Definitely not okay.

Olly eased her car forward, and the person stood. The details of her appearance came into definition. A woman, dark hair, Mediterranean complexion, and a dangerous smile similar to Olly's, but without the underlying humor and good will.

"Olly, who is that?"

"That is Gen. My sister." Olly's mouth was set in a grim line and she rolled forward at a crawl.

"Whoa," Beth muttered.

"Your sister? Were you expecting her?" Sam vaguely remembered Olly mentioning a sister, maybe. But she was pretty sure she hadn't mentioned her coming to visit.

"No. Somehow, I never am." Olly took a deep breath and visibly squared her shoulders. "Might as well get this over with."

She parked and climbed out of the car and Rampart jumped out after her. Beth climbed over the side of the Scout, landing softly on the gravel. Sometimes, the girl had the grace and fluidity of a ninja. Or a cat. A cranky, teenage ninja cat. She skirted around the front of the vehicle to join Sam.

"What's going on?" Beth asked in a stage whisper.

"I have no idea." Sam didn't bother with being subtle. Olly and Gen were right there. They could hear anything they said, whisper or not.

The woman pulled Olly into a bracing hug and clapped her hand against her back. Olly returned the embrace with decidedly less warmth and enthusiasm.

"What's happening," she said over Olly's shoulder, "is I'm here to surprise my baby sister." She released Olly and extended her hand. "I'm Gen."

Sam returned the handshake and introduced herself and Beth.

Gen clapped her hands together. "Well, should we go inside?"

"Oka—"

"No," Olly interrupted. "We need to get going."

"Fair enough. Sam, Beth, it was very nice meeting the

two of you." Gen swung an army-green duffle over her shoulder and went to the Scout. She tossed the bag into the back and climbed into the passenger seat.

"I'll talk to you later." Olly stared into Sam's eyes, her look penetrating and deep and a complete mystery.

Sam nodded slowly and said, "Okay."

Olly smiled tightly and gave her a curt nod. "Come on, Rampart."

Moments later, Olly was gone. She left a wake of dust behind her.

"That was weird," Beth said as she unlocked the lobby door.

Sam stared after the Scout, acutely aware of Olly's absence. As she followed Beth inside, her earlier weariness returned. Nothing about life in Bitterroot had been as simple and easy as she had hoped.

"I know you don't feel well, but we need to talk," Sam said. "Are you ready?" she asked, not sure if she herself was.

Beth looked at her askance. "I suppose I have to be."

"You're right. You do." Sam looked around their room. The floor still awaited a coat of finish, their furniture was still in the storage container, and there wasn't a single place they could sit comfortably and chat. She sighed and hoisted herself up onto the kitchen counter. She needed to be seated for what came next. "Do you remember anything from last night?" she asked.

"I remember the party and hanging out with Rachel. She's really nice."

"I'm sure she is. What about after you got home?"

"Mom, I really am sorry about last night. I was so out of it. Olly told me that she's the one who brought me home. I don't know why I called her and not you. And I would like to check in with Rachel. She was pretty wrecked when

I called her earlier."

"You can do that after."

"Okay." Beth drew the word out and turned it into a question.

"You don't remember saying anything to me?" Sam asked the question again, worded slightly differently than the first time. She couldn't quite wrap her head around the possible reality of Beth being pregnant. Saying it out loud was just beyond her at the moment.

"I don't remember much." Beth tugged on her lip, a new nervous habit that Sam hadn't noticed before.

She stared at Beth, looking for signs that Beth was different, as changed as her confession the night before implicated. She looked like the same kid, a little belligerent and snarky, with threads of sweetness throughout. Sure, Beth had some bad habits, like talking back, rebelling against everything, and smo—

"Did you quit smoking?" Sam asked, dreading the answer. She didn't want Beth to smoke, but she also didn't want to think about why she might quit.

"Yeah, about a week ago."

"Why?"

The blood drained from Beth's face, and she looked at Sam with wide-eyed fear. "Mom..."

"Why, Beth?" Sam started to tremble. What the hell was her fifteen-year-old baby going to do with a baby of her own? "I need to know."

"Christ." Tears pooled in Beth's eyes and then slid slowly down her face. "I'm not even sure if I'm going to keep it."

"So it's true, what you said to me last night. Whether you remember it or not."

Beth nodded and whispered, "Yeah, I'm pregnant."

"Fuck."

"Please don't be mad. I didn't do it on purpose." Beth sounded truly panicked. Her tone, like a cornered animal that was about to bolt, jolted Sam out of her own head. She looked and sounded terrified, and it was Sam's job to help. If she'd been more present, better at communicating, maybe Beth wouldn't be in this situation.

"Oh, sweetie, I'm not mad. Okay, that's a lie. I was mad. Really mad. But more upset than anything else." She slipped off the counter and opened her arms.

With a sob, Beth crushed herself against Sam and buried her face in Sam's shoulder. Sam hugged her and whispered nonsense words until Beth's tears subsided. As she held her, all the obvious clues Beth had dropped since they'd moved landed with a thud in Sam's mind. The terse, crying conversations with Denmar. The vomiting. The smoking. Even the change in appetite. It all made sense and Sam felt like the worst mom on the planet for not realizing how much her daughter needed her.

Beth eased away from her with a loud snuffle. Her eyes were rimmed with red, but she managed a timid half-smile.

"Denmar?"

"Yeah, he's being an asshole about it, saying awful things to me about how I'm a whore and it's all my fault."

"That little bastard."

"I know, right?" Beth laughed and wiped her nose on her sleeve. "He's the only guy I've had sex with, so it's his."

Thank God there was only one. Sam would take that as a slice of good news in this.

"He said he'd send me money to pay for an abortion, but he wants nothing to do with being a dad. I told him if he didn't want to be a dad, then he needs to think about where he sticks his dick."

Sam's eyes widened and Beth's face fell.

"It's my fault," Beth said. "I had the condom out and then things got..." she looked at the floor. "I forgot, and by the time I remembered, it was too late."

"It's his fault, too. Sex is a huge responsibility for the people having it. I'm sorry I didn't make that clearer, or really sit down and talk about it more with you." Her throat tightened.

Beth sighed. "All the talking in the world wouldn't make his reaction any easier to take."

"What do you want?"

"I don't know. I'm fifteen. I don't want to have a baby. But I can't even think about...you know, terminating it or whatever. I get this rolling knot in my stomach, and it feels like my skin is stretched too tight and all my insides are trying to get out. I have no idea what to do."

"Is this why you asked to do school online?"

"Yeah, mostly."

Sam nodded, understanding.

Beth closed her eyes and pressed her fingers against her eyelids. After a moment, she looked at her with bare vulnerability. "I'm really scared, Mom. What am I going to do?"

"You want me to decide for you?"

"Not really. But I guess I need to know what you'll do if I decide to keep it."

"What do you mean?"

"Like, will you kick me out?"

She stared at her, horrified. "God, no." Sam pulled Beth into another tight hug. "Never."

Beth clung to her, thankfully without the tears and the snot this time. "Will you help me?" Beth asked, her voice small and insecure as though she thought Sam would actually refuse.

"Jesus, Beth. I'm your mom. I know I've screwed up, but I will always help you however I can. I know what it's like to be a young, single mom. I wouldn't let you face that alone."

"Promise?"

"I promise." Sam had a million questions, a million things she wanted to discuss with Beth. Had she thought about all her options? Abortion seemed to be off the table, but Sam couldn't tell for sure. What about adoption? That would be emotionally more difficult than abortion, probably, but it would give Beth the time she needed before becoming a parent, and it would help another couple realize their dreams.

If she decided to have the baby—and keep it—had Beth considered everything she needed to do now in order to prepare? Such as no more parties. Prenatal vitamins. Doctor visits. Sam was overwhelmed by the possibilities, so Beth was probably drowning in them.

For now, however, it seemed to be enough for Beth to know that Sam would support her, no matter what.

"What the hell are you doing here?" Olly had waited until they were on the highway to speak. As much as she loved her sister, she hated the things she did more.

"I told you, I wanted to see my baby sister." Gen smiled in that charming way of hers that disarmed most people but left Olly with a cold pit where her stomach should be.

"Bullshit. You told Linda about this place, didn't you?"

"Now, Olly, why do you automatically go there? I—"

"You did, didn't you? And she sent you here to case it. Un-fucking-believable."

Gen continued to smile half a beat longer and then her expression sagged. "No, I promise. She just kept poking for information about you, so I bailed. I've spent the last three days stowed away on those intermodal train cars and hitchhiking. I'm tired, hungry, and I smell like things I don't even want to think about."

"That's really fucking unfortunate." The longer Gen talked, the angrier Olly got. It wasn't a reasonable response, she knew, and she wanted to believe her. History, however, told her it would be stupid to do that.

"Come on, Ol, don't be like that. It's not all bad. You missed me. I know you did. And I missed you. So, why is it so bad for me to be here?"

"Because you're going to fuck it all up."

Gen sighed. "Can't we just head back to your place? I could sleep for about a year."

Olly's foot slipped off the accelerator. She just realized that she couldn't take Gen to George's farm, and that's exactly where she was headed. She flipped around in the middle of the road and headed back toward town.

"I don't have a place."

"What? I thought you worked something out."

"Nope. That fell through. The Scout isn't big enough for you, me, and Rampart, so you'll have to get a room. There's a hotel by the college." If Olly got lucky, she'd be able to get herself back to George's. If not, she'd sleep on the side of the road somewhere rather than turning Gen loose on a guy like George. The idea that she should call George, let him know she might not be home tonight, crept to the front of her mind half-formed. The implications of the thought disturbed her almost as much as Gen showing up unannounced. At what point had she started

Bitterroot Queen

casually thinking of the loft as home and George as someone she checked in with?

"But what about... Look, I don't have any money."

Olly glared at her. "Of course you don't."

"What's that supposed to mean?" Gen sounded believably insulted, but Olly knew her too well to fall for it. This was the part Gen had been cast in for this town and this time. Olly was consigned to a role opposite her, a puppet in an act she wasn't interested in.

"It means that you better check your bra or your shoe or wherever else you're hiding it, because there's no way I'm paying. You came here. You figure it out."

"Don't be like that. I don't have any money."

"Stop it." Olly pounded the steering wheel with the palm of her hand. "I was trained by Linda, too. Remember? You have money. We both know it. And pretty soon, that hotel clerk is going to know it."

Olly drove fast, well above the speed limit, too angry to care about potential speed traps and tickets. All she wanted was Gen out of this town. With her arrival, all the things that Olly had thought of as beautiful and green were now tarnished, tainted in some inexplicable, yet irreparable way. The hotel marquee came into view, and Olly slowed. She pulled into the lot and then into the valet drop off and pick up zone.

"Get out, Gen. Maybe we'll talk tomorrow. After I've had a chance to cool down."

"Olly, I know you think I'm here to hurt you in some way. That's not the case. Linda's worrie—"

"Don't bother finishing that sentence. The only thing Linda worries about is herself. And sometimes her cat."

"Fine. Well, then, I was worried about you."

"Are you kidding me?" Olly had been on the road since the day she turned sixteen and passed her driver's test. "The first time you so much as say boo in the same time zone as me just happens to be the one time I say I think I found the place. That's one hell of a coincidence, don't you think?"

"Well, when put like that, it does sound a little suspicious."

Olly shook her head. The only thing she'd gotten from Gen so far was a mouthful of half-truths and the beginnings of a migraine. With anyone else, Olly would question how Gen found her so easily, how she knew to look at the Queen. With Gen, though, it was a given. Her sister had a ready smile and easily charmed information out of others. Olly had told her Bitterroot, not expecting Gen to do anything with it, and that had been enough.

"Out." Olly pointed at the building.

Gen looked like she was considering another approach, but finally snapped her mouth shut and climbed out. She collected her bag from the back seat and said, "I wish it wasn't like this."

"Yeah, me too." She pulled out of the lot before Gen made it inside the building.

Chapter Nineteen

Olly paced the length of the loft. The place already had so many little pieces of her, as if her belongings had already decided to put down roots in this town. What the hell had she been thinking when she told Gen about Bitterroot? She loved her sister, and part of her was really happy to see her. But that was snuffed out with the implications of what her arrival really meant.

Frantic energy, verging on panic, buzzed through her. She couldn't talk to Gen while she was like this. As was her habit, Olly went to work. She'd sweat out the negative vibe that was wrapped tight around her chest.

She gave herself a moment to breathe. Deep inhale, calm exhale. Even in her agitated state, Olly knew working on the stairs while distracted was dangerous. A broken bone would only make matters worse.

When she felt calm enough to focus on the work rather than her family, Olly climbed down to the ground. Through great foresight, George had installed a pulley system that helped move heavy objects, such as bales of hay, into the loft. She used that, along with an extension ladder, to maneuver the top set of runners into place. Normally, she preferred to use screws, but in this instance, the pneumatic framing nail gun was faster. With a few well-placed stud nails, the boards were at least temporarily secured.

She followed up with a combination of metal strapping and screws. She worked methodically, giving herself over to the process. Once, she'd ended up in the middle of a Buddhist compound. While there, she'd learned a lot, not the least of which was the value of active meditation. With that one simple life philosophy, her life had changed. She'd always recognized her need to move, but active meditation—using work to clear her mind—gave her permission to stay long enough to figure out what she really needed from a situation.

As she worked, Rampart moved with her, restless and uncertain, reflecting her own mood. When she started laying in the steps, he rested with his head on her feet. It was awkward as hell, and she stopped working long enough to pull him into a hug.

"Sorry, Ramp. I'll figure it out soon. I promise." She buried her face in his fur, and he sighed.

After that, he let her finish. She inserted the last screw in the safety railing just in time to head inside to fix dinner. Her body was a lot sweatier and, as predicted, her mind much clearer.

George was seated at the kitchen table with an assortment of hunting knives and a sharpening stone laid out in front of him. "Hey there. How was Missoula? Find anything good in that old building?"

Olly washed her hands in the sink. "Yeah. There's a ton of useable shiplap and hardwoods, plus the fixtures and some of the windows." As she talked, she washed and peeled the big russet potatoes George had set out on the counter for her. "Do you want these mashed, steamed, or fried?"

"You pick." George shrugged and started in on the next knife.

"Well, what kind of meat?"

"Steak. It's in the fridge," George said. "I'll throw it on the grill outside when those are near to done."

"Fried it is." She sliced the potatoes thin and dropped them into a pan with some olive oil, basil, salt, and a bit of pepper. "I'll make some gravy, too."

They had some leftover sausage from that morning, and that was the perfect starter for some hearty country gravy.

"Do you have a good knife?"

Olly glanced over her shoulder. "Yeah, I keep one in my pocket."

George nodded once, and the set of his jaw seemed to say that she'd passed an important test. "Good."

"How would you feel about a wall of windows separating the living areas from the bedroom?"

"What do you mean?"

"That hotel has a wall of Tiffany windows. They're gorgeous, and I'd like to use them in the loft. They're not quite tall enough to reach the ceiling, but I thought I'd do a short stub wall, frame in the windows, and then put a header along the top."

"Hmm. Will that reach?"

"Nah, but I'll think of something. Maybe I'll wall it in with that shiplap. Or maybe I'll find some other windows to put in the gap. It can stay open for a while until I do, don't you think?"

"Sure." George more grunted than said the word, but that was enough for Olly. She liked him because he didn't have to fill the air with the sound of his voice. Silence was better than other nonsense.

"My sister is here." Olly didn't mean to say that. She had no reason to bring George into her family drama.

"Here?"

"In town. I took her to the hotel."

George continued to sharpen his knife without responding.

"She...is hard to explain." Explaining Genevieve had never been a problem before because she'd never felt compelled to do it. She typically didn't give a damn what others thought about the total dysfunction of the Jones family.

"Okay."

Olly went back to her cooking. "She won't be here long." She hoped. "So, you probably won't even meet her."

George set his knife on the table and said, "Do you want me to meet her?"

A flutter of panic rose up in Olly's throat. "Why? Do you want to?"

"Olly, why don't you say what you need to say? But first, stir those potatoes."

She did as she was told and used the time to collect her thoughts.

"She showed up without announcing it, and I'm worried that she's going to do something to ruin things here. I like it here. I don't want... I don't want to leave because of her." Olly twisted a dishtowel tight in her hands.

"Why would you?"

Olly took a deep breath. "Gen is a lot like my mom. They...take advantage of people. They use people."

"How so?"

"They're grifters." Olly glanced at George to gauge if he understood what she meant. Grifter was a term most people weren't familiar with.

"Like snake-oil salesmen?"

If the situation wasn't so serious, Olly would have laughed. "Yeah, something like that."

"Well, it seems to me like you need to live your life and

stop letting them decide things for you."

She'd done just that when she'd hit the road all those years ago. This time, though, maybe it was time for her to take a stand without leaving.

"Maybe you're right."

George snorted. "Usually am."

Later that evening, after the dinner had been eaten and the dishes done, Olly went back to the hotel where she'd left Gen. The desk clerk, a twenty-something guy with a tragic amount of acne, gave her the room number for the price of a smile. She stood outside her door for several long moments, tried to knock more than once, and then finally sucked in a deep breath and rapped her knuckles against the door twice. Sharp and quick. If Gen didn't hear her, then she'd just have to come back later.

As she waited, counting silently to ten under her breath, she rested her hand on Rampart's head. He leaned into her side and issued a soft, happy dog sigh.

The door flew open just as Olly reached nine, and Rampart came to alert, sitting up straight, his nose forward, ears up.

"Olly? What's up?" Gen held her cell phone to her chest.

"Can I come in?"

"What? Oh, yeah, of course, sure." Gen stepped to the side, and as Olly entered the room, Gen lifted her phone to her ear and said, "I'll call you back."

She disconnected the call and set the phone on top of the hotel stationery on the desk, obscuring the writing on the top page, something Gen had scribbled down quickly, judging by the sloppiness. Gen sat on the end of the bed and motioned toward the chair. Olly sat and Rampart curled up at her feet.

"So, what's this about?" Gen asked.

"I was really mad earlier, about you being here."

"Yeah, I got that."

"I'm sorry about that. I should have asked why you're here."

Gen raised an eyebrow. "What about a hug? Being happy to see me? You know, the way normal people greet their siblings."

"We're not normal."

"No," Gen conceded. "We're not."

"As I was saying, I should have asked why you're here, but I didn't. Now I'm asking."

"I'm here to see you, of course." Gen waved her hand, a breezy gesture meant to dismiss and disarm, but Gen's tactics didn't work on her.

"No bullshit, Gen. Did Linda send you?"

"Not really."

"What does that even mean?"

"It means that she knows where you are, but the idea to come was mine." Gen dropped the performance. Her voice was clear, concise. No nonsense, reminiscent of Linda as she recapped their performance after a job.

"Why?"

"You know why." She looked at Olly, a dead-eyed stare that made Olly shiver.

"You used to hate this stuff. Hated Linda. Now you're setting up your own marks?"

"People change."

"Who's your mark, Gen? Me? You don't know anyone else here."

"That's not true. I know Bobby at the front desk, the

guy who owns the gun shop across the street, and tattoo Barbie at Bitter Ink. I'd say I know plenty of people."

"I'll warn them about you."

"Will you? Take out a notice in the town paper?"

Actually, she'd put a notice on the bulletin board. "Gen, please. Pick a different place. I like it here."

"I know. You told me, remember? You found it. That's what your text said."

"Is that why you're here? Because you can't stand the idea of me being happy?" Jesus, Olly hated the sound of her own voice as she said those words. The tone and message were straight off of trashy daytime television. The calm that she'd worked so hard to achieve was completely broken.

Gen laughed. "Believe it or not, Olly, you are not the center of my universe."

She remembered a time when Gen made her feel like the most important person in the world, but that seemed like a lifetime ago, back when Olly was too young to understand anything at all.

"Can you just tell me what you want?" Her shoulders slumped. She'd almost forgotten how exhausting it was to simply be in the same room with her family.

Gen relaxed incrementally, the tension visibly draining from her body. "Truth? I just wanted to see you. See what about this place is so perfect."

"That's it?" Olly remained skeptical.

"Yeah, that's it. I miss you."

"You're not working some angle with Mom?"

"No. She doesn't even know where I am. I left without telling her." Gen looked and sounded sincere, and Olly hated that she couldn't be sure. It sucked not to trust her sister, but experience had taught her it was better to approach with caution than to jump in with her arms open. It could mean the difference between surviving the swim or being used as a flotation device.

"You're not really casing the people you mentioned?"

"I'm really not."

"So how long do you plan to stay?"

"Dunno. Depends on a lot of things, like whether or not my kid sister stops treating me like the enemy," Gen said, her voice deadpan.

"Your kid sister would be less inclined to treat you like that if you hadn't ambushed her."

"That wasn't an ambush, Olly. It was a surprise. Most people like surprises."

"No one over the age of six likes surprises."

"God, you're a cynic. When did that happen?"

"When I realized that my mom had been grooming me my entire life to be a part of the family business," Olly said.

"Yeah. You always were braver than me."

"Remember that time Mom ran that scam on that rich guy in Boston? He thought she was actually talking to spirits." Olly had been ten at the time, so the memory was clearer than she generally liked.

"Yeah, and she had you do crazy shit like flicker the lights and bump tables. You thought it was a game."

"I did. Until he caught me."

That man had twisted her arm so hard she'd gone home with a spiral fracture to go with her already long list of injuries and broken bones.

"Mom lifted his wallet while he was distracted. That sucked," Gen said, a wistful quality to her voice.

"She always was more interested in money than her kids. Parent of the year, our mom."

"I always thought that's the way all parents are."

"Not so much," Olly said.

"I'm sorry," Gen said softly, her voice so quiet Olly could have missed it if she hadn't been paying close attention.

"For what?"

"Coming here."

Olly stared out the window. Under the blanket of darkness, Bitterroot looked the same as every other crap place her mom took them when she was little.

"I'm sorry too. Are you staying?"

"Yeah, have to."

"How long?"

"Depends." Gen laughed humorlessly. "Are you going to make me stay in this hotel?"

"Yeah, have to," Olly mimicked Gen's earlier answer, wishing things could be different, but unable to imagine how to make that happen. She patted Gen's shoulder and stood to leave. "Please don't wreck this for me."

She left then, Rampart at her side, her stalwart companion no matter what kind of shit the rest of the world had to offer.

Chapter Twenty

Sam watched Olly working on the antique cash register. In the past week, she had finished stripping and refinishing the floors in her apartment, helped empty out the storage container so that it could be removed, salvaged two box-trucks full of materials from Missoula, and had just started on the main lobby area. When it was done, she'd move to the rental rooms.

"I'm really glad you answered our ad." Sam hadn't said that out loud to Olly until now, but for some reason, she really needed her to know.

"Yeah. Me, too." Olly smiled in that way she had, lopsided and sexy, as she moved the antique register from one end of the counter to the other. She grunted with the strain of it, which made her that much sexier, and Sam wondered what she would do when things were finished at the Queen. Would Olly stick around? Or would she hit the road again?

"Too bad that register doesn't actually work," Sam said, more for something to say than because she wanted to use it. The computer system was scheduled for delivery next week, and that included keycards for the rooms, along with fancy registration software that cost a fortune but didn't come close to the functionality of the system she'd used in Vegas. The difference between small-town America and the Strip.

"Yeah, but polish it up and it'll make a beautiful decoration."

Beth entered from outside where she'd been washing the exterior windows. Rampart followed behind her, staring at her with loving devotion. Beth started on the interior, and Rampart sat next to her feet.

"What do you have planned for this area, Mom?" Beth asked.

Since she'd confessed her pregnancy news, Beth had been a changed person. She looked worried more often than not, but she approached Sam with a newfound respect.

"First, clean. Then we'll paint, put in that awesome bar top that Olly picked up, deal with the hardwood floors like our apartment, and shiplap on the front of the counter. Then we'll have to find some durable, affordable furniture."

"What about breakfast? Most motels like this serve something," Olly said as she wiped down the soon-to-be counter, a genuine saloon bar top reminiscent of the Old West that she'd salvaged from the hotel in Missoula. According to her, it only needed a good sanding and a coat or two of finish. It fit the property.

"Yeah, I thought perhaps we could set up a station in that corner, with a few small tables and chairs."

The lobby extended past the check-in area to a large open space that would be perfect as a staging area for guests to meet up with the rest of their party, as well as providing space for serving a meal.

Beth stopped and studied the wall, a small crease lining her forehead. She tilted her head to the side. "Can I have that wall?"

Sam hesitated. Yes, she believed in Beth's talent, but that didn't mean she'd produce something that was appropriate for a public area. "I don't know…"

"Mom, I won't embarrass you. I know which walls

should get what. I promise."

"Okay." She could always paint over it if it wasn't appropriate or didn't work.

"It'd be a nice touch to have a fireplace or woodstove in here, too," Olly said. She was working on the shelves beneath the counter, filling bag after bag with debris and detritus from the previous owner.

"How long would it take to put in something like that?" Sam didn't even mention the money or the permit process for that kind of addition.

Olly stood, clapped the dust off her hands, and said, "Depends. We can talk about it later, after we get some rooms up and available for use." She hefted three full large black trash bags, making her muscles flex hypnotically. Sam swallowed, staring at her.

"I'll be right back."

A moment after the door swung shut behind Olly, Beth tossed a wadded up newspaper—she was using vinegar and newsprint to prevent streaks on the glass—at Sam's head. "Seriously? Don't you have a girlfriend?"

"What?"

Beth was looking at her, half-teasing, half-disapproving. "After telling me I needed to finish things with Denmar, and here you are, lusting after—"

"First, I'm not lusting. Second, if you're referring to Karen, she's not my girlfriend."

"I know you keep saying she's not, but she sure spends a lot of nights in your bed, so…"

"We're friends," Sam reiterated.

"Oh, okay. Does she know that?" Beth asked, succinctly getting to the crux of the matter.

Sam huffed. She loved Karen and loved sharing sexy times with her, but it seemed more and more as though

Bitterroot Queen

Karen's feelings had deepened beyond strictly friends. She'd known that after her disastrous date with Alan and hadn't done anything to dissuade her. Shit. She wasn't being fair to either of them.

"You know it shouldn't take that long to answer that question, right?" Beth went back to cleaning the windows. The view of the mountains just beyond the lot and stretch of highway was spectacular.

"You're right. I should talk to her."

"Yeah, especially if you plan to do more than just stare at Olly."

"Do—what?" Sam sputtered, unable to defend herself and completely flustered by the implications.

Beth laughed. "Don't strain yourself, Mom. Not like it isn't obvious."

Sam started to retort just as Olly returned to the lobby and a car Sam didn't recognize pulled into the lot.

"That's Rachel," Beth said.

"Rachel? The girl—"

At that, Olly spun around, went out the door, and marched up to the car.

"Oh, shit," Beth muttered. She and Sam stared out the window, at Olly talking and gesturing emphatically. Something about it warmed Sam's heart, because she knew Olly was talking to Rachel about the party and probably demanding answers.

Beth sighed, breaking the moment. "I should probably go talk to her."

"Do you want to?"

"I mean, I kinda have to. Don't I?"

"Not really." Sam would be happy if Beth said she never wanted to see her again. Anybody who took her daughter to a party like that didn't deserve further attention.

"I need to give her a chance to explain." Beth shrugged. "I like her, but I'm beginning to think that I have crap taste. I want to be wrong about that."

"Honey, you're fifteen. You don't even know what your taste is, yet."

"Well, so far, it's bad."

"Speaking of, have you heard from Denmar?"

"Not yet. I don't know what to say. He hasn't called me, either. I might have to break up through text."

"I wish you wouldn't. I wish you'd call him and do it. Or at least leave a phone message with the option to talk about it." Sam gave Beth a hug. "Sorry."

"So, how long should I let Olly yell at her?" Beth asked when she pulled away.

"I don't know. I'm usually the one yelling, and you hate when I do that, so maybe not much longer?"

"Yeah." She stared thoughtfully out the window. "It's really sweet that she cares enough to do it."

"Yeah, it is." Sam watched her, too. Olly's gestures slowed to a less angry energy, and Beth visibly relaxed.

"Maybe it's not as bad as I thought," Beth said.

A few minutes later, Olly turned back toward the building. Beth set her supplies on the counter and met Olly at the door. As she passed, Olly squeezed her shoulder and smiled.

"Good luck, kid."

With Rampart trailing behind her, Beth went to Rachel's car.

"What did she say?" Sam asked. She had repressed most of her mama-bear instincts when it came to the events of last Saturday, in favor of focusing on Beth and her needs. Now, however, with the culprit sitting in her lot, the instincts were back full-force.

Bitterroot Queen

Olly shrugged. "Okay, she's not a bad kid. When she realized how messed up Beth was, she locked her in an upstairs bedroom and wouldn't let any of the guys in."

That actually tracked with Beth's drunken rambling about kissing Rachel. A locked bedroom with nothing else to do? Sam had been in a similar situation the first time she'd realized that kissing girls was better than kissing boys.

"Do you believe her?"

"I do." Olly turned back to their work, leaving Sam to watch her, caught in a place where she wondered how exactly Olly had gotten to this point in her life, that she was taking on a pseudo-parent role with Beth. She turned and watched Beth, assuring herself that Rachel wasn't doing anything stupid.

"We're at a crossroads in this room," Olly said. "We need to paint before doing too much more. I'll start taping things off."

"Sure, I guess." Sam watched for a moment longer before turning to help Olly. As much as she wanted to solve all of Beth's problems, her daughter needed to do some things herself, and, unfortunately, her choices so far meant that she needed to grow up sooner rather than later.

Olly worked at a steady, measured pace, her movements deliberate, like a well-choreographed dance. She made the mundane—like paint prep—fun to watch. That, and the fact that she was seriously sexy, provided quite a show.

"How's your sister?" Sam hadn't asked since the evening she had arrived unexpectedly, and Olly hadn't mentioned her again, either, which was odd. Normally, people liked to talk about their families.

"Fine." Olly didn't slow in her work.

"Fine? Is she still in town?"

"Yes."

"Where is she staying?"

Olly sighed. "I don't usually talk about my family."

"Yeah, I figured that out. But I'm curious. So I'm asking. Would it really be so terrible if I knew more about you?"

"Maybe." Olly shrugged. "It usually is."

Sam frowned. What was so bad? "What's her name? Remind me."

Olly looked at her out of the corner of her eye. "Genevieve."

"Right. So, where is Genevieve staying?"

"With me."

"Really? At the apple farmer's?"

"Yes. For now."

"How do they get along, George and Genevieve?"

Olly stopped working and set her tape on the counter. "Can we please talk about something else?" She enunciated each word.

"Like what?"

"How about your pregnant fifteen-year-old daughter." Olly looked at her levelly, a clear challenge in the set of her jaw.

Okay. Sam took a physical step back. Maybe Olly was right. Maybe they shouldn't talk about some things. "You know about that?"

Olly lifted one shoulder in a shrug.

"Did she tell you?"

"No. But it wasn't hard to figure out."

"Oh."

How was it that Olly, a virtual stranger, was able to discern the signs of Beth's pregnancy when Sam had been caught completely off guard? Was she really that oblivious? Yet another tick in the shitty parenting column. Her stomach clenched.

"It's easier, sometimes, to see things when you're not

emotionally attached to the information," Olly said, her tone more gentle than before. "You'd probably have my sister nailed in a matter of minutes."

"Thanks." Sam smiled wanly. "Maybe we should call it a day?"

"I can finish up." Olly gestured toward the tape. "That way, I can start on the paint first thing in the morning."

It was Friday afternoon, and they hadn't actually talked about the upcoming weekend. "Are you working tomorrow?" Sam asked.

"That was the plan, assuming that's okay."

"You going to charge me overtime?"

Olly laughed, a sharp bark of amusement that cut through the tension. "As if."

Sam smiled and relaxed a little. They worked together to finish prepping the lobby for the next day. Eventually, Beth returned, smiling, and finished cleaning the windows. At the end of the day, with their projects completed, the three of them were almost back to normal. Still, when Olly left, she gave them a polite nod and said a curt goodbye as she held the door open for Rampart to lead the way to her vehicle, and it left Sam a little empty.

"Hey, can I borrow the Scout?" Gen got up from the overstuffed beanbag Olly had picked up secondhand. She slipped her phone and wallet into her pocket and held out her hand, presumably for the keys.

"No," Olly said flatly. She rarely ended her workday grumpy, but Sam had pushed just hard enough to set her on the wrong side of that line. Near as she could tell, Gen hadn't done a single damn thing while Olly had been at work. If she wanted to loll around like a slacker, Olly couldn't stop her, but she sure as hell wasn't going to reward her, either.

"Come on. I want to hit the casino. Check out their tables. I need a ride to get there."

Olly stuffed her keys into her pocket rather than dropping them on the makeshift table as she normally did. She looked at Gen for a moment then started toward the stairs. Rampart, who had been circling his favorite spot on the floor, followed her with a heavy doggie sigh.

She was crafting a wooden platform of sorts for the pulley system and preferred to work on that rather than argue with Gen about keys. When it was done, she'd be able to use it to move heavy items up to the loft with ease. She'd finish up tonight and hopefully start on the docking mechanism.

Gen, of course, followed her. "Olly, don't be a jerk. Let me use the car."

Olly sucked in a deep breath and forced herself to count to ten before she responded. "I'm almost out of gas. No."

She would have plenty of gas if she hadn't said yes the last two nights when Gen asked to borrow her car.

"I'll put some in. Fill it, even." Gen stuck out her hand again.

This—a demand that would be seen as rude by others but was normal for her family—was high on the list of reasons Olly hadn't wanted Gen to stay. As always, after two days of Gen at the hotel, with Gen promising anything and everything, Olly had given in and brought her here. She'd cleared it with George first, hoping he'd say no. He'd smiled at her sadly and commented on how families could be difficult and that there was no point to avoiding hers any longer.

"Fine." She slapped the keys into Gen's palm. Hard enough for them to bite into her skin, but Gen didn't flinch. "Just be careful. No more door dings. And stop riding the clutch."

Gen laughed. "What are you worried about? That thing is a beast."

"I'm serious." Olly made a grab for the keys, but Gen jerked them out of reach.

"I'll treat it like a goddamned princess, okay?"

With that, Gen made a run for the door, leaving Olly to fume. So far, Gen had spent every night at the casino, working the tables. She was an excellent gambler, but it was only a matter of time before she asked Olly to come with her. Grifting at the tables was always easier with a partner, and like Gen, Olly had learned very early.

However, Gen would have a harder time convincing Olly to go with her than she had getting those keys tonight. The casino was on tribal land, which meant tribal laws. As good as Gen was, she was playing with fire on this one. She was foolish to think she wouldn't get burned.

"Come on, Ramp." Olly patted her leg. As long as Gen was leaving, she'd head inside and say hi to George, catch up on his comings and goings, and fix them both some food. Her platform project would keep until later.

Chapter Twenty-One

As she woke, Sam automatically went over her list for the day. The storage container was empty and still sitting in her lot. She'd check in with the company and then start painting. Again. After a stop in the bathroom, she went to the kitchen. Beth was already there, sipping a cup of coffee and staring at a pack of cigarettes. She didn't look up as Sam poured herself a cup and then sat on the other side of the counter. The box of Marlboro Reds rested midway between them.

"Do you want me to get rid of those?" Sam asked, trying like hell to keep her voice conversational.

"I'll do it." Beth met Sam's gaze and gave her a sad smile.

"Everything okay?"

"Yeah." Beth pulled a Zippo from her pocket and set it next to the cigarettes. "I actually talked to Denmar last night."

"Oh? You finally called him?"

"No, he called me. It was a pretty short conversation. He's met someone else, and she doesn't think he's an asshole."

Sam kept her tone level. "How do you feel about that?"

Beth shrugged. "Okay. I mean, I was going to break up with him, eventually. It had to happen. Doesn't matter who actually said the words, does it?"

Sam took Beth's hand. "No, it really doesn't."

"That's what I figured."

Bitterroot Queen

"Did you talk about..." Sam let the sentence trail off. She still wasn't sure what Beth planned to do, keep the baby or terminate the pregnancy. Until she made her intentions clear, Sam didn't want to say the wrong thing. Tough as it was, it was Beth's decision, and all Sam could do was hope she'd ask for advice before taking action.

"Yeah."

"And?"

"He sent me some money on PayPal, for an abortion. But he still says there's no way it's his, and I can't ruin his life with a kid. Direct quote. Asshole."

"Is it good or bad, that he sent the money?"

"I haven't decided. The money is good. But what if she wants to know her dad?"

Sam's stomach clenched. "She?"

"I'm just saying that. I don't actually know."

"Does this mean you're going to have the baby?" Sam asked.

"Yeah. It's stupid and I hate myself for being this stupid. But that's not her fault."

"And later, if she does want to know Denmar, you can always do a DNA test."

"Yeah, I guess. But I hate that I'll have to. It's not like I've had sex with anyone else. For now, though, I need to figure out a way to earn some money. That's step one. Babies are expensive. Who knew?"

"Beth, we'll figure it out. Until you have a driver's license, it makes more sense for you to work here."

The gravity of that statement hit Sam square in the gut. Beth was pregnant at fifteen, before she could legally drive. That meant Sam would be a grandmother at thirty-four, possibly thirty-five depending upon which side of her birthday the baby was born.

Beth took a deep breath, and her eyes grew wet with unshed tears. "I really fucked everything up. I'm sorry, Mom. Really, really sorry."

Sam circled the island and pulled Beth into a hug. "Yes, but at this point, all you can do is prepare for what's coming. Having a baby is hard. I'm not going to lie. And it doesn't end after the child is born. So you need to be really, really sure, and not simply motivated by guilt or some romantic notion of doing the right thing. There's no clear line between right and wrong in this situation."

"I know."

She backed away until she held Beth at arm's length. She wanted to see her daughter's face for what came next. "Do you? Do you have any idea how exhausting it is? This beautiful little creature who you are willing to sacrifice everything for will suck the very life out of you and make you feel guilty that you don't have more to give. She will make unreasonable demands and take all your time. You won't be able to sleep, to eat—hell, you'll be lucky to shower regularly when she's born. Forget about parties and dating and all the fun things you should be doing as a teenager.

"You're going to be up to your ass in nasty diapers and snot and baby puke. You'll be so tired you won't remember your own name. And that baby won't care. Three in the morning and all you'll want is sleep, and she'll be screaming her lungs out over something that you can't fix. You'll feel like the world's worst mom, and you'll want to scream right along with her.

"On top of that, you have school. Do you have any idea how hard it is to think when you're drowning in baby formula and strained carrots? She'll be three before you graduate. That means finals and term papers with a toddler running around. It takes an act of God to keep a toddler from destroying the furniture, their toys, the walls, hell, even themselves. Toddlers are fearless. They will walk off a cliff or grab a hot pan off the stove or any number of other things."

"Wow." Beth stared at her, shell-shocked.

"Wow is right. Parenting isn't for the weak of heart. So think long and hard about this." She picked up her cup, watching as Beth got up and refilled hers, then went to the back patio.

The loft was beginning to look more and more like an apartment, but there was still a lot of work to be done. For example, Gen slept on the floor in a sleeping bag, and that's where she currently was, cuddling Olly's keys like a precious lover.

Olly needed those keys, dammit.

Quietly, so as to not wake her, Olly tried to peel her fingers away one by one. Gen refused to loosen her grip. Rampart sat patiently next to her, watching with a serene look on his face. Finally, after several failed attempts, Olly gave up and shook Gen's shoulder.

"Gen," she said sharply, "give me my keys."

Gen grunted and rolled over.

Olly shook her harder. "Dammit. Let go."

Rampart whined and licked Olly's hand. As a natural extension of his attention, he also licked Gen's cheek. That got Gen's attention better than any shaking or yelling on Olly's part.

Gen sat up, groggy, and pushed her hair out of her face. "What's going on?"

Olly pointed to her keys, still gripped tight in Gen's hand. "I need those."

Gen looked down and seemed to only then realize that she still had Olly's keys. "Oh. Yeah, sure." She tossed her the keys.

"Thanks."

"Where you going?" Gen asked.

"Errands."

Gen started to get up. "Like what?"

"First the motel, then Bitter Ink, and ending with groceries." Olly didn't mention the gas station, but she was pretty sure that would also have to happen sometime today.

"I'll come with." Gen stretched and yawned. "I need to pick up a few things, too."

"I'm leaving now."

"Okay, I'm good." Gen pushed her hands through her hair and headed toward the stairs.

Surprisingly, Gen had returned the Scout with a full tank of gas, as promised. As they settled into the front, with Rampart in the back, she asked, "How'd it go last night?"

Olly didn't really want to ask, but needed to keep track of Gen to some degree. If she was building enemies in the community, eventually there would be fallout. And history taught her that, regardless of her involvement, she would be affected. She started the Scout and headed down the driveway. George was working in his orchard, and she waved on her way past.

"It was great." Gen laughed. "I stuck mostly to blackjack. Tonight I'll go back and not have as much luck."

What Gen meant by that was she would still count the cards, but she would bet against herself, purposefully los-

Bitterroot Queen

ing so the house wouldn't suspect her. That was something Olly appreciated about Gen. She was smart about her cons and played the long game whenever possible.

"In fact," Gen pulled a stack of folded bills from her front pocket, "this is for you."

She peeled off a third of the bills, mostly twenties with the occasional fifty mixed in, and offered it to Olly. By the look of it, there was several hundred dollars there. Olly took it as she pulled onto the highway toward the Queen.

"Thanks." Olly tucked the bills into the pocket on the front of her shirt, an oversized men's work shirt that she'd picked up for next to nothing at a yard sale.

"Don't sound so happy about it," Gen said.

Olly kept her gaze trained on the road. Gen already knew how she felt about earning money this way. There was no point in arguing with her. "You should use it to find a place." She paused. "Or to get back home."

After a prolonged moment of silence, Gen sighed and said, "I don't want to go back. I told you that."

"I know. And I told you that I like it here. I don't want to blow it."

"I'm not going to blow it. I'm just building a little bit of capital while I figure things out."

As the Queen came into view, Olly turned to Gen and said, "I really hope so. Just remember where you are. This isn't Atlantic City."

"Which is run by the mob."

She had warned Gen about the dangers of running a con while on the reservation. Tribal lands had their own set of laws and their own way of doing things. It she got caught, it would be the equivalent of being arrested in a foreign country. U.S. laws and protocols didn't apply and local law enforcement couldn't cross the border without an invitation. Even then, they had no authority.

"Just be careful." Olly pulled into the parking lot of the Queen. "Wait here. I'll be right back."

Before she could get the door open, Rampart barked happily and jumped over the side. He waited for her at the front door, wagging his tail. In spite of her mood with regard to Gen, she smiled and moved to catch up with him. At the door, she patted him on the head and used her key to let herself in.

"Hello?" Olly called out before she went in.

"Olly!" Beth bounded out of the apartment and met her halfway across the lobby. She gave her a brief hug and then dropped to her knees to give Rampart loves.

"Hi," Sam said, leaning against the doorjamb that led to the apartment behind the lobby. She offered Olly a soft, sexy smile and sparks shot all the way to her toes. "What are you doing here?"

Olly smiled back, hoping she looked less goofy and smitten than soft and sexy, but she wasn't sure how it worked. "I'm on my way into town to do some errands and I thought I'd see if Beth wanted to ride along."

Sam's smile faltered. "Oh, okay. Beth?"

"I'm in. Let me get some shoes." She ran back into the apartment, squeezing past Sam as she went.

The sun filtered through the large picture windows and haloed her in light. Backlit as she was, her long auburn hair drawn up in a messy bun, she seemed to glow with ethereal life. She was beautiful and Olly was helpless to do anything other than go to her.

She stopped just short of Sam, took a long, deep breath, and simply looked at her, something she generally tried to avoid. "So. Um...hi."

Sam met her gaze, her eyes a beautiful play of light brown with dark specks throughout. Her smile returned, and it held an edge that Olly had caught glimpses of before. This time, though, it lingered and hinted at a lot more than just a warm greeting. "Hi yourself."

For a moment, Olly let herself daydream about closing the distance between them and kissing her right there. Before she could do anything more than dream, Beth returned. After a prolonged moment, Olly followed Beth out with a glance over her shoulder at Sam. Something shifted in the air between them, like an intangible thread drawing her in. When the door closed between them, Olly fought the urge to go back inside.

Sam let the door close behind her, and collapsed against it with a sigh. She dropped her head into her hands. What the hell was she doing? Sure, Olly was charming and clever and a goddamn miracle for the Queen, but she was also young and closed off and had no intention of staying in Bitterroot. At least that's how it seemed. The last thing Sam needed was to fall for a flight risk.

She thought about working on the Queen's new website. They were closing in on an opening date faster than she'd expected. Hopefully, by this time next week she should be ready to launch the website and wait for the reservations to come in. Assuming, of course, that they continued to make progress on the motel at the same rate.

That was another reason pursuing a relationship with Olly was a bad idea. She needed her, more than she cared to admit, to stay focused and on task. Sam hadn't realized how invaluable she would become, couldn't have imagined the person she first found hanging out in her parking lot could possibly play such an important role in the success of the Bitterroot Queen. Without her, the Queen would be sunk, even with the lawsuit slowly moving along. She'd probably be old and gray before that got resolved. Besides, would Olly even stick around once the motel was open?

And why did she care? It's not like there was a future for her with Olly. She barely knew anything about her, after all, except that she had a tense relationship with her sister and an even worse one with her mom. And she no doubt had all kinds of wild oats to sow.

But damn, the way Olly looked at her. And the way the air seemed to heat up between them, and the way even a light touch from her made her feel like she was on fire. Messy, she thought. Too messy.

Website development, at least, was something Sam could do on her own. She went over to her desk—a monstrosity of a thing that she had brought from Vegas that was too large to fit in her current living space—and sat to resume her work. She shook the mouse to wake up her computer and stared at the design screen for her website. This, she understood. The bones of the work, of the structure she was trying to create, were clearly visible to her. There was no guesswork as there was with the renovations of the Queen.

So far, she'd created the landing page, but the stock images she'd found online would have to be replaced with professional photos of the Queen at some point. The stock photos were nice and gave her a good visual representation of where she was going, but they didn't do the job she needed them to do. The website needed to show the beauty and the charm of the Queen, and the only real way to do that was to make sure that the photos captured the pieces that made this a unique motel. Also, who wanted to stay at a property that didn't share pictures on the company website?

She wasn't trying to create a five-star resort in the middle of the mountains of Idaho. All she really wanted was something that made it feasible for her to stay out of the big business environment of Vegas and other such cities. She didn't need the Queen to make her rich. She just needed it to not make her bankrupt and to keep her and Beth comfortable.

In addition to the landing page, she'd also populated the "About Bitterroot" page, which included links to local sites and activities.

Bitterroot was the kind of place where people could come to relax, to enjoy the scenery and to simply get away from modern-day life. There was whitewater rafting, hiking trails, biking, kayaking, camping, and skiing. Plus, every summer the town hosted a banjo festival, an apple festival, and a folk music festival. In the fall, the college hosted an independent film festival. It wasn't Sundance, by any means, but it brought in some traffic.

Sam had fallen in love with the place all those years ago, when she'd come to visit Karen. Beth had still been a baby, and Sam had just started her rise up the corporate ladder in Vegas. Back then, she'd seen Bitterroot as an odd, quaint place, where she could bring her daughter, see her friend, and escape work pressures.

That trip had been her first vacation in too many years to count. She'd just been promoted to pit boss, which meant she was in charge of all the tables on the gaming floor, keeping track of the dealers, the money, and players.

She'd funded that trip with a bonus she'd received after breaking up her very first card-counting ring. There had been many others after, and the excitement waned for her. By the time she made it to the big office and the title of property manager, she was happy to leave those kinds of details to her staff.

The Queen, however, needed more of her attention in the minutia. The details in any business venture could make or break an operation, but she'd never felt the pressure so acutely as she did now. So, as attractive as Olly was, and as much as she had come to depend on her in some ways, she needed to put that out of her mind and focus on why she'd come to Bitterroot in the first place.

Chapter Twenty-Two

Bitter Ink was closed when they arrived. Olly parked in a space across the street, between the butcher and a vacant storefront. It looked as though a new business was moving in, but it was too early to say what.

"It doesn't look like Ava is here yet," she said. "Do you guys want to hang out here or wander around?"

"I'm going to explore. I haven't seen much of the town," Gen announced without any actual enthusiasm for the prospect.

Olly looked around, trying to decide what to do. Ava should arrive in a few minutes, assuming she was on schedule. Olly hadn't spoken to her in a while, since she finished her work on the shelves in the back room. It would be nice to see her again. In the meantime, however, she'd check out the butcher. Last time she'd gone in, he'd had a decent selection of meats, including some really good pepperoni sticks, one of her guilty pleasures.

She stepped away from the car. "Going into the butcher. You guys can come with or you can stay here. Come on, Ramp."

Fifteen minutes later, a bag of pepperoni sticks and a few samples of seasoned elk and deer jerky in her hand, she went to Bitter Ink. Beth was sitting on the stoop waiting for her, and Gen caught up with her just as she reached the door. The door was unlocked, and music—

some smoky nightclub number—came from within. Clearly, Ava had arrived.

"Why are you waiting out here?" Olly asked.

"I don't know." Beth shrugged. "I didn't know if I could go in without you."

Olly shook her head, but didn't comment. She opened the door and held it, indicating with the tilt of her head that Beth and Gen should go in front of her. Rampart ran ahead and barked, happy to return to his beloved courtyard. Ava appeared, pushing open the saloon-style swinging doors that separated the front of the house from the back office.

"Olly!" Ava greeted her with a happy smile. "What are you doing here? I didn't know if I'd see you again."

"Hi. Good to see you." She gave Ava a polite half-hug. "Rampart missed you."

"I think he's happier to see my courtyard."

She grinned. "Ava, this is my sister Genevieve and my friend Beth. Guys, this is Ava, the owner of Bitter Ink."

"We met the other day, actually." Ava shook Gen's hand.

They made polite small talk for a moment until they all turned in unison toward Olly, clearly waiting for her to take up the conversation.

"So, as you know, someone bought the old motel out on the highway, and they're remodeling. That someone is Beth's mom, Sam. As a surprise for her mom, Beth sketched a sign that she'd like to have made for the front of the building." Olly pulled the folded paper from her back pocket and opened it to show Ava. "It's a suspended metal sign that uses negative space and lighting for full effect. George said that you might be able to hook us up with someone who can do metalwork, a blacksmith or something?"

Bitterroot Queen

Ava took the paper and studied it. "You drew this?" she asked Beth.

"It's not my usual style, but this is for my mom, so I made an exception."

"It's very good. What do you normally do?"

"I sketch, just not usually something so formal. I like to do portraits, and lately I've really been into trash polka-style paintings."

"Hmm. I'd love to see some other samples of your work." Ava raised her eyebrows.

"Yeah, I can do that." Beth looked at Olly, a question in her eyes. "Maybe Olly could bring me back again sometime?"

"Sure. But for now, about that metalworker..."

Ava laid the drawing out on her workstation and smoothed it down with her hands. "If you leave it with me, I can take it to her. She doesn't really like to meet new people."

"That'll work." Olly smiled. This whole sign-making thing looked like it was going to work out after all. She was excited to see how Sam reacted once all was said and done. "Do you still have my number?"

"Yup, assuming that my kids haven't deleted you from my phone."

"Excellent. Let me know either way what she says." Olly motioned for Beth and Gen to move toward the door. "Come on, Rampart."

He emerged from where he'd been resting in Ava's courtyard, his nails clicking on the wooden floor. She heard him long before she saw him. "Say hello to Valentina and the girls for me."

"Will do. And seriously. She does want to have you over for dinner."

"Well, you've got my number."

Ava smiled. "Talk to you soon."

Olly made her exit, happy to have one less thing on her to-do list for the Queen.

"You okay?" Beth asked Gen as soon as they were back on the road. "You didn't say a word."

Gen smiled like she couldn't be bothered. "I was just checking the place out. No need to comment."

"Gen, no." Olly placed a heavy warning in her tone. "Do not even go there."

Beth looked at her, puzzled.

"What?" Gen said. "I'll be good."

Olly stared at her sister in the rearview mirror. For some reason, she'd opted to sit in the back with Rampart, leaving the front seat to Beth. She shouldn't have brought Gen with her today. That was a very bad idea on her part. God only knew what kind of con she had rolling through her mind at the moment.

"I'm serious."

Gen met her gaze levelly in the mirror. "You always are."

"I don't know what all this drama the two of you have going on is," Beth said, "but Olly, did you hear the part where she asked me if she could see more of my art? I just about peed."

"Yeah, kid. That was pretty cool. I'll take you into town again soon, okay?" As worried as she was about Gen's intentions, she was equally excited about Beth's chance to share her talent with someone who knew the true value of it. From what Olly had seen of Ava's work and Beth's paintings, the two of them were kindred spirits.

"What else are you doing today?" Gen asked.

"Grocery shopping. Remember?"

Bitterroot Queen

"And after that?"

Olly hesitated. As much as she wanted to talk to Gen about her life, she needed to guard the pieces very closely. Especially anything to do with Sam.

"What's that smile for?" Gen asked with a chuckle.

Olly hadn't even realized she was smiling. She schooled her features into something more neutral. Gen was a goddamn bloodhound when it came to opportunity and vulnerability.

"Why do you ask?" she said, redirecting the conversation back to Gen's original question about her plans.

"I was thinking about hitting the casino again today," Gen said.

"I need the Scout. You'll have to find another way to get there."

"Come on, Olly. All you ever do is work on that damn loft apartment. You don't need the Scout for that."

Olly pulled into the parking lot of the Red Barn Market and came to a stop toward the back of the lot. She turned off the vehicle, put the keys in her pocket, and gave Rampart the command for him to stay put. As she opened the door, she said, "No, Gen. I'm not going to change my mind. If you want to go there so badly, you'll have to find another way."

Beth hopped out her side of the vehicle. "While you two are arguing, I'm going to go see Rachel. That's her car, so she must be working."

"You sure?" Olly said.

"Yeah. It's cool."

As Beth headed into the store, Olly closed her own door and said to Gen, "Maybe you should just stay home tonight."

Gen didn't respond, and Olly hurried to catch up with Beth.

"Hold on a minute." Gen hopped out of the car and ran

to beat Olly to the door. She stopped Olly from entering. "What's going on with you? Why are you making such a big deal out of this?"

"Gen, it's my car. You don't get to just take it whenever you want to. I have work to do and things I have to take care of. I need my car. So if you want to drive, then get your own damn car. Now, get out of my way. I need to go inside."

Gen glared at her, but stepped aside.

Rachel was working the main register, and Beth was standing next to the postcard rack, occasionally giving her a shy smile.

"Hi, Olly," Rachel said. She looked at Gen, a question in her eyes.

"This is my sister, Gen. Watch out for her." She was only half-kidding. She grabbed a handheld basket from the stack by the door and set about her shopping without waiting for the introduction to play out between them. That Gen had invited herself along and then turned it into a platform for making demands pissed her off. It was better if she didn't talk to anyone at the moment.

She selected a few staple items for her and Rampart, such as cheese, deli meat, and an assortment of fresh veggies and fruit, but gave up after that. She couldn't focus enough to remember what she and George had discussed for meals in the upcoming week. She'd have to make another trip, and that pissed her off further.

Halfway through checking out, a bolt of realization struck her. Unlike her usual patterns, she didn't feel compelled to leave a difficult situation like the one Gen was creating for her. She wanted to stay. Gen, on the other hand, needed to go.

Chapter Twenty-Three

Beth opted to hang out at the market until Rachel got off work. After she assured Olly she would call Sam and let her know, Olly drove back to Randolf Farms with Gen, who pushed about needing the Scout at the beginning of the ride. Olly bit out an angry reply that stymied any further comment. The rest of the ride was made in tense, yet welcome, silence.

She handed the bag of groceries to Gen with directions to put them away in the loft and then drove away. She didn't care what Gen did, as long as it was on her own time and didn't involve Olly. Now, Olly sat in front of the Queen. She'd driven here entirely without meaning to. Somewhere along the line, this had become her safe space, and she hadn't even realized it until now.

She stared at the building, wondering what Sam was doing and if she would welcome Olly showing up. She could go in and pretend she forgot something earlier. Once inside, she could walk right up to Sam and kiss her the way she'd wanted to earlier.

Except she couldn't. Not yet. And besides, Sam had Karen in the background. For all she knew, Sam enjoyed all the flirting but didn't want anything more.

And so far, she had managed to keep Sam off of Gen's radar. How, she didn't know, but she didn't want to push her luck and act impulsively, no matter how sweet it would be in the moment, generally led to disaster in her experience. She liked to measure her steps and move with purpose. Sam made her want to abandon all of her reservations and self-control, and that was dangerous. Doubly so with her sister lurking behind her, looking for whatever con she could get away with.

Rampart barked softly and jumped over the seat from back to front. With a sigh, he leaned against her with his head on her shoulder. She pushed her fingers through his fur.

"I know, Ramp. I like it here, too."

He dropped his head and nuzzled closer.

"Sam is..." she couldn't finish the sentence, even with just Rampart to listen. She switched gears. "Beth loves you. And George, he just gets us. It's weird, isn't it, to feel more at home in a barn than in any house I've ever lived in. But that's how I feel, and he understands."

George, she'd decided, was her soul mate. Not her perfect lover kind of soul mate. Rather, he was her guy, the friend she was meant to have. More importantly, he seemed to think so, too. But he didn't need to say it or need her to say it. They just understood each other.

"Do you want to stay?" She whispered the question in Rampart's ear, half afraid that saying the words would make the comfortable feeling flee.

"Beth's pregnant, you know. We haven't talked about it, but that's a big deal. If we make this our home, I won't be able to stay away from Sam, and I'm not sure I'm ready to be responsible, even peripherally, for a baby." She stroked his fur.

"Jesus, I learned about parenting from Linda, who sucked at it. That's the kind of influence that can totally fuck up a kid. But maybe it'll be different here. Sam is good, you know? She'll help and be good to Beth and the baby. I might like being a part of that. If Beth keeps it, that is. I don't know what I would do if I were her. Not that Linda would have given me a choice. She would have married me off to some sweaty middle-aged dude who owned a car lot or something."

Rampart whimpered and she patted him reassuringly.

"Don't worry. She can't do that anymore." She hugged him. "One thing is for sure, staying or going, I need to get Gen out of this town."

Driving away from the Queen filled Olly with a weird, unfamiliar burning in her chest—heartburn or deep longing. It could go either way. She was used to the tightening bands of tension pushing her to keep moving, but this was something else entirely.

Rather than heading home right away, she drove. She let the miles disappear under her tires, drawing comfort from the familiar growl of her engine. She needed to get back, to talk with Gen, but odds were she wasn't there. That thought allowed her to justify going just a little farther, and a little farther, until an hour and then two had passed.

Her thoughts stretched and relaxed, lining the road with neat precision rather than the jumble she'd grown used to. The road was her friend, her confidant, her therapist. In the past, all she'd needed was a long strip of blacktop with Rampart as a travelling companion. Today, however, as the sun dropped in the sky and the shadows lengthened, she found a primal, undeniable truth. The road would be here for her if she needed it. She could follow it, so long as she remembered to turn around and drive back home.

She didn't have to constantly chase the next town. She could stay in Bitterroot, at George's. She could let whatever was happening with Sam happen, baby and all if necessary. And she could be okay with all of it. It didn't need to terrify her into motion. She could, for the first time, trust the stillness.

With that moment of clarity, she turned around and headed back to Bitterroot.

As she drew closer to Randolf Farms—a place she'd been thinking of as home more and more recently—a red truck that looked an awful lot like George's pulled onto the highway in front of her. It had the same rust spots on the tailgate, the same wooden sides, and the same handmade wooden boxes that George used to keep his produce under control on the way to the farmers' market.

But George hadn't mentioned any errands, something he liked to keep Olly apprised of, and he generally drove much slower. Olly hit the accelerator and closed the gap between her and the truck. Maybe everything was okay, but there were enough anomalies to make her worry. She squinted, trying to get a better view of the driver. George normally wore a beat-up snapback cap similar to Olly's. Not now, however, and his hair was a lot darker. And thicker. And he looked slimmer, more delicate—

"Oh, shit."

Gen was driving George's truck.

Olly eased off the accelerator. There was no reason to follow so closely now. She needed the few extra seconds it took for her to pull into George's long driveway behind Gen. As she came to a stop, Gen slipped the keys—George's spare set—into the space between the visor and the ceiling of the cab and climbed out of the truck, whistling all the while.

Bitterroot Queen

"Did you have a good night out?" Olly started talking before she even had the door fully open. In a graceless, angry stop-and-start motion, she muscled the door open and rushed to cut Gen off before she made it to the barn. Rampart barked and hopped out behind her.

"Oh, hey, there." Gen spun on her heels to face Olly. A flash of surprise and guilt were quickly replaced by the cool gambler's facade that Linda had taught them both long ago. "I didn't expect you back this early."

"Did you ask George before you borrowed his truck?" Olly overemphasized borrowed.

"What? Oh, sure, yeah, of course." Gen tried to sidestep her.

Olly gripped Gen's arms and held her in place. "And George will say the same thing when I ask him?"

"Olly, have a little trust. I'm your big sister, after all."

"That's exactly why I don't have trust. You know better than to ask me to do it." She didn't mention how hurt she was by the lie. She'd thought, if nothing else, she could count on Gen to be essentially truthful with her. Small white lies didn't count. Grand theft auto, on the other hand, was not small. Instead, Olly added the hurt to the pile of bruises and scrapes she'd accumulated since Gen had shown up in Bitterroot. "Tell me the truth. Because George will."

Gen's face fell. "Okay, no. I didn't. But, come on, it was just sitting there. He didn't even notice I was gone."

"It's time for you to leave." Olly spoke softly, each word clipped with precision.

"Come on. That's not necessary."

"It is. It's long overdue, actually. I like it here. I want to stay, make a life. I can't do that with you here. Not like this."

"Like this?"

"Stop working marks and we can talk about it."

"I'll stop. Done. I'll be good, quiet as a mouse. You won't even know I'm here." Gen's voice returned to something close to the soothing tone Olly associated specifically to setting up a grift.

Olly shook her head. She loved Gen, would love to share more of a connection with her, but not now. Not under these circumstances. "That's great, but you're going to do it somewhere that's not here."

"But you said—"

"You have to prove it before I can trust your word on the matter. Call me in two years."

"Two years? What the hell?"

"Two years. Not a minute earlier. Then, if you can convince me you've changed, you can return. I might even help you move." Olly didn't mention that her original instinct was five years, not two. Frankly, it didn't matter. Gen wouldn't last two weeks. Two or five, they were both completely unattainable goals.

"Where will I go?"

"I don't know. Don't care, either. I'll take you as far as the bus stop. Or train station. You choose."

"Olly, come on." Gen's shoulders slumped.

"You can pack or not. Either way, I'm taking you tonight."

"Fucking nice way to treat family." Gen started toward the barn.

Olly trailed behind. She didn't care about any of the things she had in the loft, but George's stuff was another story, and Olly didn't trust her not to pick up something else of his on her way out.

Gen packed quickly, stuffing her clothes in her bag with stiff, jerky movements. She helped herself to two new packages of beef jerky and a handful of protein bars, pulled a

Bitterroot Queen

two-inch-thick roll of cash from her hiding place behind Olly's laundry detergent, and stomped down the stairs.

When they came to the Scout, Gen tossed her bag in the back and started for the passenger door.

"Wait. We need to go inside first."

"What the hell? If you want me gone so badly, let's leave already."

"It'll only take a minute." Olly signaled for Rampart to wait and turned toward the house. Gen would follow or she wouldn't. Either way, George deserved to know that his truck had gone out without him.

Hopefully, he would let her stay, but she'd understand if he wanted her to leave. It wasn't every day a man had his truck stolen, after all.

She found George relaxing in front of his TV, recliner pushed back all the way with a big bowl of popcorn resting on his belly. Some news program played at a low volume and he muted it completely when he realized she was standing there.

"Olly. I didn't figure you'd be out tonight when you missed dinner."

"Sorry. I had to sort some stuff out."

"Not that I'm not happy to see you, but what brings you by?"

"Right." Olly took a deep breath. "I just wanted to let you know that Gen is leaving tonight."

George nodded and said, "Any particular reason why?"

"Gen took your truck out earlier. It's back now, undamaged, but that is not okay." She heard a movement behind her and knew it was Gen, in the kitchen.

"Did she?" George looked surprisingly calm, as if this news wasn't news at all.

Gen remained behind Olly, partially hidden in the shadows of the kitchen. Olly paused half a beat to see if

Gen would respond. When she didn't, Olly said, "Yeah. She drove it to the casino."

"Ah."

Olly waited. She needed more from George than a two-letter sound that wasn't even a word. Like Gen, he said nothing else.

"I'll understand if you want me to go."

"You?" George looked concerned for the first time since the conversation started. "Why would I want that?"

"This wouldn't have happened if I weren't staying here."

"True. But a lot of other things wouldn't have happened either, like all the work you've been doing on my barn."

"Does that mean I can stay?" Olly asked.

"You'd better."

Olly almost hugged him. It was a gesture that he was less comfortable with than she was, she knew instinctively, but the urge was still there, sharp and bright like a summer apple. Holding back, however, didn't stop the rush of tears from blurring her vision. She blinked a couple of times until it passed.

"But I'm still taking Gen to the train."

"If you're sure that's what's best." George nodded, his expression once again neutral. He hit the button to restore the volume and resumed watching his show.

Olly paused at the break between living room and kitchen. "I'm really sorry about the truck, George. I never should have let that happen."

Gen snorted, a derisive, judgmental sound that made Olly wonder if she'd ever be able to trust her sister.

"You're not your sister's keeper, Olly." George didn't turn to look at her.

Olly made her way outside. "Thank God for that. I'm a

total failure at it," she mumbled under her breath as she turned. "Did you pack everything?" Olly asked, more to have something to say than because she needed the answer. Gen always got hers and often Olly's as well.

Gen nodded tightly and moved to the door. Olly sighed and got into the driver's seat. Rampart jumped in, and they made the drive to the train station in silence. When they arrived, Olly didn't get out of the vehicle. Gen grabbed her bag and marched up the steps, back stiff, shoulders squared.

And just like that, Gen was gone as quickly as she'd arrived.

Chapter Twenty-Four

When Olly arrived at the Queen the next morning, she felt light. Free. Unencumbered. It was nothing short of a miracle. And instead of pushing aside her attraction to Sam, she let it build. By the time she made it inside to Sam, all the negative voices that swore she was unworthy of happiness faded into static white noise in the background of her consciousness, replaced by an intense desire to get to know Sam better, to take her in her arms, to feel the warmth and energy of her skin.

She went into the lobby, surprised to see Sam standing at the counter, sipping from a cup.

"Hey," Sam said, eyes lighting up. "I wasn't sure what time you'd get here."

Olly stood, staring at her, and something sparked in Sam's eyes. Slowly, deliberately, she put the cup down, and Olly closed the distance between them, following her instincts.

She stopped inches away from Sam, heart hammering. Sam glanced at Olly's lips then back to her eyes. She inhaled, a slight hitch in her breath, and exhaled in the moment before Olly kissed her. It was a simple light brush of her lips against Sam's, an introduction and tentative exploration. It was soft and gentle and possibly the best kiss of Olly's life. At the moment of contact, a thrill shot through her, along with a sense of wonder and belonging. It was perfect.

Bitterroot Queen

Long before she was ready to relinquish the beautiful whisper of a kiss, Olly regained control and just like that, the kiss ended. She pulled away slightly, but stayed close enough to rest her forehead against Sam's, eyes shut, and just breathed her in. She needed a moment to calm the pounding of her heart.

"Wow," Olly finally said, a little breathless.

"Definitely wow." Sam touched Olly's face, her fingers a light caress that charged Olly with a purpose so clear and precise she couldn't understand how she'd missed it until now.

Olly opened her eyes and took a step back. She met Sam's gaze, uncertain what to say next.

"Uh, hi," Olly managed, the picture of eloquence.

Sam looped her arms around Olly's neck and smiled. "Hi."

Panic lapped at the edges of Olly's mind, but it didn't sweep in as it had in the past. Instead, it gradually receded. Olly focused on the moment in front of her. No matter what else happened, she really liked that kiss and wouldn't mind another, but rather than fall head first into the moment, she pulled herself together.

"Okay, so I, um—I'll get to work." She gently extricated herself from Sam's arms, though it was really hard to do. "And I guess...later. We can talk. I mean, if you want to. About this. Or whatever." Jesus. She sounded like a teenager.

Sam laughed and leaned in so she could kiss her lightly on the cheek. "Okay." She picked up her cup and Olly turned to leave.

"I'm holding you to that conversation," Sam said. "And a lot more."

Olly's face flushed with heat, and she tripped over her own feet on her way out the door. She was a true charmer, no doubt.

Throughout her workday, every time she remembered the feel of Sam's lips against hers, she stopped and stared stupidly at whatever she was doing, a huge grin on her face.

After far too long, she finished with the floors in the first five rooms. She'd been working on them in chunks, cleaning, painting, refinishing, restoring five in a group. After this second coat of polyurethane dried, she'd start moving furniture in. Assuming, of course, that the order Sam had placed arrived on time. If not, she'd start on the next block of five rooms.

Finally, satisfied that she'd worked hard enough to deserve a break, she went back to the lobby. And Sam. She hoped.

The kiss they'd shared had been simple and perfect and overwhelming and beautiful and terrifying. She wanted to do it again, over and over, for the rest of forever, and that thought didn't scare her nearly as much as it should have. They needed to talk, she and Sam, but where would she find the words? What if Sam simply thought that she was a nice—but ultimately expendable—distraction?

As the lobby door closed behind her, Sam appeared in the doorway that separated the lobby from her apartment. She smiled and waited.

On autopilot, Olly closed the distance between them.

"Hi again," Sam said simply and leaned in to kiss her.

Like before, the kiss was soft and easy and sent tingles of electricity all the way through her body, from her head down to her toes. She made a happy humming sound in the back of her throat and threaded her fingers through the hair at the base of Sam's head. She forced herself to move slowly, to be gentle, to not assume, but God, Sam's lips felt so good against hers, a simple truth she'd been searching for her entire life.

When Sam ended the kiss, Olly chased after her with a whimper. A full-on, loss-of-control, pathetically needy whimper. Jesus. She closed her eyes and tried to collect herself.

"I'm glad you came back." Sam smoothed her thumb over Olly's cheek, and Olly pressed into the touch.

"Of course I did. I was just a few doors down."

Sam laughed, and it filled Olly's chest with a light, fizzy energy that made her feel like she could float to the sky and beyond. "Yes, but you looked terrified when you left."

Olly got caught up in the moment, in the dark flecks that peppered Sam's eyes, and somewhere between the lobby and the apartment, Olly's hand found its way into Sam's. Her skin was warm and soft and their fingers laced together perfectly, and Sam pulled her into the kitchen. Once inside, Sam led her toward the bedroom, but Olly stopped and tugged gently until Sam turned to face her, and then she cupped Sam's hand between both of hers.

"I really want to follow you into your room and do… everything with you. But, um, I think we need to talk about what this means before that happens." Olly's voice shook as she spoke, and she took a deep, calming breath. "Because I have no idea what you're thinking."

"You don't know what I'm thinking?" Sam's voice rose, along with her eyebrows.

Sam pushed Olly back until she bumped up against the island that separated the kitchen from the living room. She pressed her body tight against Olly's and cupped her cheek with her hand, fingers barely touching as she brought wave after wave of excitement to the surface of Olly's skin. She tilted her head and kissed Olly hard and fast and demanding, a complete counterpoint to their earlier kisses. Olly slumped against the counter, her knees instant liquid, incapable of holding her up.

"That's what I'm thinking. That's all I've been thinking since you kissed me this morning."

Sam clung defiantly to the sexy, flirty vibe she had going with Olly. Sure, they needed to talk about it at some point, but that didn't mean they needed to do it right now. Kissing Olly was fun, way better than kissing anyone else. The instant Olly's lips touched hers, it was as if a switch had been flipped. Her insides quaked and pulsed. The idea that she'd been satisfied with her hookups with Karen was laughable in comparison. If kissing felt this good, sex would be of the life-changing variety.

Olly's eyes were dark and stormy, a moonless midnight sky that drew her in with the fathomless intensity of her gaze. Then, as if compelled by Sam's inner thoughts, Olly leaned close enough to press her lips against Sam's. With the hot breath of promise between them, Sam waited, eyes closed, head tipped back, and a sigh of happiness bubbled up inside her.

Instead of completing the kiss, Olly rested her forehead against Sam's and said, "I really want to kiss you."

"What are you waiting for?" Sam tried not to sound as though she was crumbling and on the verge of begging Olly to do just that. It didn't work.

Olly gripped Sam's biceps lightly and eased back until there was a heart-breaking amount of space between them.

"First, though, I need to know what we're doing here. I can't..." Olly's mouth moved silently as she searched for the right words to continue the sentence. "I can't..." She threw her hands in the air and gave Sam a helpless look. "I need more."

"More?" Sam hadn't let herself think about more. Olly was a drifter, destined to leave, so Sam had convinced herself that this moment, feeling Olly in her arms right now, would be enough. Anything more was too much to think about.

"More." Olly stepped around Sam and moved to the other side of the room. "You stay there. I can't think with you that close."

Sam grinned and took a step toward Olly. "Really?"

Olly stepped back rapidly. "Really. Stop."

The look on Olly's face, as if she was on the verge of losing all control, enchanted Sam, and made her feelings come alive. She wanted to see what came next. So far, she'd seen Olly mildly annoyed, bemused, and confused (during their first meeting), and she'd seen her focused, intense, and determined (while working on the Queen), and she'd seen her excited, nostalgic, and brimming with energy (when touring the hotel in Missoula). She'd even seen her angry and ready to lash out (when she brought Beth home from the party). The expressive nature of her face, her eyes especially, made Sam want to see every other possible emotion flit across her face. Moreover, she wanted to be the cause of all of them.

Sam stared at Olly's lips. They were so damn kissable, soft and smooth and barely parted. Olly would give in, she knew, if she pushed the issue, if she slipped her arms around her waist, her hands under her shirt, if she drew Olly tight against her and kissed her until the need to breathe burned in her lungs. Instead, with a force of will she hadn't realized she possessed, she stopped herself and relaxed against the kitchen island.

"Okay, let's talk."

Olly took a deep, shaky breath and moved closer to Sam. "What is this?" She gestured between them. "To you? What do you think we're doing?"

Way to start with a softball question. Forced to think about all the things she didn't want to think about, Sam hesitated.

"I—I want…"

"Yes?" Olly moved closer still, her body leaning in as if what Sam said next would define her entire existence.

"I really want to take you in the bedroom and talk about all this later."

"I want that, too," Olly said. "But that's a really bad idea."

"Why? It sounds like the best idea ever." Sam tried for flirty again, hoping Olly was more open to it now.

"Right now, it's not," Olly said. "Because I really like Bitterroot. For the first time in my life, I want to stay. I don't know what that looks like. I've never done it. And what happens if we sleep together and it doesn't work out? What if I want more from you than you want from me? Will I have to leave? What if you want just as much as I do and I can't handle it? What happens then? If I drive away, will I come back? Will I keep going? Will you wait for me to figure my shit out? Or will you move on? You're beautiful and smart and so fucking sexy and amazing. What in the world makes me think I'm special enough for someone like you? You are so far out of my league—"

Without thought, Sam moved closer and placed her fingertips on Olly's lips.

"Shh. We have time. We don't have to answer all those questions tonight." Sam followed with a soft, sweet kiss, not aggressive enough to make Olly think she'd forgotten the earlier request to stop. Rather, it was a gentle caress

Bitterroot Queen

meant to calm and soothe.

Olly relaxed incrementally. "Are you sure? Because my chest is about to explode, and it feels like the only way I can make it settle is by figuring this out right now."

"Hey." Sam took her hand. "Nobody knows those answers at the beginning of a relationship. But that doesn't mean we shouldn't try. I want to try. I want to take you to bed and wake up with you in the morning. I want to pause in the middle of the work day and kiss you just because you're there and I can't wait."

"What about—"

"What?" Sam smiled. Olly was so cute and shy about some things and overflowing with swagger at others.

"Karen, for one. I've seen you with her. You seem... close." Olly averted her gaze, her eyelashes sweeping down to block Sam's view of those beautiful, expressive eyes. "It's not my place to ask what's going on, but I don't want to get in the middle of anything."

"We've been friends for a long time." Sam maintained a careful smile. She wasn't sure what Olly was asking and didn't want to respond until she was.

"Is that all?"

"It's—Karen and I are friends. Really good friends who have shared some benefits. A very short-lived period of benefits. And we won't be returning to the benefits regardless of what happens next with you. It added a layer of complication that neither of us wanted." That was the simplified version of things and bringing Karen into the conversation dropped a whole bucket of cold water on Sam. She needed to talk to Karen. Even though they weren't actually dating, she'd grown attached to Sam in a way that surpassed friendship. She owed it to all three of them to clarify the boundaries before going further with

Olly. But damn, that was going to be hard to do.

Olly's frown slowly transformed into a smile. "Yeah? That's awesome."

"You're unbelievable." In Sam's experience, most people wanted to know about Beth and how she would impact any possible relationship. Single moms were treated differently than single women without kids.

"What? Why?"

"You're not worried about Beth?"

"No. I like Beth. She's a good kid."

"But you know she's pregnant." Sam said it out loud without puking. That was a good sign. "That's kind of a big deal."

"Yeah, but until she knows what she's going to do, it's more questions than answers. Either way, I want to try with you, Sam Marconi."

"That," Sam's eyes brimmed with tears, hardly the sexy vamp she had been trying for moments ago. "That answer is just about perfect."

Chapter Twenty-Five

The website for the Bitterroot Queen was a straightforward affair, showing the property, the rooms and rates, and information about the town of Bitterroot. Sam had launched it over the weekend, earlier than she should have, really, but the Queen was ready. Almost.

The featured photos focused exclusively on the areas Olly had declared finished, plus shots of the river from their back patio. If that didn't encourage visitors, nothing would.

Sam settled into her office chair with an oversized mug of fresh coffee. As she jiggled the mouse to wake up the machine, she took a sip and then promptly cursed herself for not waiting for it to cool.

The monitor blinked to life, and she set the coffee aside. Not expecting anything, but hoping for everything, Sam accessed the reservation system for the site. The page loaded, and there, in lettering so small it downplayed the significance of the words, were two new reservations awaiting her approval. Sam blinked. And then blinked again, frozen for a moment with excitement.

Then, with a loud whoop, she opened the first entry. One room for seven nights, starting next Thursday. Sam did some quick calculations about the work still needed and then gave up trying to figure out how long it would take to finish up. Olly could finish it, she was certain. Not because she truly understood the scope of the work, but because Olly had given her the target date to start accepting reservations. If Olly said she'd have it done, she would. On faith, Sam clicked the button to approve the reservation.

"What's going on?" Beth ran in from her bedroom with Rachel two steps behind her, looking decidedly more rumpled than when she'd arrived. Beth reached for Rachel's hand and asked, "Is everything okay?"

"Everything is better than okay. Look." Sam pointed at the screen. "We have two reservations." As she spoke, she opened the second reservation and accepted it as well.

"Wow. Really? We're not ready."

"But we will be." Olly entered from the lobby, newly arrived for another day of work. She smiled at Sam, easy and affectionate, with just a little teasing.

Sam rushed to Olly and stopped just short of throwing herself onto her like an overly affectionate howler monkey. Instead, she pulled her into a quick, celebratory kiss. Then, because it felt so good, she kissed her again. A floaty giddiness swelled in her chest and threatened to bubble over.

"Holy shit," Beth said, "when did that happen?"

Olly broke the kiss with a laugh that sounded as ridiculously happy as Sam felt. She slipped her arm around Sam's waist, allowing her to tuck herself into Olly's side. Sam melted into it. Being here, standing next to Olly with her arm around her, this was as right as Sam had ever felt.

"It's happening right now, kid," Olly said easily.

"Yeah?" Beth's voice was filled with equal measures of disbelief and hope.

"Yeah." Sam left Olly's embrace to pull Beth into a hug. "No promises, but it's definitely happening," she whispered in Beth's ear.

"What about Karen?" Beth asked.

"We talked yesterday and everything is fine. We're still friends." That was the over-simplified description of a far more complicated conversation. Ultimately, though, Karen had admitted that her feelings for Sam had more to do with wanting an easy solution to being lonely rather than actual romantic affection. "I promise."

"Good." Beth nodded once, decisively.

"I have one more surprise for you when you're ready," Olly said.

Sam, Beth, and Rachel turned to Olly at once, and Sam smiled hard, unable to contain herself. "What did you do?"

"This is actually Beth's surprise, not mine, and we need to go out front to see it." Olly jerked her thumb toward the door.

Beth grabbed Sam's hand and tugged her toward the exit. "Is it what I think it is?"

Olly nodded. Beth smiled even wider. Sam let herself be drawn along, clueless and excited.

Rachel followed, shaking her head. "You guys are all nuts."

Out front, a group of people, along with a small crane, worked to unload a large metal disk from the back of a truck. A woman with long, straight, dark hair that she wore down along with a skullcap that Sam generally associated with bikers, supervised the endeavor. Olly greeted the woman with a handshake and then promptly returned to Sam's side.

"That's Quinn. She's a metalworker who we contracted to bring Beth's design to life."

"Beth's design?" Sam turned to her daughter. "What does she mean?"

"I wanted our sign to be special and unique, so I came up with this." Beth pulled a folded paper from her pocket and handed it to Sam.

Sam opened it slowly, careful of the worn-thin creases where it had been folded and unfolded over and over. The drawing was smudged, but the image was still clear enough to easily make out. It showed a rough sketch of the exterior lobby wall, complete with a circular sign with "Bitterroot Queen" etched into the surface. Light poured out through the openings made by the letters and from around the edges. Sam stared at it for a moment longer, tears threatening to spill over. She was so damn happy, and this gesture pushed her dangerously close to the sappy, soppy edge.

"You did this?" Sam ran a finger delicately over the drawing, as if to bring the image to life in her mind.

"Do you like it?" Beth asked, uncertain and timid.

"Oh, Beth. I love it." Sam carefully folded the paper and slipped it into her own pocket. Later, she would have it properly framed and hung behind the reception desk. She pulled Beth into a hug and held her long enough for Beth to start squirming to get away.

This new life they were building was full of bumps and bruises and promised to stay that way for a while, but it had already supplied her with so much more than she'd dared to hope for. Beth had opened up and no longer seemed to think Sam was an evil demon mother. Her pregnancy certainly wasn't ideal, but they'd figure it out. The Bitterroot Queen, in total disrepair when she'd arrived in town, no longer filled her with an overwhelming sense of dread and hopelessness. It was coming together, thanks in large part to Olly.

Olly...her feelings for Olly caught Sam by surprise almost as much as Beth being pregnant. She wasn't looking for a relationship, certainly not one as potentially complicated as one with Olly promised to be, but she'd tripped her way into it nonetheless.

On cue, as if somehow aware that Sam's thoughts had turned in her direction, Olly moved to Sam's side, slipped her arm around her waist as she had earlier, and pressed a gentle kiss to Sam's temple. "You okay in there?"

Sam nodded, unable to form actual words because her throat was drawn tight with emotion. How could she properly explain what she was feeling? Everything was so new and exposure made her feel shiny and raw and a little vulnerable. But she wouldn't trade it for the life she used to have. "Mmm-hmm. So okay."

The road ahead was uncertain at best, but she was eager to meet it. Life, it seemed, was on the precipice of giving her the happily ever after she'd never quite dared to hope for. In this moment, everything was so much better than okay.

It was perfect.

THE END

Other Books by Jove Belle

Archer Securities
(The Law Game Series—Book Two)
The Job
Love and Devotion
Uncommon Romance
Indelible
Chaps
Split the Aces
Edge of Darkness

Also from Dirt Road Books

Friends in High Places
Far Seek Chronicles 1
by Andi Marquette

Outlaw Torri Rendego and her crew are working to fulfill a black market contract on Old Earth, but they have to contend with hated Coalition forces. Kai Tinsdale, a part of Torri's past she never expected to see again, shows up, and Torri's survival depends on their ability to trust one another.

Coming Soon from Dirt Road Books

Rise and Shine
by Jove Belle

For best friends Emily and Sarah, a zombie outbreak seems like a pretty good reason to skip third period. And to skip town, for that matter. The girls pack up and start out on a 400 mile road trip to a bunker Emily's survivalist dad built. With a little luck, they'll survive long enough to make it to safety and maybe fall in love along the way.

Little Dip
Garoul Book 5
by Gill McKnight

It's 1977, and Connie Fortune has an easy, freewheeling life as a wildlife illustrator. A contract with a periodical brings her to the Little Dip, but a clash with Marie Garoul ruins the deal. Next year Connie tries again—but Marie is waiting for her.

Borage
Book 1 in Sisters of the 13th Moon Series
by Gill McKnight

Astral is the last of the Projector witches on a special mission to find an evil critter that is damaging her coven. Her search brings her to Black & Blacker. A company run by the enigmatic Abby Black. But who is bewitching who?

CPSIA information can be obtained
at www.ICGtesting.com
Printed in the USA
BVHW072315070119
537198BV00020B/492/P